The Women's House

Also by Joan Lingard:

The Second Flowering of Emily Mountjoy
Sisters by Rite

The Women's House

Joan Lingard

St. Martin's Press
New York

Library of Congress Cataloging-in-Publication Data

Lingard, Joan.
      The women's house / Joan Lingard.
             p.   cm.
      ISBN 0-312-03453-9
      I. Title.
      PR6062.I493W66   1989
      823'.914—dc20   89-10340
                                                              CIP

First published in Great Britain by Hamish Hamilton Ltd.

First U.S. Edition

10 9 8 7 6 5 4 3 2 1

For Penelope Hoare
and Bruce Hunter

From 'A House of Mercy' by Stevie Smith

'It is a house of female habitation
A house expecting strength as it is strong
A house of aristocratic mould that looks apart
When tears fall; counts despair
Derisory. Yet it has kept us well. For all its faults
If they are faults, of sterness and reserve,
It is a Being of warmth, I think; at heart
A house of mercy.'

ONE

They had not thought to put 'Funeral Private' in the newspaper announcement, not expecting anyone other than themselves to attend. 'Dorothea Mary Wilberforce,' Anna had dictated to the clerk at the newspaper office, 'widow of the late Jack Wilberforce, and dear friend of Evangeline Hudson.'

It was Anna who first noticed the four men. The other two women were facing front, staring glumly at the coffin and the three wreaths lying on the shiny lid. Hearing the door squeak behind them, feeling a quick rush of cold air, Anna glanced round and saw, advancing up the short aisle of the crematorium chapel, wearing a dark suit and a blindingly white shirt and a black tie, which he was fingering just below the knot, Mr Maximo Tonelli, otherwise known (to the women) as the King of Naples, or, when the sun shone and he sported dark glasses, Papa Doc. He inclined his head to Anna and, involuntarily, she nodded in return. Behind him came his three sons, in single file, dressed in similar fashion to their father. The only things missing were black armbands, thought Anna. The men seemed uncertain as to what they should do next. Presumably they were used to genuflecting in front of the high altar when they entered a church. She supposed they were Roman Catholic. And they must have been taken aback when they came in and found the chapel so empty. It would probably not have occurred to them that some people would want to mourn their dead privately. Tonelli funerals would be large, marked by pomp and ceremony and much swinging of incense burners and the guttering of massed candles, with a densely-packed and expensively-dressed congregation, and several priests in attendance, perhaps even the bishop himself, in purple and

1

gold.

The moment of hesitation passed, and Mr Tonelli senior resolutely led the way into a pew two rows behind the women. The men dropped to their knees and buried their faces in their hands.

Anna turned back, smoothing the skirt of her flame-coloured coat. Holly was wearing a baggy, yellow T-shirt with University of Kentucky written in scarlet across the chest and a yellow ribbon in her fiery-red hair, Evangeline a peacock-blue felt hat with a long peacock's feather which flicked Anna in the eye every time she moved her head. Dorothea had asked them not to wear black. She had loved colour.

'What is it, dear?' asked Evangeline in a voice that soared above the doleful organ music issuing from the two loud-speakers on either side of the chapel. She was becoming increasingly deaf, and for her to swivel at the waist was an effort.

'Nothing,' mouthed Anna, shaking her head, opening out her hands, palms upward. She could convey much by gesture: she earned her living, modest though it was, and, indeed, it was quite modest, by performing as a mime artist. Satisfied, Evangeline settled down again.

Holly, however, did not. She twisted round in her seat and glared at the intruders, not lowering her eyes under the interested stare of one of the sons, the one whom she called Don Juan. She knew the eldest son, the plump one, Giorgio; she frequented his fish and chip shop. He gave her a little nod and she allowed her gaze to soften while it rested on him. Georgie was all right. Poor old Georgie. Just the type to kiss the girls and make himself cry. He was looking pretty miserable even now, as if he wished he weren't here. But he wouldn't have had a choice. When the King cracked the whip, his sons came running. What a nerve they had, though, to come barging in on their funeral! She was tempted to get up and tell them so, but feeling Anna's hand on her arm, she subsided and made do with wrinkling her nose to let them know that she did not care for the smell. She noticed Don Juan's mouth flickering at the corner with amusement. Shrugging her shoulders, she put her back to them.

2

A chaplain glided in through a side door and came to rest beside the coffin. Dorothea, who had been a non-believer for most of her life, would not have welcomed this development but it had been difficult for them to decide what else to do. The chaplain restricted himself, as he had said he would, to speaking in very general terms and giving thanks for the long and bountiful life of the deceased. He was a radical churchman, ready to meet everyone's changing needs; he would not insist on swinging incense or leading them in prayer or even mentioning the name of the Lord. Let us give thanks, he said, without specifying to whom, or for what.

'And now, I believe, Miss Pemberton, you wish to recite some poetry in honour of our dear departed friend Dorothea?' He smiled, showing well spaced teeth, and extended a hand which Anna was clearly not expected to take.

She stepped forward, irritated by his use of the words 'recite' and 'poetry', by his claim on the friendship of Dorothea whom he had never met, and by the presence of the four sombre-suited men who had brought with them into the room a number of currents, all of which were disturbing. And she was irritated that she was irritated. She was annoyed that these men in their black meaningless mourning should come here and see them in their bright colours and misjudge them. She saw that they saw them as eccentrics. Those oddball women. A peacock's feather in her hat! University of Kentucky written across her boobs – in scarlet! But these were fairly ordinary clothes and colours for what they were: a seventeen-year-old girl, an eighty-five-year-old and a middle-aged woman. This coat, the colour of autumn ferns blazing on a hillside, had been an unusual purchase for her. Normally she favoured muted colours, like soft greys and bleached straw and moss green. She was self-effacing, by career, perhaps partly too by temperament. If not, why had she chosen to spend her life living inside the minds and bodies of other people?

The four men were gazing at her as if she had stepped off the moon. She shut their thoughts out, not wanting to enter into them. At times it could be a curse to see the world through other people's eyes. Let them think whatever they wanted to think! They would have their stock responses to most situations. But she wished now that they had let the crematorium get on with the business and send the ashes on to them afterwards. They had discussed this option but decided that it would not do: it would seem too cold, too disinterested. And they had been immensely interested in Dorothea.

Strangely nervous for one who was used to facing an audience – though, of course, she did not make much use of her voice in public, except to introduce her acts – Anna began to speak the poem which Dorothea had selected for her funeral.

'*My Dreams*,' she began. 'By Stevie Smith.'

One after the other, like a wavelet breaking on the shore, the men dropped their eyes and stared at the spaces between their black feet.

'In my dreams I am always saying goodbye and riding away,
Whither and why I know not nor do I care.
And the parting is sweet and the parting over is sweeter,
And sweetest of all is the night and the rushing air.

In my dreams they are always waving their hands and saying goodbye,
And they give me the stirrup cup and I smile as I drink,
I am glad the journey is set, I am glad I am going,
I am glad, I am glad, that my friends don't know what I think.'

The men looked up, startled, and at the same moment Dorothea's favourite music erupted from the loud speakers: Schubert's *Trout Quintet*. It rushed and burbled through the chapel as the coffin slid backwards from their sight. The chaplain raised his hands in what might have been intended as a benediction, mouthed a few words and then made his escape back through the side door.

Evangeline blew her nose and reached for her stick. Anna came to help Holly support her out into the autumn sunshine. The four men had made it there before them and were waiting

4

on the steps, lined up to receive them like a guard of honour. Their shirts and their teeth gleamed. Their eyes were shaded with dark glass.

'May we offer you our sincerest condolences,' said Papa Doc, taking Anna's hand. 'I am sure she will be a great loss to you.'

'Who is this man, Anna?' demanded Evangeline.

'Mr Tonelli. He is our neighbour, from the house across the road.'

'Ah yes, I thought I had seen you before. You live in the Villa Neapolitana?'

'The Cedars,' corrected Mr Tonelli. 'When it was first built I believe it was called Taj Mahal but our predecessors changed it.'

'It belonged to the Wilberforces originally, you know,' said Evangeline. 'Jack Wilberforce's grandfather built your house and ours at the same time, in 1850, absolutely identical. He was a rich man, one of the richest men in town, a tea importer by trade. He liked to sit in his own house and look at the mirror-image house across the street where he had installed his son. That way he could have his cake and eat it.'

The King of Naples coughed behind the white cuff which protruded from his black sleeve. 'The houses do have a very interesting history. We Tonellis have been in our house for nearly sixty years. My father – '

'Ah yes, Antonio! He came from Sorrento or somewhere, pushing his hand-cart loaded with ice cream, is that not right?'

'You know the story?'

'He came along the street and he looked at your house and he decided that this was where he would live. The house inspired him, and lo and behold, he became rich! Yes, Mrs Wilberforce – our dear Dorothea – told us. An admirable story. The kind of story that we all like. It certainly cannot have been easy for Antonio arriving here as a poor immigrant owning nothing but a hand-wagon. And with virtually no English to speak of, I believe? Always a disadvantage in this country.'

The other three men were growing restive, clearing their throats and fidgeting with their shirt cuffs.

5

'You have an appointment at twelve, Father,' said Don Juan.

Mr Tonelli senior said, 'If there is anything we can do for you, Signores, please do not hesitate to ask. My wife also sends her sympathy.'

'How kind,' said Evangeline.

With a small bow, the King backed away. His sons, breaking rank, headed for their Alfa Romeos. Their father, walking with more majesty, went to claim his long red Ferrari.

'Smoothie,' said Holly. 'He didn't sound Italian to me, except when he called us Signores.'

'I think he had a slight intonation, if you listened carefully,' said Anna. 'But not much. He was born here, after all. In the Villa Neapolitana.'

'Why do you think they came?' asked Evangeline.

'I'm not sure,' said Anna thoughtfully. 'A neighbourly gesture perhaps.'

Evangeline snorted, then said, 'I'm dying for a fag.'

Holly struck a match on the sole of her black boots and, cupping the flame between her hands, lit a cigarette for herself and one for Evangeline. Anna was working on Holly to give up but realized there was no point in trying to change Evangeline who attributed her long and healthy life to bad habits. She had never spent a night in hospital and her arthritis appeared to be tolerable without medication. She preferred madeira to aspirins. The two women blew smoke into the crisp air, shifting to one side so that the next group of mourners could make their way in for the next funeral. It seemed a thriving business, observed Evangeline, between puffs.

'Don't see why those jerks should have come,' said Holly, as they watched the Tonelli cars grind up the gravel and go screeching out of the driveway. 'They never knew Dottie, did they?'

'I believe Antonio tried to court her when he first came,' said Evangeline. 'He was after the house, no doubt.'

'That was yonks ago. None of them have ever paid any attention to *us*, have they? Except for Don Juan when I was sunbathing in the garden.'

'I told you you shouldn't have been lying there topless,' said Anna. 'It was inviting trouble.'

'Oh, I can take care of him. And you must admit I don't have much to show.' Holly grinned and beat a tattoo with her fists against the University of Kentucky. 'Skinny as a washboard. That's what Janice's mum says.'

'Shall we go?' said Anna. 'That looks like our car.'

The car dropped them off in front of their house. The name on the gate said Shangri-la but it was known to everyone in the neighbourhood as the women's house. It was a large, imposing building of eighteen rooms plus the usual offices, standing three storeys high on a raised basement, and turreted, as was its twin across the street. Jack Wilberforce's grandfather Septimus had spared no cost, or effort. The bricks had been shipped from the Low countries, the marble for the internal staircases and the front steps from Marmara, the carpets from Persia and Turkestan, the silks and satins from the Orient. They were the first houses to be built in the street, which had then been on the outskirts of the town, well away from the gushing smoke of factory chimneys and the huddle of factory workers' cottages. Over the years the street had filled up with other large houses, occupied by other well-to-do merchants, though none was as large or as imposing as the Wilberforce houses. They dominated the district.

Following the death of Septimus and his son, Jack's father, Taj Mahal was sold. And shortly afterwards, Jack himself died, still a young man, of tuberculosis, leaving his widow Dorothea to live on alone in Shangri-la in what was then referred to as 'reduced circumstances'. The house went steadily downhill or, as the estate agents would say, downmarket, like most of the other properties in the area which, after the war, became too large for servantless families and were turned into hotels and nursing homes or broken up into flats. The paintwork on the windows and roofs of Shangri-la blistered and flaked, the marble steps dulled, weeds triumphed in the garden and burst through the gravel on the drive, yet Dorothea did not once consider selling, not even when the value of her shares dwindled to almost nothing. Instead, she

7

sold the treasures that had come from the East and when that source dried up she began to rent out rooms, giving up one after the other as her fortunes declined. All her tenants were women. She preferred women. She trusted them, felt safe with them in the house. And when she became old, they looked after her.

They kept her at home as long as they could, long after she was bedridden and incontinent, but when she began to accuse them of whispering in corners, to suspect them of plotting against her, of stealing her money, of trying to do her in, they had to let her go into the nursing home at the end of the street. There, they visited her daily, taking it in turn; they talked to her and read to her. Sometimes, she was lucid and reminisced about Jack and her journeys with him to Assam and Kashmir, something they had not heard her do before, and she smiled with great sweetness upon her visitors, reminding them of the woman she had once been; at others, she was malevolent and cackled and bubbled at the mouth like a witch.

And then she died. And when she did, the only will that could be found was one dated 1932 which left everything to her brother. She had talked often about making a new will, naming Evangeline as her beneficiary, but had never got round to doing it. During the months when it was clear that she was on her way out the women had hesitated to mention it to her, though on one occasion, when she was lucid, Anna had tried to. Dorothea had stared back at her and said, 'Plenty of time yet. Plenty of time.'

Her brother, a bachelor, had predeceased her. And so the estate would now pass to a second cousin twice removed who lived in a bungalow on the south coast and who would be unlikely to want to come and live in Shangri-la or to rent out rooms to a bunch of women whom he had never set eyes on. Dorothea's lawyer, Mr Partridge, expected to be instructed to sell it.

The fortunes of The Cedars, or the Villa Neapolitana, as the women called it, home of the Tonellis, had gone contrary to those of its sister house across the street; after being bought by Maximo's father, Antonio, it had come up in the world, had been cleaned and polished and reroofed and refurbished. Its

8

peppermint green paintwork shone, its pink marble steps leading to the front door gleamed in the afternoon sun, its gardens looked like a miniature Versailles. The Tonelli business expanded to include fish and chip shops, restaurants, boutiques, discotheques. The Tonellis went regularly back to Sorrento and returned with relatives to help man their empire. (They did bring some women, too.)

After Antonio died, Maximo lived on in the Villa Neapolitana with his family: he and his Italian-born wife, Sophia, a stout voluble woman, whose voice was well known in the street, and Sophia's mother, a black-garbed Calabrian widow, who spoke no English, inhabited the ground floor; the eldest son, Giorgio and his wife, Mary-Lou (the first non-Italian to penetrate the family) and their baby daughter, Alexis, the first; and the second and third sons, Roberto (Don Juan) and Claudio, the top. The three daughters had all married into other suitably prosperous families and were comfortably set up in rather more modern and less exotic houses in other parts of town. On high days and holidays – whenever there was an excuse – they congregated at the Villa Neapolitana, choking the street with their Lancias, Alfa Romeos, Ferraris and the occasional Fiat. In summer, they held garden parties on the billiard-table lawn and the laughter and popping of corks went on into the small hours; in winter, lights streamed from every window and the sound of pulsating music carried on the night air.

'It's getting chilly,' said Anna, pushing open the rusting gate of Shangri-la. 'Let's go in and have a glass of claret.'

'Or two,' said Evangeline.

Anna and Holly went down and rummaged in the cellar. Their fingers left streaks on the dust-shrouded bottles. They sneezed so much they started to laugh.

'Some of this stuff looks as if it's been here since old guy Septimus' time,' said Holly, filling a plastic bag indiscriminately with bottles.

'Strictly speaking,' said Anna, 'it all belongs to the Second Cousin – house *and* contents.'

'Tough beans for him.'

9

Dorothea had inherited the wine from her brother who had lived improvidently and, on dying, had left a well-stocked cellar, a wardrobe full of clothes tailored in Savile Row and two dozen pairs of hand-made shoes. Years before, he had had to sell his house to cover his gambling debts.

Clanking heavily, Anna and Holly stumbled back up the steep narrow steps to the ground floor where Evangeline had her apartments. She had lit her sitting-room fire, which was smoking wispily, and she sat on a Moroccan leather pouffe, wearing her balding musquash coat and peacock hat, holding out her hands to the feeble flames. Her rings hung more slackly on her fingers now, Anna noticed.

'A few swigs of this will warm your toes,' said Holly. Her yellow T-shirt was smudged with dirt and cobwebs clung to her head like a hair-net. Anna brushed them off with her hand.

They wiped the bottles clean and chose two which, on being held against the light, seemed less sedimented than the others – a 1953 St Emilion and a 1962 Medoc. Both excellent years, declared Evangeline, reassuring Holly, who wondered if they might not have gone off. They were both older than she was, by a long chalk. Anna uncorked the bottles, sniffed their opened necks and set them by the fire.

'We're not going to wait, are we?' asked Holly.

Anna poured three glasses of wine so dark it looked almost black.

'Well, here's to Dorothea!'

'Poor old Dottie,' sighed Evangeline.

Holly objected. 'Well, she had a good run for her money, didn't she? Ninety-five! If I live that long I'll have another seventy-eight years to go. Holy Christ!'

'I shall miss her, though,' said Evangeline. 'Just not to be able to know she still exists.'

'Let's drink to her, anyway,' said Anna, raising her glass.

They drank.

'Wow!' said Holly.

Sip it slowly, advised Anna. But Holly was a gulper, used to downing coke, glasses of milk and half pints of lager. She drained her glass quickly. Her lips and tongue purpled. Evangeline produced a packet of long slim cigarillos and she and Holly puffed, wreathing their heads in blue-grey smoke. The fire burned brightly. Evangeline removed her hat and unbuttoned her coat. Beyond the windows and the privet bushes which pressed close against them, daylight waned.

'So who do you think's going to buy us then?' asked Holly.

'Maximo Tonelli,' said Anna.

'Do you think so?' Evangeline sounded surprised. 'What would he want with us? We're sitting tenants, after all. We have our leases allowing us to stay in perpetuity. At least poor old Dorothea had the sense to do that for us. The Tonellis are certainly not going to budge me, by fair means or by foul. This has been my home for *fifty*-two years. It is a long time.'

'Very long,' agreed Holly. 'So we've got nothing to worry about?' She looked at Anna.

Anna would not go so far as to say that: she doubted that the Tonellis would give in so tamely. Their presence at the funeral suggested they were about to open an offensive and she doubted if it would be conducted by fair means. Springing up, she stood before Evangeline and Holly on the silk rug which had been transported from China by the Wilberforces in the previous century; it had been one of the few things that Dorothea had kept for herself, and as soon as she had died, they had moved it into Evangeline's room.

'Ladies, I bring you Mr Maximo Tonelli! He is at home in his parlour at the Villa Neapolitana with his wife Sophia.' Anna then closed her mouth and began to use her hands and eyes and the rest of her body.

Sophia, I am going to buy Shangri-la! I shall buy it cheap.
(She rubs her hands, rolls her eyes to express pleasure.)
Because they are sitting tenants.
(She shows Holly and Evangeline sitting.)
But they will not sit all that long.
(Up, up, her hands tell them.)
I shall remove them. Clear them out.
(Her hands clear them away.)
What are they, after all? Only women!
(She points to them and smiles a derogatory smile.)
I am a man!
(She struts around with her chest puffed out.)

11

I have silver hair.
(She points at a silver teapot and then to her hair.)
I have a silver palm.
(She rubs the fingers of one hand across the other.)
I have a silver tongue.
I have a silver lining in my pocket.
Pick pocket, pick pocket
No one will ever pick my pocket!

'Bravo!' cried Evangeline and Holly drummed her feet and clapped.

'This has certainly been a lesson to me,' said Evangeline. 'I shall make a will myself as soon as possible, I shan't die intestate. You two shall be my inheritors. Not that I have a great deal to leave, you understand.'

'That's very good of you, Evvie,' said Holly. 'But you're not going to die for a long time yet, are you?' She fastened her green eyes on Evangeline's face and, pressing her fist against her mouth, began to guzzle her nails.

'Certainly not. I don't feel at all like bowing out.'

'Nails, Holly! You'll soon be up to the elbow,' said Anna and lifted the next bottle from the hearth.

By the time they had finished it they were feeling a little woozy. Evangeline's head was drooping. They needed food, Anna decided. Holly was given money and dispatched to buy fish and chips. She went wobbling off on Evangeline's ancient upright bicycle which had a handy, if disintegrating, wicker basket, strapped to its front handlebars.

The nearest fish and chip shop was the one owned and run by Giorgio Tonelli. It was a smooth, shining place, full of chrome and glass and white formica faked to look like marble and the floor was black and white terrazzo. The menu on the back wall was extensive, offering pork escalopes and smoked trout – deep fried – along with the more usual haddock, cod, chicken and spring rolls.

Giorgio was there himself behind the counter, in a white coat and chef's hat. It annoyed his father to see him serving – 'You are the manager, Giorgio!' he would tell him. 'You will never go any further with an attitude like yours. Where would we be now if your grandfather had been content to push a hand-wagon round the streets for ever?' – but Giorgio liked being behind the counter, plunging the white chips into frothing oil, lifting them up in their basket golden and gleaming, scooping them into paper bags, spraying them with salt and vinegar, passing them into the hands of the customers, watching them smile as they anticipated popping the first hot, mouth-watering chip into their mouths. He loved the fish and chip business. He loved the smells. He loved the bright lights, the door swinging open, the hub of activity at the back of the counter. His father despaired of him. He had set him up in the shop when he was seventeen and here he still was at twenty-nine. His eldest son! It was just as well the second born was more ambitious.

'Three haddock suppers, Georgie,' said Holly, moving aside a jar of pickled onions and one of pickled eggs so that she could lean her arms on top of the glass counter and look over. She watched to see that they would be given large pieces of fish. She pointed to the ones she wanted. 'And a spring roll. Curried. I'll eat that now. I'm starved. I'll fall off the bike if I don't eat something first. We've been having a booze-up. Ta, Georgie!'

She took a large bite and shuttled it about in her mouth until it cooled. She ate quickly.

'So you came to our funeral?'

'A sad occasion.'

'Yeah, funerals aren't much in my line. My dad died when I was two but I don't remember him and I don't suppose they took me to the funeral.'

'You should go home to your family, Holly.'

'You've gotta be joking!'

'Salt and vinegar?'

'One without. Anna tries to keep Evangeline off salt, says it's bad for her arteries, don't know why she bothers though. Evvie's a tough old bird. She'll make a hundred, I'm sure she will. Hang on, I tell her, and you'll get Lizzie's telegram yet.'

Giorgio shook the salt shaker enthusiastically over the other two suppers.

'It's no life for you in that house, with one woman old enough to be your mother and the other old enough to be your great-grandmother.'

'I thought you were in favour of the extended family? Anna says that's what you've got over there at the Villa Neapolitana.'

'There's nothing like your own flesh and blood, though.'

'You're dead right. Nothing but trouble.'

'Why don't you come over and see Mary-Lou sometime? She likes company, she gets fed up being in with the baby all day. She only has my mother to talk to and, you know, that is not always so easy. My mother is a strong woman. You could talk to Mary-Lou about your problems. She likes to hear about people's problems.'

'I haven't got any, Georgie. Ain't I lucky?'

'I think maybe you would like to live in a nice modern flat, no?'

'No. I like junk.'

Giorgio placed the three bagged portions of fish and chips carefully in the centre of a sheet of brown paper and wrapped them into a neat parcel. Holly passed over the money. In this moment of exchange, bordering on intimacy, during which each received what they coveted, and their hands brushed slightly, it was easy for Holly to slide in her question.

'Is your pa planning to buy our house, Georgie?' She engaged his eyes.

'Yes, well, it's a good property, prime situation. At least that's what they say,' he added limply. He looked away, into the bubbling vat of oil.

'What's he going to do with it?' Holly's breath filmed the glass counter top.

Giorgio shrugged and began shovelling freshly cut chips into the fryer.

'Come on, Georgie, you can tell me.'

'You'll keep it to yourself?'

'Cross my heart.' Holly licked her finger which tasted of salt and vinegar.

'He wants to open a casino.'

'A casino? You mean roulette wheels and all that jazz?'

Giorgio nodded unhappily, already aware that he should have kept his mouth shut. If word got out Roberto would take

14

him by the neck and squeeze him. Giorgio coughed and felt his throat.

'You won't say nothing?'

'Nothing,' said Holly, and leaping back on to Evangeline's cycle, sped off under the star-spangled sky to bring the news and the ambrosial package to Shangri-la.

TWO

Maximo Tonelli arrived as the inlaid mahogany grandmother clock in the hall was striking two. He was expected, having phoned beforehand to make the appointment. He took his silver watch (which he had inherited from his father, Antonio) from his pocket, clicked open the lid and checked the time.

'*Bene!* It is exactly right.' He clicked the lid shut, looked the clock over. He fingered the back. 'It's a nice piece.'

'Worth a penny or two,' said Anna and their eyes met. Mr Tonelli, who had removed his sunglasses on the front step as she had opened the door, glanced away first. His gaze travelled over the marble-floored hall with its two marble pillars, up the walls, whose covering was hanging down, limply, in strips, and then to the ceiling, which, of course, needed repainting, badly, and to the cupola, which was obviously leaking. Once Anna had decided to redecorate but had been unable to find a ladder long enough and Dorothea had refused to let her set a plank on top of two step-ladders and stand on top. Anna might have excellent balance, she had said, but if she were to fall she would break her neck on the marble. It was unforgiving stuff.

His inspection finished, Mr Tonelli said that he would prefer to talk to each of them separately: for one thing, he wanted to have a look at their rooms and see what was what. He did not say what the other thing was, did not need to, for that was self-evident, but they were not worried about being isolated; they could each stand as firmly alone as when they stood together.

'Come into my parlour first,' said Evangeline, waving towards her door with her stick.

'After you, Miss Hudson.' He inclined his head.

16

Anna and Holly went off up the pink marble staircase with Holly singing, 'Who's afraid of the big bad wolf?'

Evangeline invited Mr Tonelli to take the armchair to the left of the fireplace, where he would be facing the light. Seated on the other side, she would have her own face in shadow. A glass of madeira? He accepted. She poured the wine from a cut-glass decanter into delicate, matching glasses. He admired the set.

'Early Waterford. I bought it forty years ago in a junk shop for two-and-sixpence. Such bargains are not easy to come by these days, at least so I am told, for I don't get out and about much now. I suppose you are interested in bargains, Mr Tonelli?'

'Who isn't? If they are honest.'

She smiled. 'Your health!'

'And yours, Miss Hudson!'

He took a small sip and nodded appreciatively. He unbuttoned his jacket. Then he shifted the angle of his chair a little so that he could survey the room.

She watched his dark eyes as they moved under their heavy crocodile-type lids. They were making an inventory. Chaise longue and matching chair in bottle-green velvet, shabby, but basically sound, would fetch a bit if re-upholstered, two leather armchairs, somewhat scuffed and scored, Moroccan pouffe, inlaid mahogany coffee table, roll-top writing desk (the genuine article), glass display cabinet filled with glass paperweights in need of dusting (as was everything else in the room), a number of rather heavy Victorian-style landscape paintings in heavy gold frames, one portrait of a girl looking pert in a green dress (Evangeline herself, aged twenty), one Chinese rug, two very nice Persians, bow-fronted mahogany bookcase (possibly Georgian), open mahogany bookcase from floor to ceiling stuffed with books. Books everywhere. On top of the roll-topped desk, under the coffee table, in stacks on the floor. She watched his eyes shift from the piles of books to the yellowing cardboard boxes full of old photographs and old postcards and old theatre and concert programmes to the teetering mounds of newspapers and magazines which looked as if they might slip and slide at any moment.

17

She was a hoarder, always had been, was not prepared to make any apology for it.

'You have a lot of things.'

'All my own possessions. Mrs Wilberforce's effects are in her apartments across the hall. Perhaps, though, you would permit us to dispose of her clothes? To the Red Cross or Salvation Army?'

'Well, naturally. I would prefer that you did.'

'Most considerate.'

'You are aware then that I have bought the house?'

'Indeed. Lock, stock and barrel, so we understand. You signed the contract yesterday.'

'You seem to have good lines of communication?'

'Very good.' She lifted the decanter. 'More madeira, Mr Tonelli?'

He brought his glass to be refilled.

'You are a literary lady, I believe?'

'I don't know that I would describe myself in those terms exactly. I used to do a fair amount of journalism, literary reviews and so forth, and I have also published a number of novels, well in the past.'

'Under your own name?'

'Well, yes. But don't trouble yourself if you haven't heard of me. I'm sure you are a busy man and have no time for reading.' He admitted that he had not and she went on, 'For a long time, anyway, I was dead, and then they revived me.' She laughed and he did too, although she suspected that he had no clear idea of what she was talking about. Their terms of reference meant nothing to one another. She explained. 'My books were out of print for a long time – fashions change, as you, a man of business, will know – and then along came a publishing house called Virago, a feminist publishing house.' She saw him blench slightly at the mention of the word 'feminist' but he was good-mannered, he recovered quickly. She went on. 'They resurrected a number of forgotten women writers and when they had done all the obvious people, the front runners in the forgotten stakes, if you like – people like Antonia White and Rosamund Lehmann, names which will also mean nothing to you – they came further down the barrel

18

to people like me. I like to think they did not find me quite at the bottom.'

'I cannot believe that you would ever be there, Miss Hudson.'

'Thank you, Mr Tonelli.'

He confessed that he regretted not having had more time for things like books. Sometimes he felt he had missed out on too much. 'But we can't have everything in life, can we?'

'I would have thought you might have considered that one could?'

'I am not a stupid man, Miss Hudson.'

'No, I can see that.'

'What have you written about in your books? Or should I not ask that question?'

'I would have to refer you to the books. One is set in Rome. I lived there for a few years, before I knew Mrs Wilberforce.'

'You speak Italian?'

'Only moderately. I haven't been in Italy for some time.'

They talked about Italy for a bit, an enthusiasm they could share, and it left Evangeline feeling nostalgic and with a strong desire to go back one more time to Rome and Venice. And, of course, to Florence. Perhaps, in the spring, she might go with Anna and Holly, if Anna could be bothered with an encumbrance such as herself. And if they could raise the money. Maximo Tonelli went back every year, at least once, he told her. 'It draws me, even though I was born here. Sometimes I think I might spend my last years there, though I don't suppose that I will.'

'I can't imagine you retiring, Mr Tonelli?'

'Perhaps not.' He made a steeple with his fingers, which he contemplated for a moment. He frowned, causing his forehead to become ridged right up to the balding patch on the crown of his silver head. The lids of his eyes slid so far down that he appeared to have closed them. Then he came alive again and sat up to take another look around the room. His eyes came to a halt on the long knitted sausage at the back of the door.

'It must be cold in here in winter with no central heating?'

19

'Are you considering putting it in for us, Mr Tonelli? How kind.'

'Don't you think, Miss Hudson, that at your stage in life you would like to have a few more comforts – a modern bathroom, a nicely set up kitchenette?'

'I have no objection to some modernization, not in those offices. I am not a stick-in-the-mud even though I may be eighty-five. But my parlour cannot be touched. Or my bedroom.'

'I was thinking that you might be better off in something tailored more to your requirements. Say in sheltered housing?' He leant forward so that the bottom half of his face sank into shadow. His eyes glowed in the light from the fire. Rembrandt would have liked to have painted those eyes, she thought. 'I can arrange it. There is a very nice block of apartments only a mile away and each one has the same accommodation as you have here: bedroom, sitting room – '

'A quarter the size, no doubt.'

'A bit smaller.'

'Boxes!'

'But very comfortable. And warm, very warm. There's a warden who comes round to see that you're all right and haven't fallen out of bed or anything like that and there's a string hanging over your bed to pull in an emergency and one in the bathroom. Everything's been thought of for your comfort and well-being. You would have your privacy but if you wanted to you could find friends in the recreation areas.'

'You sound as if you've swallowed the brochure, Mr Tonelli.'

'I know it takes a while to get used to the idea but I want you to think about it. The gardens are beautiful and you'd get an excellent meal in the dining room every day. These places aren't easy to get into, you know, there are long waiting lists, but I've managed to fix it up for you, through a friend.'

'Well, you can just unfix it. I am not going anywhere. My dear man – I do not wish to be sheltered, to have a string above my bed, to eat in a communal dining room, to sit in a communal recreation room with my peers. I like the tenants in this house. I like this house. I have inhabited it for more than

20

half a century and I shall not leave it until I am ready to go, feet first.' Reaching for her stick, Evangeline stood up and escorted her landlord to the door.

He was sorry, he said, before going upstairs, that she should take it this way; it would really be so much better for her to live in a modern flat than in this house which, if it was not gutted and refurbished soon, would collapse around their ears.

Anna's room was a surprise to him; she saw it reflected in his face. He stopped in the doorway, startled by the room's lightness. The walls were white, the high ceiling the colour of faded pink roses which was picked up in the design on the grey, pink and white curtains. The same fabric had been used on the two small settees and on the table lamps. A soft dove-grey carpet covered the floor. The furnishings were sparse: a low smokey-glass table on which stood a vase of pink chrysanthemums, a simple desk and chair, a white bookcase, modern paintings set in narrow silver frames.

'Very nice. It has a kind of' – he was searching for a word – 'quiet feel to it.'

Tranquil, like a placid lake: that was how Evangeline, who could never live with so much space and light around her, described it. It was the largest room in the house, the original drawing room, with three long windows facing south. It was too exposed, too open for her, Evangeline said, although she enjoyed coming for a visit; she was one of those creatures who needed a burrow in which to live. The brightness made her blink.

'Did you do it yourself?'

Anna nodded.

'All of it?'

'Yes. I went to evening classes for upholstery. One has to learn to do such things when one is short of money.'

That he could appreciate. He began to tour the walls, to examine her paintings, which gave her the opportunity to examine him. He was a stocky man of small to medium height, an inch or so shorter than she, with an immense energy in his body which she could sense even when he stood, immobile, lips pursed, unsure whether he liked a particular picture or not.

'I like that one.' He pointed to a painting of a girl swimming overarm.

'It's a bit David Hockneyish. Although any painting of a swimmer is almost bound to be compared to his now. But it's rather good, I think. It was painted by a friend of mine.'

Maximo Tonelli confessed that he did not know much about painting, though he knew what he liked. And he did not like the brightly coloured abstract beside the swimmer. Too splotchy for him. What was it meant to be anyway? Sunburst, she told him. He shook his head. He could not see it himself; he did not think it sufficient that a lot of yellow and orange was splashed about. To his mind it could just as easily be called Broken Eggs.

'I suppose you think I am a Philistine?'

'Not at all. You don't *have* to like it.'

He moved on to the next painting and she excused herself to go to the kitchen to make some coffee, needing an excuse to escape so that she could make an attempt to get the measure of her visitor. He appeared to be a curious man who sought clues when trying to understand how other people ticked. She could not blame him for that. She did so herself, was doing it now. But what did surprise her was that he *wanted* to understand her: she had expected him to ride roughshod over them, to make his demands, and waste no time. So many people were not interested in anyone other than themselves, she had found; while they made a pretence of listening they were merely thinking of what they themselves would say next and when one paused for breath they jumped in.

When Anna returned with the coffee, Maximo Tonelli was sitting on one of the settees reading a dance and mime magazine. He looked up. His eyes, under those hooded lids, were penetrating.

'Are you interested in this?'

'I work as a mime.'

'Is that so? I saw Dario Fo perform once, in Italy. My cousin took me. He was amazing, this man Fo. In one act he was miming swallowing spaghetti – yards and yards of it – and on and on he went, stuffing it into his mouth, his throat glugging, his eyes bulging, until you expected to see him burst in front of

22

your eyes. We were all starting to gag with him. Do you do things like that?'

'Perhaps not quite the same. Everyone has his or her own style.'

'Tell me! Good coffee, by the way, very good.'

She explained that she was the kind of mime who takes on the character of her characters, leaving no impression on her audience of what she herself is. People would not recognize her in the street even if they had seen her perform the evening before. Her appearance was unremarkable: mid-brown hair, long, worn in a knot at the nape of her neck but easily transformable into other styles, grey eyes, pale skin. Once seen, easily forgotten, she often said of herself, but not to Maximo Tonelli.

'Then there are mimes like Dario Fo and his wife Franca Rame who project their own personalities. Fo is ebullient and outrageous and zany – and political. Franca Rame has a very forceful personality, too. She is tall with brilliant red hair and she wears flamboyant clothes, black fish-net tights, high black boots – '

'She is very sexy then?'

'Yes. Would you like some more coffee?'

'Thank you. I could drink coffee all day though Sophia – my wife – is trying to make me cut down. She says it is bad for my heart.' He smiled, as if he did not believe it. 'So you take these characters – who are they?'

'Anybody. Male or female.'

'You could do me?'

'I would need to study you more,' said Anna evasively.

He sat back, unbuttoning his jacket to show a shirt of the same whiteness as he had worn at the funeral. His suit was dark, too, but he had changed the black tie for a blue silk one. His black shoes were of a very fine leather, and well polished.

'I find all this very interesting. When you have your character, what then? What do you do?'

One-woman performances, she told him, anywhere she could, in small theatres and halls, sometimes even in rooms, for private parties.

'It can't be very lucrative?'

23

'Not particularly. I do a little teaching as well.'

'You teach here?' He was quick to put the question and she wondered if she should have asked their lawyer if using the premises for commercial reasons complicated their leases. Tonelli would be sure to think of everything, to seek out every loophole. 'In this house?' he added, as if he needed to be absolutely sure.

'Yes, here,' she said. She had three rooms, one of which she used as a studio. He said that he would like to see the other two. She presumed she could not refuse. They crossed the hall to her bedroom – another quiet room, with more shades of grey, and touches of yellow. She drew back, allowed him to stand in the doorway by himself, not wishing to see the room through his eyes, resenting his right to look into her private life. Earlier, she had warned Holly to stay calm and not let herself be provoked; now, she needed to caution herself.

'Very nicely done, too.' He nodded approval.

They then went to look at her studio, which was painted white, with a long mirror running along one side. The only furniture was a table, an upright chair and a barre.

'Is that for ballet?' She watched his body move in the mirror as he gesticulated.

She told him that she had trained as a dancer, with Ballet Rambert. He told her that he had thought she walked like a dancer.

'I damaged my knee in a skiing accident when I was twenty-five and had to give up.'

That must have been traumatic for her, he said, pivoting in the mirror so that now he presented his back to it. He was looking at her. His voice had been soft, and sympathetic, when he had spoken. His eyes sought hers but she lowered her head and moved towards the door. He followed. They returned to the sitting room to sit opposite one another.

'You have very little security in your life. Does that not worry you?'

'When you work freelance you don't expect security. Your grandfather didn't have security, did he, when he came here selling ice cream from a hand-wagon?'

24

'But he had a vision of something else. He didn't intend to sell ice cream all his life.'

'And I do.' She smiled.

His eyes raked her left hand. 'Have you been married?'

'Once, yes, a long time ago. It only lasted five years. He was an artist.' She glanced at the back wall.

'Your friend who painted the swimmer? You might have been too much alike?'

'Perhaps,' she said, amazed that she was allowing herself to discuss her personal life with this man. Her ex-husband had subsequently married a woman who had an artistic temperament but no artistic ambitions; she appreciated his work and supported him. It had proved to be a good marriage. At Christmas-time Anna received a card from them, designed by him, and when he had an exhibition in London she went to see it.

'I think you are a loner?' said Maximo Tonelli, whom she presumed never spent a week under any roof on his own. He had never lived anywhere but in the house across the road which was always full of people. 'It seems to me that is even more reason for you to think about security and about your future.'

She sat very still, something it was easy for her to do. Mime was half movement, but the other half was stillness.

'You have put a great deal of effort into your room,' he went on. 'It's a very beautiful room but you don't own it.'

'Owning or not owning doesn't bother me.'

'But in your old age it might.'

'Evangeline has survived without being a property owner.'

'Because the rents here have always been very low, I suspect. But I'm afraid you can hardly expect to go on paying such small amounts.'

'I realize that you have bought the house as a commercial proposition, Mr Tonelli.'

'Mrs Pemberton . . .'

'It is my maiden name.'

'Miss then – or Ms? How is anyone supposed to say that?'

'Miss will do fine.'

'Very well. Miss Pemberton, would you not like to own your own flat? Then you could do what you liked with it and know that you would never be put out? It would be better to pay a mortgage than to pay rent. It would make more economic sense.'

No one would give her a mortgage, she said; her income was not secure enough and she had no deposit to put down. Her parents had lived equally improvident lives – her father had been an inventor who had had brilliant ideas which had usually turned out to be inviable – and so they had had nothing material to pass on by way of inheritance. For the last year of her life her mother, who was by then a widow, had come to live here in this house with Anna.

Mr Tonelli, though, had a solution, as she had expected. He could arrange a mortgage through a finance company, and a deposit, too, at very favourable rates.

'But I like it here, Mr Tonelli. It's my home. You of all people must appreciate what that means. I have been here for more than ten years.'

He rose. 'Think it over, Miss Pemberton. If you are ever going to make a move and buy a place of your own then this is the time to do it. Otherwise, it might be too late. And remember – I am willing to help you.'

She went with him out on to the landing. Before making his way up the next flight of stairs, he took a quick look at the three rooms standing empty on this floor. Until six months ago they had been inhabited by an Australian woman who had left to return home. At that stage Dorothea had not been interested in new tenants and the other women had agreed to allow those rooms, and three others on the top floor also recently vacated, to lie empty. Anna wished now that they had filled them. They could be doing with all the support they could muster to help them to stand up to the Tonellis. She was certain that the docility with which the King had appeared to accept rejection was misleading.

When his feet had ceased to ring on the marble, she went back into her room and sat down. She felt curiously drained.

The first thing that confronted Maximo Tonelli when he

stepped inside Holly's room was an outsize grainy reproduction of Elvis Presley's face. He stared at the slickly glistening black hair and the thick lips curled into a half-smile then he shifted his gaze to the poster alongside it. It was a second world war recruiting poster for the United States Navy. A saucy looking girl wearing a sailor suit with a plunging V-neckline was saying, 'Gee!! I wish I were a man. I'd join the navy.' Underneath the caption read: 'Be a man and do it.'

Maximo Tonelli turned to look quizzically at Holly.

'It must be great to be a man,' she said.

'You think so?'

They were shouting at one another; the strains of 'Jailhouse Rock' were belting through the room.

'Sure,' she yelled, raising her thumb.

'Can you turn that down?' He indicated with his hand and she went to the tape recorder and flipped the switch. The silence took a moment to adjust to. Holly spoke first.

'If you're a man you'd get to fight in the war and things.' He glanced pointedly at an anti-nuclear poster and she grinned. 'Did you fight in the war?'

'I was too young.' He answered curtly, as if he did not like to be questioned himself. 'So you're an Elvis Presley fan?'

'I find half of him yucky, the other half turns me on. The music's O.K., the face isn't.'

'Why look at it then?'

'I like to annoy myself.'

He raised his thick black eyebrows then he put his back to her again and resumed his patrol. She folded her arms across her chest to stop her hands trembling and hummed 'The Yellow Rose of Texas' under her breath. One of these days she would go to Texas. She tried to picture the wide open spaces and the hot sky above but she couldn't fit the image over the one of the silver-haired man with the black eyebrows prowling up and down her walls. She didn't have to feel nervous of him, she told herself sternly; he couldn't do anything, Anna had said so. But those hooded eyes frightened her. And he did own the place. People who owned things could usually do what they wanted.

Tonelli passed the Golden Gate and the lights of downtown

27

New Orleans and stopped at Mae West, head cocked to one side.

'I think she's great,' said Holly, who wished she didn't have to keep talking. How great it must be to be the strong silent type. 'Is that a gun you're carrying?' She laughed. Cool it, you dumb cluck! Fancy saying that to him! He might get ideas. And she must have sounded like a hyena with that laugh. Though what on earth did a hyena sound like? She must ask Evvie. She knew everything. *He* was still standing there. 'Do you like Mae West, Mr Tonelli?'

'I've never thought about it.'

'I'm crazy about old movies. I don't like colour. Lucky, isn't it? Because I can't afford a coloured telly. On my old black-and-white box everything looks like an old movie. Even *Dynasty*. What do you think of Alexis, Mr Tonelli – Joan Collins? Your granddaughter's called after her, isn't she? Georgie's daughter. Do you think she's sexually attractive? Joan Collins, I mean, not your granddaughter. It's O.K. – I guess you haven't thought about it.' She was prepared to bet that he had – she could imagine him watching *Dynasty* and *Dallas* and she could imagine him watching the women closely – but he wasn't going to tell her. He wasn't going to tell her anything about what was going on inside his head. Now Anna, she could read people's minds. She said you had to stay very still and absorb every movement they made, every flicker of their eyelids, but Holly found it difficult to stay still, or silent. Old Rattlemouth, she called herself. She narrowed her eyes until she could see Tonelli only as a kind of blur. He appeared to be floating.

With one arm behind his back he skated past the New York skyline, the Grand Canyon, Ronald Reagan embracing Margaret Thatcher, the cactus-dotted desert of Wyoming, black-clothed Menonites riding home from church in a black carriage, an advert for the Sunset Motor Inn somewhere in Idaho, a huddle of American football players closing in on a tackle. He stopped again. She had to open her eyes; they were hurting.

'I'm crazy about American football. See those shoulders –

six feet wide! Wow! They're like space men, real way out. They turn me right on.'

'You seem to be crazy about America?'

She shrugged. 'I'd like to go there. I guess I will, sometime.'

He stood in front of the window now, with his back to the light, looking into the room, at her assorted bits of furniture ancient and modern (but none new), at the old cash register, the wooden rocking horse with a missing ear and docked tail, the stack of china plates (mostly chipped), the bakelite clock with one hand, the piles of old damask curtains and tablecloths with bobbled ends and candlewick bedspreads that nobody wanted now that they slept under continental quilts. He made no comment. Bending over, he lifted the top book from a pile and held it edge on in front of him to read the title. '*The Member of the Wedding*. Is it romance?'

'You've got to be joking!'

'You don't like romances?'

'Boy meets girl and all that stuff! Used to read them when I was twelve. Even then I didn't believe them. But that's a great book, that one. It's by a woman called Carson McCullers. She's a Yank.'

'Do you read a lot?'

'Yeah. Didn't have the chance to read too much before I came here. Evvie – Miss Hudson – lends me books. She's trying to educate me!'

He picked up another book. '*On the Further Shore* by Evangeline Hudson.' He flipped through the pages. 'Is it good?'

'I don't know,' she said and immediately felt disloyal to Evangeline. 'Yes, it's pretty good. It's about two women and it runs on for quite a long time, about their feelings and things and the ripples on the shore of this lake. I guess it's how they wrote then. Not too much happens, at least it hasn't so far. I haven't finished it yet.'

He was glancing around as if searching for a chair. She uncovered a green-and-gold wicker one and dragged it forward. She loved these old wicker bedroom chairs, was always on the look-out for them.

29

'Take a pew,' she said and throwing a leg over the rocking horse, seated herself on the saddle. 'Giddy up!' She rocked gently to and fro.

'What age are you, Holly?'

'What's it to you? And don't bother telling me to go home to me mum for she wouldn't want to know.'

'How long have you lived here?'

'A year.'

'Have you got a job?'

'I work in a pizza joint, six to midnight, five days a week. *Pavarotti's*. I guess you know it? He's Italian, too.' She liked working in the evenings, coming home when everybody had gone to bed, and it gave her the days to herself to roam around the junk shops and yards and to sit curled up in her gold wicker chairs reading or watching old movies.

'You seem to be a very self-reliant girl.'

She kept rocking, to and fro, to and fro, each time pushing the horse's head a bit further forward, so that her own head moved with it, up and down, up and down, going nearer and nearer to the floor in front. She was irritating him but he didn't want to annoy her by asking her to stop, not yet, at any rate. He was trying to butter her up. Soft soap her. Well, she wasn't going to let him get her in a lather, ha, ha! Silly old thing thinking she didn't know what he'd come for! She laughed.

'Something amusing you?'

'Just a joke inside my head. I often have jokes inside my head, don't you?'

'I want you to listen to me, Holly.' He spoke softly. 'A young girl like you should be leading a different kind of life –'

'Is that a fact? Why should you try to tell me what way to live? I don't want to tell you. You can sit starkers in your front garden counting your gold bars for all I care.'

'Wouldn't you like to live with some young people of your own age? A nice hostel perhaps – '

'Cut the cackle, Mr Tonelli!' Holly brought the horse to an abrupt halt by putting both feet down on the floor. 'You don't give a shit about me. I know why you've come – you want to evict me but you ain't gonna.'

'We shall see about that.' He smiled.

30

'I know my rights.'

'But perhaps you will be persuaded to see reason.' He stood. 'I shall have to raise the rent, you know.'

'If you raise it too high we'll go to the Rent Tribunal.'

'You've got all the answers, haven't you? What's so marvellous about living here? Most girls of your age would want to be in a flat with other girls having a good time.'

'I like it here,' she said fiercely. 'I've been happier here than I've ever been anywhere else.'

When he had gone, Holly ran down to collect Anna and together they went to see Evangeline, who was standing by her sitting-room window with the curtain held back to the side.

'He didn't look too happy,' she reported. 'I waved to him as he was going out. I could see he was bristling!'

'Looks like it's round one to us.' Holly raised her thumb.

But only round one, Anna reminded them; the King of Naples was not going to be so easily defeated. He would be at home now talking to Sophia.

He is in a rage. He stamps up and down.

He addresses Sophia.

Don't worry, Sophia! They will not get away with it!

Three women like them! Who do they think they are to defy me – the great Maximo Tonelli!

Soon we shall proceed to round two! I have plenty of other tricks up my sleeve!

THREE

Evangeline remembered her vow not to die intestate and summoned her lawyer the next day.

'I kept telling you you should make a will,' said Mr Partridge 'and you kept telling me you had nothing worth leaving.'

'I'm sure I didn't say *nothing* worth leaving. I would never have regarded my books as nothing.'

'You have a few other bits and pieces that must be worth a penny or two. And then there's your annuity, small as it is, and your royalties – '

'Small as they are.'

'And your Public Lending Right. It all adds up.'

'Why did you keep telling me then it was a pittance?'

'It's not exactly a fortune. And you can't live very high on it.'

'I don't require to live high, as you well know. As long as I can afford my madeira and cigarillos and a few small but nice things to eat, I don't want much else.'

People like herself were a trial to him, she knew, for he, who earned a fortune compared to her, had a struggle to manage, and was continuously overdrawn, by the time he paid a thumping big mortgage for a thumping big house, school fees and ballet lessons and music lessons for his three children, and two holidays abroad every year, one at Easter to Austria or Switzerland for the skiing, the other in high season to a high-priced Mediterranean resort. Apparently, two holidays abroad per year were now *de rigueur*. Evangeline enjoyed hearing about other people's habits and customs: it made her feel happy to live her own life. She and Dottie used to travel on the continent, but in very modest fashion, staying in cheap

32

pensions that had no private bathrooms and certainly no swimming pools and poolside bars. Mrs Partridge had started to bring home brochures on the Caribbean and the Seychelles and to talk about friends who were just back from the Maldives, or Bali. When Mr Partridge sat by Evangeline's fire, relaxing with a glass of madeira, he liked to unwind and talk out his troubles. He enjoyed her room, he said, even though he did think she ought to throw out all those old newspapers, and he found her easy to confide in, even though he was not a man who spoke easily of personal matters. It must be because she was a writer. He expected everyone told her their life histories. She listened but was not so foolish as to give him advice, such as that he ought to change his way of life – or his wife. Either course would involve more upheaval than he would be willing to endure.

'Ah well!' He sighed and yawned. The fire and the wine had made him sleepy.

'You should tell your wife you're going to Butlin's this year, that holiday camps are in.'

'She's not that naive,' he said, becoming defensive at a hint of criticism towards his wife from someone else. He unbuckled his briefcase. 'Now are you sure you want to leave everything to these friends? Haven't you got any cousins or great-nephews or nieces anywhere?'

'I might have one or two but I haven't seen them for years. They send me cards at Christmas with their love on although I don't think they can be hopeful. I was always known in the family as the improvident one. They thought that if I was going to spend my time writing the least I could do was to get married. But marriage had no appeal for me.'

'Blood's thicker than water, remember!'

'That's easily tripped off the tongue.'

He held up his hands in an attitude of surrender. 'All right! So you want to leave your estate to Miss Pemberton and this girl Holly. How long have you known her?'

'You sound suspicious, Mr Partridge! Do you think that Holly might be a fortune hunter? The next thing you know she'll be plotting to do me in!'

'As long as *you* know what you're doing.'

33

'I'm sorry, I do realize I test you sorely.'

'You're not the easiest client I've got.'

'I'm sure not. Though who would want to be that?'

He smiled and shook his head.

On his way out, after he had taken down the details and promised to return the following week with the will ready for signing, he crossed in the porch with Mr Maximo Tonelli, who was coming in to see Miss Hudson. Evangeline, standing at her half-closed door, heard the rise and fall of their voices and caught disconnected words and phrases like stubborn, commonsense, sheltered, old age. Mr Partridge then said, rather more loudly, 'I'm afraid, Mr Tonelli, I can do nothing to help you. Miss Hudson will do exactly what she wants to do, that is my experience.'

Mr Tonelli did not spend any time today contemplating her literary life, he came straight to the point. He had come to make her an offer. He was prepared to give her a thousand pounds to vacate her rooms, and the other offer of a place in a sheltered housing block still stood.

'Goodness me, Mr Tonelli! Two handsome offers which I'm sure you feel I can hardly refuse. But I shall, thank you so much all the same. I have no need of a thousand pounds, strange as that might seem to you.'

'Two thousand? It would buy you a few extra comforts for your old age.'

He did not persist for long, he must have known he would have little chance of buying her. But they were both aware that if he could crack even one of them he would be on his way to getting what he wanted. He stood at the door for a moment with his hand on the knob, his lips pursed in a manner she was coming to recognize.

'I hope you'll leave the other two free to decide for themselves, Miss Hudson. It would be very selfish of you to try to influence them to stay on for your sake. They're a lot younger than you are and deserve the chance to spread their wings. Especially a young girl like Holly.'

He went upstairs to Anna.

Evangeline wondered how much freedom he had given his daughters before their marriage; if they had attempted to fly he would have nailed them firmly to the nest, she fancied. She pottered around the room switching on the lamps and closing the velvet curtains which had faded almost to white at the edges; the afternoon was drawing in. It had been dark and wet for most of the day and she had not ventured out for her usual walk to the end of the street. The days were shortening, with the approach of another winter. Whenever she moved pain flashed like forked lightning through her hip. She stayed still for a moment to catch her breath. She supposed she should have that hip operation but then there were her knees, too. Falling to pieces, Evvie old girl, that's what you're doing!

She thought of what Maximo Tonelli had said. He was right: she should not be selfish, she should think of Anna and Holly, for she was old and they were not. Anna was still in mid-life and should seriously consider buying a place of her own so that she would be free of landlords and the threat of eviction. But if Anna were to go what would become of her? She laid a hand against her throat and felt a pulse jump under her fingers. I must *not* be selfish, she told herself, I must tell Anna to do what is best for her, I must release her from any obligation towards me. I cannot bind her to me like a nurse-maid, she did enough for Dottie. And I myself might not have many years left. Indeed, she could not hope to have, and did not wish, anyway, to end up like poor old Dottie. Most definitely not! But by the time she did depart this world Anna might have lost her chance.

And then there was the child Holly on the top floor. She, however, had no need yet of flats of her own or to think of security; she was young, and a free spirit, and could afford to stay here for a while – if she wished. Holly had years ahead of her in which to manœuvre and move on to other things. Cheered by the thought, Evangeline took *Middlemarch* (her favourite novel) and a packet of cigarillos and went to enjoy both by the fire.

The King of Naples was tired: Anna saw that he was as soon as he entered her room. When she had opened the door to his knock and seen him standing there she had resolved not to offer him any refreshment, or detain him in any way. They

35

might stand up to conduct their business. As far as she was concerned, five minutes should suffice. But whenever someone came to visit her, no matter for how short a time, she felt impelled to offer something. Because she didn't feel she was sufficient in herself? The thought had occurred to her.

'A cup of tea?' she said now and Maximo Tonelli accepted, settling himself on the settee exactly where he had sat before, going back to it as if it were his accustomed place. He sank down with a sigh and passed his hand over his eyes. His day had been tiresome: he had driven a long way to find that one of his managers had absconded, taking the previous weeks' takings with him. 'He was not a member of the family. That was the mistake I made.'

'I suppose, though, even your family must have its limits?'

'That is very true.' He smiled briefly, put his head back against the settee and closed his eyes.

Anna switched on two low-set lamps and went to the window to draw the curtains. As she looked out, a light sprang on in the ground floor of the Villa Neapolitana, and then she saw a woman's arm come up and catch hold of the edge of the curtain and pull it across the window. The movement was a quick, decisive one. She saw the woman's face for only a moment but was sure that it was Sophia.

They drank their tea, Tonelli sipping his slowly with the air of one who intended to stay for a while, Anna silently scolding herself for having given way to the impulse of offering hospitality. She felt guilty – here she was taking tea with the enemy! Evangeline had taken madeira with him, she reminded herself. Evangeline maintained that it was easier to disarm the enemy by charming rather than riling him. Anna suspected that the King of Naples thought likewise. Holly said that if she were to give him anything she would spike it with arsenic or ground glass. While Anna and her visitor sipped they listened to Dennis Brain playing Mozart's *Horn Concerto*; she had just put the record on the turntable when he knocked on the door.

'A great performer,' said Tonelli, when the record ended. 'A pity he died so young. Can you play the other side?'

Anna found herself getting up and turning the record over.

Tonelli moved his head a little, keeping the rhythm of the music.

He liked classical music, he told her, Mozart, Bach, Vivaldi, Verdi; he was no good with modern composers, they all sounded jangled to him. A common complaint, said Anna, though not unsympathetically. He liked to listen to music in his car, especially to opera; he had to drive many hundreds of miles in a week, visiting his businesses in other towns. That was one of the secrets of success in business: to keep an eye on everything personally, never to think that you could relax and leave it to others.

'I expect, though, your sons are a great help to you?'

He nodded. 'Roberto especially. He has a good business head. Giorgio likes his fish and chip shop, Claudio his restaurant. It is an excellent restaurant, by the way, very fine cuisine. You must go there one evening, all three of you ladies – it will be on the house. But it is Roberto who will succeed me when I retire. Which will not be for many years yet.' He set aside his cup. 'That was good.' He appeared refreshed, sat up straight and turned the full beam of his stare upon her. 'You know, I'm curious about this mime of yours. I would like to see you perform.'

'I doubt if you would be interested,' said Anna quickly and picked up the teapot to refill their cups, thinking again how ridiculous it was to be playing at tea parties with someone whose intention it was to destroy the very structure of their lives. The tea overflowed into the saucer. She put down the pot. 'What was it you wanted to see me about, Mr Tonelli?'

He asked if she had remembered their conversation of the other day? Well, naturally, she said, but she had not changed her mind, and would not, so there was no point in his trying to persuade her. She did not tell him that she had lain awake the previous night thinking about the idea of having a place of her own. And had been tempted. She loved this house, but if Evangeline were to die and Holly to move on – and both events must be expected sometime – she would be left alone here. She was in her mid-forties, not so young any more. There was to be no question of her giving in, however; the

37

three of them had agreed to stand together and she would not be the one to collapse, bringing the other two down with her. In addition, she was attached to them: they were her family. How would he like it if he had to break up his family home? She put the question to him.

'That is different. We are all related to one another by blood. And I do own the house.'

She had no answer to make to his last statement. Possession so obviously meant much to him.

He said, 'But listen, Miss Pemberton, I have come to offer an extra inducement. A gift of a thousand pounds.'

'Bribery and corruption!'

He did not see it in that way. It would be in the form of compensation, for any inconvenience caused, and to help with removal expenses, though when it came to the move itself he would be happy to arrange free transport.

'Have you got every area of life sewn up, Mr Tonelli?'

'Hardly! What do you say then to my offer? I am prepared to go to two.'

She spread open the palms of her hands and shrugged her refusal.

'You are very sure for someone who has so little security.'

She refused to be drawn any further on the subject. He continued to sit on the settee, the lids of his eyes pulled half way down, making no effort to go. It was almost six when he finally drew himself up and said he had better move on. He must go upstairs to see Holly and then get back across the road. They were having a party tonight, for his daughter Guilia, who was twenty-five today.

'You've missed Holly, I'm afraid,' said Anna. 'She'll have gone to work by now. But I'll tell her you called. Shall I tell her also about your offer?'

He knew that he could not prevent her but she could see that he was irritated. He should have worked his timetable out better, not sat so long drinking tea and listening to Mozart, for now he would lose the advantage of surprise with Holly. She suspected it was unlike him to fudge a battle plan.

'Holly's a free person,' said Anna. 'I shan't attempt to influence her.'

38

Tonelli paused on the threshold of her room. 'Do you really expect to be able to stay on in this big house, just the three of you? Don't you think you're being unrealistic?'

'We would be happy to have tenants in the other rooms – as long as they were women.'

'What have you got against men?'

'Nothing. But we've found that the house has run smoothly with women.'

'Never any disruptions?'

'Well, of course. But seldom anything insoluble, or else the person involved has left. We keep for the most part to ourselves, we don't live in one another's pockets.'

He shook his head. 'I could not imagine living in a house of men.'

'Women enjoy the companionship of other women.'

'And I of men. I am close to my sons. But I like women in my life as well.' He went down the stairs.

Anna withdrew to her room. Two thoughts preoccupied her. The first was that he might move some of his male subjects into the vacant rooms by way of irritation factor, and she was distressed to think that, by stressing their preference for women tenants, she might have put the idea into his head. And then there was Holly and a thousand pounds. Perhaps even two. It was a lot of money for any of them but, to Holly, it would seem like winning the pools. On that she could go to America.

Anna realized that she had no real idea what either would do; both Holly and Tonelli were unpredictable. It was said that she could get inside other people's skins but that was true only in a fairly superficial way. When it came to discerning their deeper or more devious thoughts, she was as lost as anyone else.

That evening, she was restless, which was unusual for her. She heard the Tonelli cars arriving in the street and the slam of doors and the call of voices. Drawing back her curtain, she saw the doors of a car opening and a man and a girl emerging from either side. The girl's black hair shone under the street light. She was wearing a short fur jacket, possibly mink, and gold high-heeled shoes. She laughed and the man came round the back of the car to join her, and putting his hand under her elbow, guided her across the road. They moved together in perfect unison, like two people dancing. When the door of the Villa Neapolitana opened, the girl went into the embrace of the person who had opened it. It was the King himself. The door closed behind the couple.

Anna sat down with a book. She was rereading *A Room with a View*. She had been to Florence last month, had gone afterwards to Rome and then to the coast south of Sorrento. It was Sorrento that kept forcing its way into her thoughts now, pushing Florence out. She had stayed in a small fishing village huddled at the foot of a cliff and when there had thought idly of the Tonellis of previous generations, imagining them mending their nets and setting out into the shimmering Bay of Naples in small boats as the sun was spreading an orange glow across the horizon, returning in the cool quiet of early morning to their sparse dwellings. And now they sat in their luxurious villa drinking champagne and eating smoked salmon and caviar. What a leap they had made! She herself had made no great leaps in life, had moved from one stage to the other, from childhood to adolescence to adulthood to marriage to divorce without greatly breaking her stride. The end of her marriage had knocked her out of kilter, of course, but even then it had happened gradually and by mutual consent and, therefore, with the minimum of bitterness. Her feeling had been one of relief, mostly, when she had abandoned that life and come to live in Shangri-la. Here she had refound her own space.

While on the Sorrento coast, she had stayed in a small hotel next door to a bar where she liked to drink a nightcap before going up to bed. The manager of the bar, Eduardo, an older and puffier looking version of Dario Fo, worked desperately to try to attract custom to his terrace. He accosted tourists as they strolled past enjoying the night air, sometimes taking hold of their arms, saying, 'Come in, come and join us! How do you do? Eduardo welcomes you! Come in!' If there was no response he tried German or French. He had a few phrases in a number of languages. When the holidaymakers passed on, he called after them, 'Good night, good night! Enjoy the bed!', then he would turn away muttering, 'Fools!' He made a beeline for unmarried women, alone or in pairs, of a certain age. Young girls he left alone. He had made a beeline for Anna. He had come to her with his arms outstretched. 'How do you do, lady? You are beautiful, I have never seen anyone so beautiful.' He bent his head and kissed her hand and she blushed and laughed and although she knew that he must say the same things to many women she could not help but feel a little flattered. It was seldom that anyone at home told her she was beautiful. Rather to be told that with less than total sincerity than to be ignored. 'Ah yes, Anna, you are *bellissima!*' She accepted Eduardo as another component of the Italian evening. He sat beside her at the white wrought-iron table. He told her he was in love with her. He said that when she went away his heart would break. On going to bed, she thought of his words even though she did not believe them. She would have been a fool to believe them. But while she sat at the white table under the coloured umbrella and drank brandy and soda and watched the promenaders come and go she suspended disbelief.

He was a widower; his wife, before her death, had been ill for many years, but even before that their marriage had been empty. 'No sex, Anna! She was not interested in the bed. She had no passion. Now you, you have passion, I could see that the first time you walked on to my terrace.' She found him attractive in spite of the air of failure that beset him and was tempted to go to bed with him but knew that she would regret it afterwards. He would parade on his terrace like the cock of the walk. The bar boys would snigger at her. 'I would like to go away from here,' he told her. 'Far away, across the sea. I am tired of running this bar, I am tired of having to be nice to idiots. Would you take me home with you?' He would miss Italy, she told him – the food, the wine, the balmy warm evenings. 'No!' he cried. 'Not at all.' 'I have no money, Eduardo. I could not afford to take you home.' When they had said goodbye on the last morning, he stood waving until the bus turned the corner and left him behind. She took the memory of his defeated face with her all the way to the airport.

She put down *A Room with a View* and went back to the

41

window. The Tonelli party was in the big front room on the ground floor – the one, which in their house, Dorothea had used as a sitting room – and the curtains were open. The room was packed. People were moving around with glasses in their hands; some held plates. They were talking and laughing. Anna saw Maximo near the window with his head thrown back, as if he were enjoying a good joke. Perhaps the time he had spent in her room had helped him to recover his energy. Suddenly, he turned towards the window, away from the company in the room and looked out, and up. She drew back, afraid that he might have seen her. She felt like a child standing gazing into a sweet shop window, whereas she doubted if she would want the sweets on display were she to try them. With a quick flick of the wrist, she pulled the curtain into place and returned to her own world.

She stood in the centre of the room, uncertain as to what she would do. And then she decided: she would take a bus downtown and go and see Holly.

It was a slow night at *Pavarotti's Pizzas*. There was never a lot doing on wet nights, mid-week. Everyone but Holly moaned about coming in to work with wet feet and about customers leaving trails of footprints across the floor. Holly loved rain, the sound and the sight of it. 'Barmy, if you ask me,' said Jackie, the chief chef. When the drizzle swelled to a downpour, Holly went and stood by the door and watched the rain bouncing off the pavement. It mesmerized her, made her shiver with pleasure. She couldn't explain the sensation to Janice, the other waitress, said it was a bit like having it off with someone. 'You're terrible,' said Janice, giggling, covering her mouth with the corner of her orange nylon apron. Holly loved rain especially at night; it soothed her to drift into sleep to the sound of it falling. On those nights, her dreams were less lurid. Evangeline said she should go to India in monsoon-time. Dottie, when she'd been ill, had talked about monsoons in India, how streets had run with mud-coloured water. There was a heck of a lot to see in the world, thought Holly, as she stood at the door gazing into the shiny wet street.

Trade, when it did materialize, came in rushes and sent

Jackie's hands flying, working so fast with the dough that they seemed almost not to touch it, and then he'd toss it up to the ceiling where the hole had been especially cut out and all the while Steve would be chopping peppers and onions and mushrooms and whistling and Holly and Janice would be weaving in and out of the orange plastic tables in their orange uniforms scribbling down orders on their little white pads and balancing giant plates of pizza on their arms. And then it would go quiet again: the chefs would slouch against the wall behind the counter, the girls would perch on a table and chat. They discussed *Dynasty* and *Dallas* and *EastEnders* and both lamented that they couldn't see them more often. (They could just manage to see a bit of *Neighbours* before they came to work since it was on early.) Janice had a friend who owned a video and sometimes she would tape a programme and invite them round to view on Saturday afternoons, but mostly they had to rely on Janice's mother to keep them up with current developments in the soap world.

'I'm thinking of getting a daytime job,' said Janice. 'Well, you miss all the best things, don't you, by working nights?'

Holly sighed. She didn't like the idea of missing anything. Catching sight of herself in the mirror on the opposite wall, she straightened her orange hat which had the slogan *Pavarotti's Pizzas* printed in white across the front. She hated the uniform; the nylon was slippery and on hot nights made her sweat like a steamed duff, and the colour clashed nastily with her hair. Orange was her least favourite colour.

The door opened, and the girls looked round.

'It's Anna!' Holly launched herself off the table and went hurtling towards the door, panic jumping in her chest. 'Is anything wrong, Is Evvie all right?'

'She's fine.' Anna smiled. 'I just wanted to talk to you.'

There were booths down the right-hand side of the room. Anna slipped into one of these, near the door, and eased her coat off her shoulders.

'Want a coffee?' asked Holly.

'Do you know, I rather fancy a pizza?'

'One nine-inch with the works and double cheese,' Holly ordered and leant against the counter while Jackie made it.

'And make it real good 'cause this is for my aunt.'

Anna's pizza flew up in the air and landed neatly. Jackie had learned to throw pizzas in America; he'd spent a year in Miami, had started by cooking hot dogs on the waterfront but after his stand had been overturned by a bunch of hoodlums one night he had turned to pizzas. He had knocked off work at four in the morning, had lived in a rooming house sharing a room with another guy who worked days; he'd got up and Jackie had gone to bed and slept all day. How often had they changed the sheets? Holly had wanted to know and Jackie had said she wanted to know funny things. She objected that he couldn't have slept all day but he maintained that he had, more or less, except to go to the corner store to buy groceries and to cook himself a burger or a steak before going to work. He'd gone once to Disneyland, on his day off, but claimed he couldn't remember all that much about it. 'Just what you'd expect, really. Lot of people.' He exasperated Holly who had to drag information out of him, bit by tiny bit. 'You're not a lot of use to me,' she told him. 'Now come on, tell me *everything* you can remember! Think, Jackie, joggle your brain box!' Jackie said he didn't like thinking.

Holly carried the pizza and cup of coffee to Anna's table and slid into the seat opposite.

'So, what's new?'

Anna told her.

'A thousand quid! You've got to be joking. Do you *mean* it?'

'He might even go to two. It would be worth it to him to get us out.'

'Two thousand . . .' Holly's voice trailed away and her eyes went past Anna, into space.

'You are now arriving at John F Kennedy airport. Welcome to New York!'

The gangway is going up and the silver doors are opening and she is emerging into the open air, the open air of the United States of America! A band plays the Stars and Stripes and she waves and starts to walk slowly down the steps to the outstretched hands . . .

She is strolling down Fifth Avenue. It is night. The golden-spangled skyscrapers rake the sky far above her, their summits spinning when she throws back her head to gaze up at them.

44

*It's warm. Her arms are bare; she is wearing a white dress cut low
at the back to show her smooth bronzed skin. Her hair no longer
screams like a beacon; it has darkened and glistens like a polished
chestnut and it has been exquisitely cut so that it curls around her head
like a shell.*

*She is walking with a man, she has her arm through his. She
cannot see his face but he is tall and he is wearing a deep blue shirt and
white trousers and he is carrying his white jacket over his shoulder
with one finger caught through the loop . . .*

'Holly!' said Anna.

Holly saw that Anna had finished her pizza and was holding
her coffee cup between her hands and looking at her over the
rim.

'You must feel free to accept the money if you want to. It's a
lot of money and you might never be offered a thousand
pounds again.'

Anna left soon afterwards. Holly sat on in the booth.

*She is sitting on a Greyhound bus. They are in desert country. The
soil is red and the sun blistering overhead. The cactuses stand ten feet
high, the buzzards wheel . . .*

'Hey, Holly! Customers!'

She blinked. Steve was waving at her and making a face. For
a moment she could not think who he was, then the room with
its orange tables swam into view and she got up and went to
serve two women who took ten minutes to decide what
combinations they wanted. She was furious, too, when she
saw that while she'd been on the Greyhound bus travelling
through Arizona Janice had picked up a prized customer.
Janice wiggled her hips as she moved through the tables taking
his order to the counter. He was a boy of about eighteen or
nineteen, and both Holly and Janice fancied him. Holly
thought he was absolutely beautiful. He had thick blond hair
and round, china blue eyes and a pink and gold face. He looked
as if he'd been lying on a beach in Hawaii. She could imagine
him riding a surf board, the waves parting on either side to
throw up a halo round him. There was a kind of fresh,
untouched look about him. She had never seen such a perfect
face on a boy before.

'Missed your chance over there, didn't you? Sitting dream-

ing and letting Janice land lover boy,' said Jackie, whose face
was slack around the jowls and whose nose was peppered with
blackheads.

'Two mushroom and ham,' said Holly. 'And Janice hasn't
landed him. He's still swimming, as far as I can see. Hey, how
much is a ticket to New York, Jackie, do you know?'

'I hear you can get some real cheap deals these days, as low
as ninety-nine quid.'

'Ninety-nine! That settles it then.'

'Come into money?'

'Matter of fact, I have. That's what my aunt came in to tell
me. My grandmother's well connected, you see. Her father
had a title. He was a lord.'

'Janice says she writes books?'

'She used to, when she was younger. Novels.'

Holly served the two women then went back to take up her
stance by the door where she could gaze into the street. When
the boy with the perfect face passed on his way out he smiled at
her and cut through her dream of New Mexico which was
where she had just arrived.

'He smiled at me,' she told Janice afterwards.

'He did at me, too. *More* than once. I had a feeling he was
trying to ask me out but he seems kind of shy.'

At five minutes to twelve Janice locked the door and turned
the CLOSED sign out and then they sat down to their own
pizza suppers. Holly had bacon and pineapple and green
peppers with triple cheese. She was starving. She usually was.
Janice's mother thought she might have worms, she was so
skinny, but Holly thought Janice's mother thought that
because she and Janice were plump, like butter. They didn't
speak while they ate their pizzas and drank their cokes. Holly
was thinking about steaks. She was worried about them.
Everywhere you'd go people would give you steak: rib,
sirloin, Chateaubriand, filet, T-bone. Two inches thick, with
the blood oozing out of them seeping across your plate to stain
your baked potato and sour cream pink. Holly shuddered and
Jackie asked what was the matter and didn't she like her pizza?
'It's great,' she said. But even to think of steak made her want
to throw up. She couldn't stand the idea of eating flesh and

gristle and bits of bone and clots of blood. In an American novel she'd read the people had eaten steak at every meal; that was how she knew about all the different kinds.

'Jackie, do you think it'll matter if I say I don't like steak?' He looked blank and she added, 'When I go to the States?'

'Naw, they won't think nothing of it. There's no law says you gotta eat steak. You like pizza, don't you?'

'Sure do.'

'There you are then! They make great pizza.'

They tidied up and took off their overalls. Steve sang, 'Show me the way to go home, I'm tired and I want to go to bed.' Janice yawned showing the maw of her throat down to her tonsils. A taxi came to pick up Jackie and Steve and Janice. Holly wheeled Evangeline's bicycle out of the backyard. She preferred to come and go by her own transport and she liked the night ride home.

The rain had stopped and a low pall of mist hung over the town. The sodium street lights threw their glare into the oily puddles. The centre was deserted; it was a town in which people lived as far out as they could afford. Steve, who was married with a baby, coveted a cottage in one of the outlying commuter villages, with a green and a nice school his kid could go to when she was old enough and a pub where he could play darts and swig pints in front of the fire.

Holly cycled up the High Street, past the record shops and clothes shops and the hi-fi centres, all shuttered and dark, except for the odd spotlight that illuminated their windows (in New York the shops would stay open all night), going through the red lights since there was nobody about. She felt like an idiot waiting alone at a stoplight. A drunk lurched out of a doorway and zigzagged across the road in front of her making her swerve. She pealed her bell at him noisily but he paid no attention. Further up, she stopped at a leather shop and picked out a white leather jacket which she thought would be great to travel in. In the next window she inspected cameras on display. She would have to buy a camera; nobody would ever travel without one.

At the top of the High Street she turned left into a narrow street, the location of a number of restaurants, upmarket ones

47

that served high-class food, not like their two-bit joint. Claudio Tonelli's was amongst them. There it was, with the name painted in green and gold: CLAUDIO's. Even the lettering looked expensive. A far cry from *Pavarotti's Pizzas*, that was for sure. As she approached, Claudio himself backed out of the doorway, locking the green door behind him. He did not see her, would probably not have recognized her if he had. He walked on to the next corner where a man was waiting for him. Claudio slipped his arm through the man's and they went off together.

So that was the way of it! Holly wondered if the King of Naples knew that one of his princes was bent. Anna said she shouldn't use that word, not in that way. Anna was careful not to speak offensively of anyone. Now, Jackie, he still talked about niggers. He couldn't stand the niggers in Miami, he said; that was why he had left. Holly didn't believe that; she thought it was because of having to share a bed with another guy.

She stopped off at Giorgio's chip shop. It was about to close but there was a scoopful of chips left in the basket which Giorgio let her have for nothing. He was wearing his dark suit tonight, and a wide yellow silk tie, picked out for him by his wife Mary-Lou. She bought all his ties. And his socks and his Boxer shorts. She loved shopping. Holly told Giorgio he looked dead spivvy. He'd been at his sister Guilia's birthday party earlier.

'Guess what, Georgie? I'm going to go to the US of A!'

'You're not! When?'

'Soon as I can get myself sorted out. It's true, though, I'm not kidding you this time.'

She couldn't keep up with Giorgio's bolide on the way home; it streaked off away up ahead of her, its rear lights gleaming, and by the time she reached their street, it had vanished inside the six-car garage at the side of the Villa Neapolitana. There were lights on Giorgio's floor, none on the ground or top.

There was a glimmer of bluish light at Evangeline's bedroom window. She must be awake, and reading. She slept badly, though was cheerful about it, said it gave her a chance to pack in some extra reading, or to listen to the World Service on the radio. It gave her extra time for living. Why waste time sleeping at her age? Often, when Holly came home and saw Evangeline's light on, she would go in and sit on the bed and they'd talk, about all sorts of things. Books, films, Evvie's life, Holly's life, the state of the world.

Tonight, Holly got off Evangeline's bike at the gate and carried it to the front door so that the tires wouldn't scrunch on the gravel. She opened the front door carefully and took her time closing it. She waited for a moment and listened. Evangeline mustn't have heard her. Sometimes, if she did, she would call out.

Holly tiptoed up the stairs.

FOUR

In spite of her difficulties in hearing, Evangeline heard the quiet click of the front door; she had been anticipating it. Sitting up in bed, hands clenching the book on her lap, she listened, and waited. What was Holly going to do? Would she come in, or go straight up the stairs? Evangeline heard no other sound coming from the hallway, even though she held her breath and concentrated hard. All she did hear was the stupid buzz in her ears, which, if she paid any attention to it, mounted in volume until its noise resembled a boiling cauldron. She missed the pleasure of low-keyed sounds: the patter of soft rain, a gently spoken word, a quiet passage in music. It was like being in a fog, when one knows that there is something out there but cannot quite discern what it is. One of these days she would have to get around to seeing if she qualified for a hearing aid. She hated outings to the doctor's surgery for he always took the opportunity to harangue her on all the things she was doing and shouldn't, like smoking and drinking, and all the things she should be doing and wasn't, like coming to him for regular blood pressure check-ups.

Holly must have gone upstairs. She was probably tired, and no wonder, after all those hours on her feet running after tiresome people. But it was unlike her not to put her head round the door and say goodnight. Evangeline was disappointed, but more than that, apprehensive. She could see only two reasons for Holly's behaviour: either she had not decided what to do about the money and didn't want to discuss it, or she'd decided to take it. Evangeline inclined to the second view. Holly was not a dilly-dallier; she made up her mind quickly. Evangeline moved sharply, knocking the book from

50

her lap, and before she could retrieve it, it had slid to the floor. She cursed.

Now she would have to get up; there was no question of her sleeping for a long while yet. Turning back the bedclothes, she eased her legs carefully over the edge of the bed and felt around with her feet for her slippers. Then she pushed herself upright. A fall, when getting out of bed, resulting in lying on the floor until morning and Anna's arrival, had taught her to move cautiously. She hated caution, it went against her nature. She hated much of what constituted old age but still treasured enough of it to want to hold on grimly. When she didn't, she would let herself go. Like a balloon soaring up into the sky. At the thought of such lightness, she smiled.

She pulled on her dressing gown, switched on the electric fire and then the kettle for a cup of camomile tea. She and Dottie had first acquired a taste for camomile on a skiing holiday in Austria; they'd drunk it each day when they came back from the slopes. The landlady of the gasthof had said it was good for calming the nerves, which had made them laugh once she had gone out of the room. There was nothing wrong with their nerves! They loved the exhilaration of gliding down the smooth, white slopes, through the dark fir trees, feeling the sun on their faces. Evangeline remembered the sensation now and put her hands to her cheeks. And felt the sag of the flesh beneath her fingers. She let them drop. The resort she and Dottie had gone to had been small and fairly disorganized, unlike the ones she read about nowadays. But it had been fun. Yes, great fun. They had laughed a lot. 'You have millions of memories,' Holly had said to her, Holly who was greedy for memories – of a kind she would want to remember. Memories, even good ones, could be both consoling and disturbing, Evangeline had told her.

Anna, as always, was first to stir in the morning. She rose, did a few minutes of limbering up exercises at the barre in her studio, then she showered and dressed, and by eight o'clock was sitting at her window eating wholemeal toast and drinking coffee and half listening to the radio news. She was also watching the movement in the street.

51

Two women in headscarves, their shoulders pulled down by shopping bags, passed after their early morning cleaning stint at the nursing home. One had a cigarette hanging from the edge of her mouth and with each few steps she took she coughed and her chest twitched, jerking her head forward as if it were controlled by a string. They would have entered the street around six, these two women, when it was still dark and quiet, and their heels would have rung out on the pavement. A motor bike roared through, swerving round the parked cars, going much too fast, causing the women to lift and shake their scarved heads. And now, on the left-hand side of the frame, a large dog was appearing, its snout pushed forward, its body elongated, as it towed along a small, elderly man, who was bent backwards with the effort of holding the animal on its leash.

Then the door of the Tonellis' garage slid up and back, and the gleaming, red nose of the King's Ferrari eased out. It was a beautiful machine, thought Anna, moving her head back to make sure it would not show at the edge of the curtain. She could see the appeal of the car even though she had little familiarity with machines, owning neither a clothes nor a dish washer, nor a personal computer. She had never even learned to drive. There had been no point since she could not afford a car. It did not irk her; she liked travelling by public transport, it gave her time to study people. But she realised that by many people's standards, her life would be accounted a failure. By the King of Naples, for example.

The glossy car stood now in the street, throbbing gently, ready for take-off. Its driver was pulling on his gloves (pigskin, she thought), adjusting his driving mirror, fixing his seat belt. The noise of the engine swelled and the car began to move and quickly to gather speed and in the next instant was flashing along the street – a red streak – and was gone. The sound lingered in Anna's ears. Five minutes later, Roberto's silver Alfa Romeo slid out and swept away in the wake of the Ferrari. Maximo was always five minutes ahead of his son.

Anna knew the makes of the cars through Holly, who loved speed and coveted a Lamborghini. It was partly the name, she admitted, which she enunciated slowly, lingering on each syllable, after Anna had taught her how to pronounce it. Anna wondered if Holly still slept. There was no sound from upstairs. Holly slept often until mid-morning, as did the Tonelli brothers, Giorgio and Claudio. The curtains were closed on the top floor of the Villa Neapolitana.

At half-past eight, the postman appeared in the street. Outside Shangri-la he stopped to shuffle through his letters, then came up the path. Anna ran down to meet him.

He had a letter for Evangeline, from Egypt; two for Anna, one with a Devon postmark, the other, London; nothing for Holly. There was seldom anything for Holly, unless it was a circular. She appeared to have no tangible ties to any part of her past. Though she longed to get letters. Once, Evangeline had written her a long letter, of a dozen pages, and posted it in the box at the end of the street. Holly had been delighted. And on her seventeenth birthday they had sent their cards to her through the post.

Anna laid Evangeline's letter on the hall table and took her own up to her room. She opened first the Devon letter, which was from her friend Charlotte. She and Charlotte had been students together and danced in the *corps de ballet*. Charlotte had been exceptionally talented and been tipped to go far, and then in her early twenties had married a farmer and whole-heartedly given herself up to country life, without any regrets for what might have been. She gave birth to two sets of twins, one lot female, the other male. Charlotte had always been able to get things to work out neatly for her. She wrote, with verve, of country and familial matters. The writing looked as if it had been dashed down while she stirred the apple jelly with the other hand and watched the cows through the window. Charlotte's letter brought the smell of the country into Anna's room and made her yearn for the sight of a cow in a meadow. 'You must come down and stay,' Charlotte finished up, 'and get some colour in those cheeks.'

The other envelope contained a card; an invitation to Julian's next exhibition which was to be held in London in two weeks' time. He had written on the back, 'Hope you can make it.'

She propped the card up on the mantlepiece and began to

make preparations for her day. This evening, she was to perform in a town thirty miles away and so would set off in the middle of the afternoon to give herself time to see that everything was in order: that the chairs had been put out and the hall had been cleaned and the heating turned on. On the occasions that she played within the framework of an arts centre she could arrive an hour beforehand, confident that the details would have been taken care of; she would have nothing to do but perform. But, tonight, she would be her own stage and box office manager. When Holly had an evening off that coincided, she came with her. Holly loved organizing the audience.

Around ten, Anna went down to see Evangeline, who was awake but still in bed.

'Stay where you are, while I make your tea and toast.'

'You spoil me, Anna!'

When Anna brought the tray and sat down on the edge of the bed, Evangeline said, 'Anna, you must take the two thousand pounds and the chance to buy your own flat. Now don't say anything! Or I shall get upset and spill my tea. I've been thinking, and I want you to think again. It may be your only chance. And I don't want you to worry about me, I shall be fine in the sheltered home. Perhaps I shall even get to like it. Human beings are infinitely adaptable, you know.'

'You're not thinking of going into sheltered housing?'

'Indeed I am. It will be nice to have somewhere that is properly warm in winter instead of having to sit huddled over the fire. I'm beginning to feel the cold dreadfully. And I want Holly to take the money, too. The poor child hasn't had many breaks in life. I've written a letter to tell her to go ahead. You might put it on the hall table for her.'

'Oh, by the way,' said Anna, 'there's a letter for you, from Egypt.'

Evangeline saved her letter until after she'd bathed and dressed; it was something to look forward to with her mid-morning cup of coffee. She believed in lining up treats to help structure her day. The letter would be from her old friend, Augustus; they'd kept up a lifelong correspondence. They had played together as children, kept one another company at the ghastly parties which they had both detested, escaping the moment they saw a gap in the organizational set-up to go running round the garden or scrambling through the woods, to return with grazed elbows and scuffed velvet knees and mangled organdy bows. And then, when they reached adolescence, they learned to dance together, treading on each other's toes, and laughing until they thought they would burst so that they had to excuse themselves and retreat to the corridors.

When she was eighteen, Evangeline had gone up to Girton to read English, which was not what her mother wanted for her, and Augustus to Oxford, to read anthropology, which was not what his mother – or father – wanted for him, either. A career in the city or in law would have been preferable, from their point of view. The parents of Evangeline and Augustus exchanged commiserations, which made them feel a little better. While at Oxford, Augustus developed a passion for the Pharaohs and decided to become an Egyptologist. Evangeline set her sights on a literary career. They corresponded between the two cities and met up in vacations.

At her coming-out dance, Evangeline was partnered by Augustus. Their parents hoped for a match but kept quiet, knowing that they might do more harm than good if they were to speak out.

Eventually Evangeline's mother decided that she must say something. Her daughter might be considered intellectually bright but she could be dull when it came to more practical matters. 'A match with Augustus would be highly suitable, dear,' she said. She had become anxious after the passing of her daughter's twenty-fourth birthday. 'We would all be exceedingly happy, on both sides. You are fond of him, aren't you?'

'Very fond.'

'Well then! Don't wait too long – he might find someone else.'

Evangeline and Augustus discussed marriage and at one stage almost decided to go through with it, to keep their families off their backs. But then Augustus met a young man who did not fancy the idea of Augustus married, even if it was only for convenience, and the idea was dropped. After Augustus settled in Egypt, Evangeline visited him regularly, and her mother, right up to her death, spoke wistfully of the possibility of a marriage between them.

Evangeline paused in front of the sepia photograph on her bedroom wall of her parents, in their thirties, and of herself, aged nine, with her long, thick, fair hair tied back by a dark bow, and her brother George, aged five, in a sailor suit. They all looked grave, as if to smile might suggest a lack of seriousness. She and George smiled, and laughed, in the nursery, but at table their father would not tolerate any behaviour that he considered to be unseemly, which meant that one kept one's mouth shut except to put food and drink into it and to say please and no thank you. At seven, as was the custom, George, stifling his sobs, was driven off to boarding school, leaving Evangeline to continue with the long procession of governesses who, if they did not find her father too much, found her much too much. Her intellectual curiosity cowed them. They had come to teach her a few refinements which would stand her in good stead when she became a wife: singing to the accompaniment of the piano, reciting a few French phrases, embroidering cushion seats. What if she wanted to become a governess instead of a wife? she asked them. Or a coal miner? Or an intrepid traveller?

Beside the photograph hung another, of their house, a vast, ugly pile, which George, dead these twenty years, had inherited and passed on to his son Evelyn, who had been forced to sell to pay death duties. Evangeline thought that Evelyn had been immensely relieved to get rid of the place. It was now used as a training centre for the Post Office.

She made her coffee and carried it to her sitting-room fire, which Anna had lit for her. What *would* she do without Anna? Well, she would just have to manage. She had no intention of going anywhere, in spite of what she had said; she would dig in here, until she was ready to be shipped out in a box. Hudson's Last Stand. There was a great deal of life left in her yet, she was relieved to find.

Holly was swimming in the ocean. The waves were high –

56

ten, eleven feet high. She had never seen such waves. They pulled back with a monstrous sucking sound then they curled over, frothing and hissing, and went crashing and streaking in long fingers up the deserted shore. There were no footprints on the sand, which stretched for miles to meet the sky.

She was swimming overarm, ploughing through the waves. When she opened her eyes she saw green water. And then she felt herself being pulled under and swept up in a wide arc. She screamed. And awoke.

She sat up in bed. The covers were on the floor, the pillow bunched up against the headboard. Her pyjama jacket stuck to her chest, with sweat, not sea water. She hated the sea, couldn't swim.

When she went to Big Sur she would have to be careful not to go too near the water's edge.

The Egyptian letter was slim, unlike the bulky ones Augustus tended to write, although, recently, his hand had been getting shakier and the pages fewer. Evangeline put on her reading spectacles and frowned when she saw that the handwriting was unfamiliar. Her heart quivered. Trying to push back her anxiety, she quickly slit open the envelope with her ivory cutter and pulled out the single white sheet. 'My dear Evangeline,' the letter began, 'I write with very sad news . . .' She let the fragile piece of paper drift down on to her lap. So dear old Augustus was dead. She felt a part of her go fluttering out with him. Her oldest friend was gone. Her two closest friends were gone, within a few weeks of one another.

For a long time she sat before the fire, staring into it but not seeing it, until the coals dwindled so low that she had to rouse herself to save it. She was shivering and her cheeks were damp. She dried her face and drew a shawl around her shoulders. When she had gathered herself together she would write to George's friend Henry, who, like herself, sat alone, mourning. Such a pity they could not drink a good bottle of wine together and reminisce but, there, life took everyone in different directions and neither was capable of making the journey to bridge the gap now.

57

On her way out, Anna looked in to see if she wanted anything.

'Nothing, thank you, dear. Any sign of Holly?'

Anna shook her head.

After she had gone, Evangeline put on her coat and hat and taking her stick, set off for her afternoon outing. To the end of the street and back! How one's boundaries shrank. Holly said that when she won the pools – she filled in a coupon every week – she would buy a car and take her for rides in the country. But it was amazing, too, how one adapted to the shrinkage and Evangeline found that, each day, her walk revealed something different. She would watch the slow change in the trees and then one day, after a high wind, the branches would be half bare and the leaves that remained be left hanging on precariously as if suspended by a thread. As she shuffled along the pavement, she was reminded how, as a child, she loved to scuff her feet through the thin, papery leaves, catching them between her ankles and building them into piles. Then she would jump into the middle of them. She might not be able to run and jump now but she could still enjoy the sight of the leaves and watch the altering position of the sun above the rooftops and the varying colours of the sky as the year crept on towards winter.

Today, as every day on which she walked, she examined the gardens. She knew them intimately, waited for flowers and shrubs to bloom, each in their season, noted when something new had been planted. It was not the planting season now, but rather the time for tidying up, and she regretted that people were no longer permitted to burn their garden rubbish for she missed the smell of bonfires in autumn, and the sight of the wispy blue smoke coiling upwards.

She studied the windows for signs of people. None this afternoon. She looked for the ginger cat who lived two doors along in the house which had been divided into six flats. They always exchanged a little conversation and he arched his back into the groove of her palm. She stopped at the Hotel Bellevue to talk to the gardener about his roses. His garden was a mass of roses, even though summer was over. He drew her attention to some which were yellow, deepening towards the edges to a shade of apricot. They bloom for months, he said. He told her their name but it was gone from her memory almost as soon as she had heard it. 'Smell this,' he said and she bent her head.

She had smelled such a rose before, unmistakably. She took a deeper breath and inhaled the scent. The yellow flower wavered in front of her eyes. It was earlier in the year, late August perhaps. She was with Augustus, lying in long, wet grass behind a bed of roses. The dampness was seeping in through her thin organdy party dress.

They had been playing Blind Man's Buff, a game she hated. She had not wanted to play but the hostess had said, 'Come on now, Evangeline, everyone's taking a turn. You can't be a spoil-sport.' 'It's cruel, making fun of blind people,' she had blurted out. 'Don't be silly, dear. It's only a game.' The hostess had been sharp.

Evangeline hated having her eyes bound tight with black cloth – that was what they did to condemned men before leading them to the guillotine – and she hated being whirled round and round until her head went dizzy and she saw stars at the back of the dark bandage. She had screamed and the children had fled shrieking, believing this to be part of the fun, except for Augustus, who knew it was not. He had seized the end of the blindfold, untied the knot and set her free, and then, taking her hand, had pulled her away. They'd gone running, to the chants of 'Spoil-sports spoil-sports . . .'

'Don't cry, Evangeline,' said Augustus. 'People are stupid.'

She leant forward and buried her face in a large, exquisite yellow rose.

'Are you all right?' said another man's voice.

Evangeline's head jerked up and she saw a man in a navy blue jersey with blue jeans leaning on a long-handled rake. 'Are you all right?' he asked again.

'Fine, thank you.' She sniffed the rose once more, without going so close. 'Delightful! Sadly, not many flowers have smells these days, not the way they used to. Certainly not the ones for sale in shops.'

She said goodbye and walked on, a little less steadily than before.

In front of the house where Dorothea had lived out the last of her life, Evangeline paused to recoup her strength before embarking on the return journey. She stood with her back to the house. She had hated visiting when Dorothea had still been fit enough to be brought down to the sitting room. It was a terrible room, with spewed-porridge coloured walls and faded olive green drapes and the inmates had sat round the edges in ugly high-backed chairs staring at the huge television set blaring in the corner. The volume had to be kept turned up so that all the ladies and gentlemen could hear, the matron had explained. Most of them had had strokes: some could not speak, some could not walk, some had twisted faces, some were incontinent. At nights, Evangeline would wake in a sweat thinking about Dorothea and wondering how she could help her to end it all. But Dorothea had seemed determined to cling to life; she had not let go easily. For herself, Evangeline felt that she would not want such a low quality of life, not just for the sake of continuing to breathe. She wished to finish her days in Shangri-la.

She must stop coming as far as the home; it only depressed her. Tomorrow, she would turn before she reached it, at the hotel with its jolly garden of roses.

She set off back along the pavement, heading homeward. When she was almost there, she saw a woman emerge from the Villa Neapolitana and come hastening down the drive. She was stocky and she walked with her head and shoulders thrust forward. As she drew nearer, Evangeline recognized Sophia Tonelli.

Evangeline leant on her stick and waited. Sophia was crossing the road and appeared to be coming towards her. She had never seen Sophia cross the road before, had seldom seen her on the pavement at all, for she, like everyone else in that house, came and went in a car. In all these years they had never met face to face. It was not a neighbourly neighbourhood.

'Miss Hudson!' Sophia stood with her hands on her hips, recovering her breath. Her hair was a heavy grey, the texture wiry, and there were deep lines around her mouth that made the skin look as if it had been stitched. She looked ten years older than her husband, though probably was not. 'Miss

Hudson, I invite you to take coffee with my mother and me tomorrow morning. My mother, she likes company and my husband says you speak Italian?'

'In a rather woolly way now, I'm afraid. It's a long time since I've been in Italy.'

'But you still speak? You would like to come?'

'Yes, indeed. I should like to. Thank you so much.'

'Eleven o'clock?'

That would suit her very well, said Evangeline, restraining a chuckle. Wait till she told Holly and Anna – she was actually going to see inside the Villa Neapolitana!

The hall was locked when Anna arrived. After ringing the bell several times, she picked her way through knee-high rank grass and nettles and banged on the back door. Nothing happened. She peered in at all the windows that were not frosted, which were only two – the kitchenette and a store room. There was a poster on the front door saying 'Anna Pemberton in Mime', clearly stating the date and time. The caretaker must have slipped out on an errand. Or to some drinking den.

For a few minutes she paced up and down the pavement then she picked up her props case and carried it to the nearest café where she ordered tea and sandwiches. She would have had to eat something, anyway, before going on. If she went on. Of course she would; this was only a hiccough and she would not allow herself to panic.

The tea room was busy and she had to share a table with two other women, housewives, friends, who'd been shopping and were rewarding themselves with afternoon tea. Their feet were killing them, the shops had been murder, they didn't know what to get for their kids' teas. Anna had heard it all before, in similar cafés. She took a magazine from her bag and tried to read but her mind would not be diverted. The vision of the locked hall came between her and the page. It was her nightmare: to arrive and find the hall shut up, and not a sign of life. One of the women lit a cigarette and held her hand on the table so that the smoke spiralled up into Anna's face and caught her throat. The woman did not notice. Anna left, without finishing her tea.

The caretaker was still absent. It was beginning to rain.

He arrived at ten past six, smelling of beer and cigarette smoke. He said she'd said she'd arrive at six; she said she'd said nothing of the sort and had stipulated late afternoon, no later than four-thirty.

'But you're not on till seven-thirty. You've plenty of time.'

She suggested he open the door; her feet were soaked and she felt chilled to the bone. For an hour she had huddled in the inadequate shelter of the doorway. And it had been just her luck that the wind had been sweeping the rain in that direction.

The chairs had not been arranged but, at least, he had the grace (no, perhaps that was not the right word) to set to and give her a hand. She would not, however, tip him at the end of the evening and, tomorrow, would write a letter of complaint to the hall owner.

'How many are you expecting? Cast of thousands?' He had a most unpleasant smile.

They put out a hundred chairs though she would be lucky – and this was obviously not going to be her lucky day – to have half of them filled. She would be looking for an audience of forty to forty-five. She had played here many times, had a number of old faithfuls.

The caretaker departed to the nether regions leaving her to arrange the stage. She placed a table and a chair in the centre, covered the table with a lace cloth and set on it a fluted, silver vase containing a single red rose. (Artificial.) On another chair at the back of the stage she laid out several coloured scarves and some hats – a topper, a swimming cap, a stetson, a cloche. She stepped down from the stage into the auditorium to examine her arrangement: it would do. She then went to the Ladies to prepare herself.

It was only a toilet, for use by either sex. Unheated and uncleaned, it contained a cracked lavatory and a cracked wash basin. The light bulb gleamed over Anna's head, unshaded. Every 'un' word she could think of might be applied here. Unsavoury. Unpleasant. But not unbearable. She could not allow it to be that. Ignoring the dirt and the smell, she laid out on a narrow shelf, peppered with cigarette burn marks, the ingredients for her make-up, and then, peering into the diseased-looking mirror above the basin, began to apply it, first smoothing on a light-coloured base to give her a pale rather than a white face which some mimes favoured, after which she drew thick kohl lines round her eyes and reddened her lips, transforming herself from Anna the person into Anna the mime. She always felt better once her make-up was on. And now for her hair. She released it from its pins and brushed it out over her shoulders. She brushed down, too, the black trousers and loose black top that she wore. A few swings of the arms and flexing of the wrists and ankles – the only limbering-up exercises she had room for in this small space – and she was ready. Five minutes past seven. Time to go and open the doors.

She dragged another table and chair into the entrance foyer and unbolted the front door. It was still raining. Wet nights were bad for business, especially in autumn, when people had not yet got used to the idea of winter weather. Why did she do this? she asked herself. There must be easier ways to make a living.

Her first customer arrived five minutes later, a young man who was studying mime himself. She was glad to see him. They talked until other people began to arrive, in dribs and drabs. Dribs and drabs described them well, she thought, as she watched them come in darkened by rain, shaking mackintoshes and umbrellas. She tore off the tickets in her book, took their money. She hated selling her own tickets. It made her feel she was selling herself.

By twenty past seven only twenty-three people had come in. It was the poorest turnout she had ever had in this hall. It *must* be the weather. Or was she losing her appeal? She wished that she had put out only fifty chairs. The caretaker would be sniggering to himself. A small rush brought in another three. Twenty-six. Oh well. In other places she had played to as few as half a dozen. She recalled a particularly bad night in a seaside town in November; she'd had a turnout of five, and that had included a woman who'd thought she was going to give a talk on flower arranging and the caretaker, who'd been very sweet and bought her fish and chips afterwards and carried her bag to the train. Thirty-one minutes past. She could hear a slight shuffling of feet coming from the hall, and the occasional

63

cough. There was to be no reprieve now: she must shut the door, pick up the money box, walk along the corridor and enter back stage left.

Taking one last look outside, she saw, coming across the street, shielded by a large black umbrella held angled in front of him, another potential customer, a man. His walk looked vaguely familiar. He came down firmly on his heels, even in the wet. She waited.

The man stepped inside, unfurling his umbrella, discharging a spray of raindrops. It was the Neapolitan King himself.

Holly was bored, an infliction she experienced only within the confines of *Pavarotti's Pizzas*. It was quiet again. She wanted some diversion other than that which she could find inside herself. Sometimes she just had to give her head a break. At the moment it was exhausted from riding the Greyhound bus through Nevada and Idaho. She daren't read a book for she tended to get lost in it and not see Mr Pavarotti coming in. That had happened a couple of times and he hadn't been amused. She smoothed out a crumpled newspaper that someone had left behind and through smears of tomato ketchup read aloud to Janice snippets about rape, indecent assault and revelations of the famous. There wasn't much else to read in it. One item intrigued her: the story of a nineteen-year-old boy in Quebec who'd been so obsessed with his sports car, revving it up and squealing the tyres at all hours of the day and night, that he'd driven the neighbours to hiring a couple of contract killers to silence him and the car for good.

'Imagine – the lengths neighbours will go to!'

'Ours play the telly far too loud,' said Janice. 'Sometimes we can hear the sound of theirs over the top of ours.'

'Now you know what to do,' said Holly. She pointed her index finger at Janice. 'Bang bang you're dead! Could be useful.' She imagined Roberto Tonelli falling, his hands clutching the tomato ketchup stains over his heart.

Steve picked up the paper and turned to the back page. Jackie was staring into space. Holly snapped her fingers in front of his nose and he blinked.

'Five cents for them,' she said.

'I was just thinking about Niagara Falls.'

'You – thinking! And don't tell me you've been to Niagara Falls! You've never let on before. What was it like? And don't just say there was a lot of water.'

'There was a lot of spray and all. You could feel it on your face. We went over to the Canadian Falls and they were even better. They had lots of good shows there, waxworks and stuff, there was one about Jesus Christ, and then we saw Dracula standing in the street. We thought he was a dummy. We were getting all ready to have a good laugh when he starts coming towards us – he was seven or eight feet high – with his hands outstretched, dripping blood, and his eyes rolling.' Jackie made a not very convincing blood-curdling noise.

'So is that what you remember most about Niagara Falls – Dracula?'

'Guess so. Him and the spray.'

The talk of the Falls had made Holly feel restless. She could be doing with seeing some of the wonders of the world. She jerked her head at Janice and led the way into the back where the toilet and Mr Pavarotti's office were located.

'Let's make a phone call. To somewhere exciting.' Holly pushed open the office door.

'What if Mr P comes in?'

'He never shows his nose before ten. If he shows it at all.' Mr Pavarotti had other business interests around the town.

Holly opened the phone book at the section on International dialling. Janice remained near the door from where she could make a quick escape.

'Now let's see – USA . . . San Francisco.'

'You can't phone San Francisco!'

'Want to bet? You dial 010 then 1 then 415 for Frisco and then think of a number, Janice.'

Holly began dialling; Janice protested that she didn't want to think of numbers. She squirmed inside her shiny nylon overall and crossed one leg over the other as if she needed to go to the toilet. Six digits seemed the most likely, said Holly, and selected half a dozen at random. 'And one more for luck. Lucky seven, it might send you to heaven! *Heaven*,' she crooned. She waited, receiver at ear, smiling at Janice. 'If Mr P comes in I'll tell him it's a customer ordering twelve pizzas, all different – and then the line will go suddenly dead. Woops!' Her attention was suddenly taken by the phone. 'Oh, hi! Is that Mr Pavarotti speaking?'

'This is Errol Gleeson here,' a voice said as clearly as if it was coming from the next room. 'Who is that?'

'You won't know me,' said Holly in a Marlene Dietrich-type voice which caused Janice to double over into a paroxysm of silent giggles. 'My name is Marlene and I'm a friend of Janice Binkie's. You remember Janice, don't you? She's got curvy hips, a bit like Marilyn Monroe.' Janice mouthed, 'I'll kill you,' at Holly and Holly smiled back.

'Janice Bink? I can't seem to remember the name. Where are you calling from?'

'Las Vegas.'

'Vegas, eh? I was there last year, must have been when I met Janice. Hi, Marlene. Nice of you to call and say hello. Do you ever get to Frisco?'

'Funny you should ask that. I might be coming soon.'

'Great! Maybe we could get together? Why don't you call me when you're coming?'

She sure would, she said and then asked about the view from his window. 'The view?' Yes, the view. Could he see the Golden Gate or Fisherman's Wharf? 'Hell, no, honey, I haven't got that kind of dough. I can just see the apartment block across the street.' That was all right, she told him; at least it was a San Franciscan apartment. He laughed, a little unsurely.

'Hey, here comes a cable car!'

'A cable car!' she shrieked.

Janice was signalling madly. Holly said she'd have to go and would call again when she knew her plans. She replaced the receiver quietly. They heard Pavarotti's voice in the outer room. Holly scuttled after Janice, pausing at the toilet to reach in and flush the lavatory. Closing the door, she came face to face with her boss.

'What are you girls doing in here?'

'Going to the toilet.'

'Both of you at once? Better get back out there – there's a

66

customer waiting.' Pavarotti was in a bad mood although Holly did not think she was the reason for it. He was frowning and chewing on a dead cigar and not looking at her.

Janice had gone to serve the customer. It was the beautiful boy again. Holly cursed.

'What's he got that I haven't got?' asked Jackie, trying to put his hand on her bottom. She slid out of his grip.

'I'm a slippery customer, Jackie. Like an eel.'

'I could give you a good time, too.'

'Oh, yeah?'

She had to go and serve a table of four. As she passed the beautiful boy, he looked up from his pizza and smiled at her. She stopped.

'Hi,' she said.

'Hello. What's your name?'

'Holly.'

'That's a nice name.'

'Some people think it's a bit prickly.' She laughed. Don't spoil it now, Rattlemouth, she told herself, don't go on and say something really daft.

'I'm Simon.'

'That's a lovely name.' *Simon*. Simple Simon, not in the meaning of being simple-minded, but uncomplicated, like a clear running stream which you could see right through to the stones beneath.

The table of four was growing restive and looking over their shoulders. 'Miss!' One of the men snapped his fingers.

'Can you come back and talk to me later?' asked Simon.

She returned after she'd taken the order from the table of four. As she came to him Simon turned his great big lamp of a smile on her and she thought she would faint, or scorch at the edges from the heat. She sat down opposite him, not caring if Mr P should come in and bawl her out.

'I was wondering,' he said, a slow blush creeping up his cheeks, 'if, well, by any chance you might . . .'

'Are you trying to ask me for a date?'

He nodded.

'I'm off tomorrow night.'

Janice spoke coolly to her for the rest of the evening. Holly wafted between the tables as if in a trance and after Simon had gone out saying see you tomorrow evening at eight then, outside the Odeon, she wondered if she had conjured him up. She practised using his name, talked to him inside her head, telling him about Evangeline and Anna and about the books she'd been reading and how she planned to go to the States. Though perhaps she might put that off for a bit now. Another thought followed, a better one – he could come, too. She saw him in a dark blue shirt and white trousers, walking down Fifth Avenue, carrying his jacket over his shoulder, a finger caught through the loop . . .

At eleven Roberto Tonelli came in, pushing the door inward as if shoving something nasty out of his way.

'Where's Pavarotti?' he demanded.

'Out the back,' said Jackie.

Roberto strode through, the coat tails of his white raincoat flying.

'He's pretty snazzy looking, you must admit,' said Janice and Holly snorted. 'Well, I like forceful men.' Janice was a bit huffed. 'I mean, they're manly, aren't they? Who wants a wimp?'

'You've got no taste, Janice, that's your trouble. Roberto would bang you up against a wall and not even look at you while he was doing it. Nice girl like you shouldn't have anything to do with a Big Bad Wolf like him.'

'He's come for his money, I bet you,' said Jackie. 'It must be late. Mr P's pushed for dough, if you ask me. Our takings have been down. That Mexi takeaway up the street's not done nothing for us.'

Holly went to the toilet and while she sat on the lavatory she read Evangeline's letter for the umpteenth time. It was getting pretty creased looking. 'You must take the money, Holly. It's a big chance for you . . .' Holly stuffed it back in her uniform pocket. As she closed the door, she could hear the two men talking in Italian inside the office. Roberto's voice was loud and insistent. *Domani, Pavarotti – domani!*

The men came out a few minutes later and Pavarotti told Holly to take an order from Roberto. 'On the house, Holly,' said Pavarotti, wiping sweat from his forehead with a grubby handkerchief.

'Twelve-inch with the works, Jackie, and double arsenic,' she said, parking both elbows on the counter. 'And don't take it easy with the grated glass.'

When she took Roberto's pizza to him, he waved a hand at the seat opposite. 'Sit down, sit down, take a pew!' She said she wasn't allowed to sit with customers, Mr Pavarotti didn't like them hobnobbing. She spoke primly, with her feet together and her hands by her sides. Roberto had to twist his neck to look up at her.

'Smart girl like you shouldn't be working in a joint like this. I could fix you up with something a bit more interesting, say in one of our discoteques?'

'I like working here.'

'Think it over.'

'I've got plenty to think about right now,' she said and then couldn't resist adding, 'I might be going to America.'

'Ah-ha!' Roberto leaned back against his chair and flashed his white teeth. Like a crocodile smiling, she thought. 'So you're going to take up our offer, are you? Thought you would be. Like I said – you're a smart girl.'

FIVE

Once Anna had got over the shock of Maximo Tonelli's arrival and recovered her composure and self-confidence, she went on to give a performance that ranked among her best. It might even have been that his presence, since she saw it as a challenge, contributed to its excellence. She did not try to avoid his eyes but rather turned often in his direction and played directly to him. She felt in control, sure of what she was doing. She felt she was saying to him, You do not call the shots everywhere you go, this is *my* world.

She became, in turn, each of her characters. She displayed the first card: THE DATE.

She is a large woman trying to fit herself into a too-small roll-on. She tugs and squeezes, she tries to pull it on over her head, gets it stuck on her shoulders, yanks it off and flings it up in the air. She puts on a slinky dress and stilt-like high-heeled shoes. She wobbles when she walks and the dress threatens to split at the hips. She puts on her make-up jabbing herself in the eye with the mascara brush. The telephone rings. The date is off. She rips off the dress and flops down on the chair with relief, pours herself a drink and turns on the television.

The audience folded up with laughter. She put on the swimming cap, showed the next card: THE OPERATION.

She is a surgeon performing an operation. She makes a huge incision, begins to yank out innards by the mile, like a navvy hauling on a rope. She dumps them in a pedal bin. She wipes her hands off on her apron. She threads a gigantic needle with string and begins to sew up the patient with gigantic stitches . . .

For the first half of her programme she played for laughs – comedy was the easiest way to warm up and beguile an audience – and in the second half shifted into rather more dramatic mood and enacted the tale of a wealthy merchant with a blue beard and his young wife Fatima.

At the end, she brought the palms of her hands together in front of her and inclined her head. Clapping broke out sporadically at first then swelled and rang out amazingly loudly, considering the sparseness of the audience. She noticed Tonelli clapping vigorously, hands raised high, elbows working in and out like bellows. One or two stamped their feet and the young man, the student of mine, cried, 'Bravo!' And then it was over. She felt herself go limp. She sat down.

The young man who was studying mime came bounding up on to the stage to tell her how marvellous she'd been, to be followed by two bright-eyed girls and an elderly couple who had come to her performances before.

'We so enjoyed it, dear. You give so much of yourself.'

'You get better and better, Miss Pemberton, if I might say so.'

Thank you, she said; most kind. She was unable to say more.

Maximo Tonelli had remained in his seat.

Her admirers drifted away, saying see you next time, we'll be here, for sure, and she rose to gather her props. Tonelli got up then and came forward to the edge of the stage.

'Can I help?'

'No, it's fine, thank you. I haven't much to do.'

'I thought you were magnificent.'

'Thank you.' Heat flooded up into her cheeks, whereas, earlier, when she had been praised, she had remained cool and pale. Quickly she whipped the cloth from the table, folded it and put it into her case along with the vase and flowers, hats and scarves. She was conscious that he was watching her. Head bent over, she concentrated on tugging the zip across.

'You must be tired after all that? And hungry? Would you have dinner with me?'

'I'm afraid I can't, I have a train to catch,' she said and immediately felt foolish at having offered such a feeble excuse. Why didn't she just come right out with it and say she didn't want to go? She had always hesitated to offend people even when she felt they deserved it. At times it was not a virtue.

71

Once, when she was thirteen, she had suffered agonies in the cinema when a boy, a total stranger, had leant his leg against hers. It had been deliberate, she had been sure of that; he had pressed his thigh meaningfully against hers. The heat of it had seared her. She had felt paralysed and unable to move her own leg away. Part of it had been not wanting to hurt him. Was she still unable to move away? Or did she not want to?

'I can drive you back afterwards. No problem.'

She hesitated again, and was lost – no, was lost before she hesitated, for the combination of earlier events had conspired to bring her to this point of passivity whereby her will might be subjected to his. The locked hall. The surly caretaker. The drenching rain. The smallness of the audience. The arrival of Maximo Tonelli himself. And then, finally, the performance which had exhilarated her and made her feel that all things were possible, even to go and dine with the King of Naples himself.

'What do you say? I know a nice little restaurant nearby, with excellent food.'

She thought of trudging through the cold dark night to the station and of sitting for an hour on a dismal train. She thought of food and warmth and conversation.

'All right,' she said hesitantly. 'Thank you. But first I must go and change.'

She went backstage. In the chilly toilet she stripped off her clothes which were sodden with sweat and towelled herself dry. When possible, she liked to have a shower after a performance. Here, there was not even hot water. She pulled on a fresh pair of trousers and top and began to repair her make-up. THE DATE. Luckily, she wasn't fat and didn't have to squeeze herself into a roll-on. Not that she would ever consider such a thing. Trying to make herself look small for a man! Wanting to please would not let her go as far as that. She smiled at herself in the mirror as she smoothed off the top layer of her pallid make-up and put a little colour on her cheeks. She left the kohl around her eyes – she had no time to remove that, she had to be out of the hall by ten. If she were not, the caretaker would be swinging his keys and saying, 'Do you mind? I have a home to go to even if you don't.' Perhaps she might do a sketch next time entitled THE CARETAKER. She brushed her hair and decided to leave it loose.

When she returned to the hall she found Tonelli holding her case. He led the way out. The caretaker, who had come slouching in through the side door, perked up when he saw that she had an escort, 'Want a hand?'

'Goodnight,' she said and followed Tonelli into the windy street.

Holly did not stay on with the others after closing time, she went to Giorgio's for fish and chips which she ate with her fingers, leaning against the counter. Two assistants were serving, Giorgio was frying. Holly talked to him, about Roberto. 'He offered me a job and I told him to go and get stuffed.'

'Roberto doesn't like people saying no to him.' Giorgio gently stirred the battered fish swimming in their sea of hot oil. 'It makes him jumpy. He is not patient, you know, he likes to get things done.'

'And for people to do what he wants.'

'Yes. Now our father – '

'Which art in heaven. Sorry, Georgie, no offence meant. Go on. Your father – ? Doesn't he want people to do what he wants, too?'

'Sure. But he goes about it in a different way to Roberto. They clash sometimes.' Giorgio raised the haddock up in their basket for Holly to admire. 'Nice and crisp, eh? Roberto charges at things, like a bull. Yes, he is much like a bull. Our father does things more – quietly. He has style, that's what Mary-Lou says, at any rate. He knows how to turn on the charm.' Giorgio landed the fish neatly on a bed of grease-proof paper. 'He usually gets what he wants in the end.'

The restaurant was French, not Italian, as Anna had expected, quite small, and attractively furbished with glass mirrors, pink tablecloths, fresh flowers and Art Nouveau-style lampshades. The effect was of intimacy and luxury. The head waiter all but bowed at the waist. The other waiters greeted Mr Tonelli by name, and with effusion. Anna supposed it might be agreeable

73

to be greeted with such respect, if respect was what it was. They were given the best table. There was a reserved sign on it. Tonelli ordered a bottle of *Dom Pérignon* and she thought, God, what have I done? Here I am about to have a tête-à-tête, expensive dinner with this man who is not only married but an enemy. The fact that it was expensive did also bother her, for she had grown up believing that if a man spent money on you he expected something in return and if you did not intend to give what he wanted then you should insist on paying your own way. But to pay her share with a man like this to whom the price of a bottle of champagne meant nothing was out of the question. Go Dutch? He would laugh. Anyway, she did not have enough money.

'We'll have the menu *gastronomique*,' he said and asked for the wine list.

The first glass of champagne, drunk on a nearly empty stomach, had an immediate effect on Anna. She could almost feel the bubbles frothing inside her head. I shall levitate in a moment, she thought. DRUNK WOMAN ON A DATE. She must sip slowly and allow him to drink the greater share. But then he would have to drive that lethal red car up the motorway in an intoxicated state. She saw them crashing through the central reservation, striking an oncoming vehicle and rising, nose first, up into the air. And then she relaxed. She found she was enjoying the champagne, and the restaurant, and, yes, Tonelli's company. He was still talking with admiration about her performance and wanted to discuss it in detail. How could she not enjoy such praise, and even more, the *interest* he was expressing in her work? That really did warm her heart. And the food, when it came, was exquisitely cooked and presented, so that each course was a new experience.

'But, Anna – may I call you Anna? Miss Pemberton is so stiff – you are too good an artist to play in squalid little halls like that one tonight. And what you are doing is not cost-effective. You had twenty-eight people there at three pounds a head – that is eighty-four pounds only. By the time you pay rent for the hall and your travelling expenses and allow for other costs like props and make-up, you are making very little profit.'

She found it relaxing to have a man talk to her in this slightly hectoring, slightly bossy way; it reminded her of her father. She had liked it when her father had taken this tone of voice with her since it had meant that, for a short spell at least, he was thinking of her and not his own concerns. He had once decided to take an interest in her spelling, when she was about eleven years old, and while it had lasted she had started to spell badly, deliberately, but also subconsciously, in order to keep his attention.

'It was a wet night. Usually I have a bigger audience.'

'Even so. You must find it difficult to live on what you earn.'

So what was the answer? she asked, smiling; she could not expect to fill the London Palladium. Hers was a minority art. An efficient manager might help, he suggested.

'I do have an agent. She gets me some engagements. I couldn't afford to pay a *manager*. I'm not a pop singer, you know!' Anyway, temperamentally, it suited her to operate on her own, without encumbrances or obligations. 'I manage to get by.'

'By keeping your needs down?'

'Yes.'

She drank her share of the two bottles of wine; it appeared to be no problem. She shifted the conversation from herself to Italy, and they exchanged reminiscenses of Venice, Florence, Rome, Amalfi. I could go to all these places with this man, she thought; I could show him some of the great art treasures that he has never seen in the country of his own forebears and he could show me other things, the life that goes on behind the facades that I have never penetrated. And then she pulled herself up. What *was* she thinking of? Of course she could not go anywhere with him, she shouldn't even be in this restaurant with him. She must be drunk. She asked for a Perrier water and when they reached the coffee stage drank several cups, black. A brandy was set before her. 'I shouldn't really,' she said and lifted it to her lips.

He was asking if she liked opera. 'I have two tickets for *Così fan tutte* two weeks on Wednesday.'

'Maximo,' she said, looking at him directly, 'I am going to

75

stay in Shangri-la.'

'That is a separate issue. It has nothing to do with going to the opera.'

'Hasn't it?'

'I like your company.' He opened out his hands palms upward, to show that he had nothing to hide.

What was the truth of it? That she could not decide; she was neither clear-headed enough nor in the mood to try to arrive at any conclusion. For this evening she was suspending judgement, and giving herself over to pleasure. And why not? It was a stolen evening, she had been aware of that from the beginning.

They left the restaurant at half-past twelve, the last of the diners to go. The waiters straightened themselves up and wished them goodnight. They smiled at Anna. She wondered if Maximo came here with other women. He tucked his hand into the crook of her arm as if he had done it often before and guided her round the corner into the next street.

His Ferrari was parked on a double yellow line. He removed the parking ticket which had been stuck under the windscreen wipers, tore it in two and dropped the pieces in the gutter. He opened the passenger door and ushered her in. She felt as if she were lying down rather than sitting. She had never been in such a car before. The bonnet stretched away into infinity.

He put on a tape of *Così fan tutte* and they sailed off into the night, eating up the miles of grey motorway, arriving far too soon – for her, and perhaps for him? – at the edges of their own town.

As the streets began to look familiar she roused herself from her trance-like state and sat up. She considered Sophia. And also Evangeline and Holly. She suggested that he drop her off round the corner. 'It might be easier.' It might be, he conceded, if she did not mind having to walk the last part of the way?

'Of course not.' She pushed her hair back from her shoulders and twisted it into a knot at the back of her neck, skewering it with two pins from her jacket pocket.

He pulled into the street that ran parallel to their own and stopped underneath a tree. The leaves were russet-coloured in the street light. Would he try to kiss her, and if he did, what would she do? She felt fifteen again. She made to open the door and he opened his and went round to her side. He gave her his hand and steadied her as she put out a foot and groped for the pavement. Then he took her bag from the boot and set it beside her. What about the opera? he asked. It was in a city fifty miles away, less than an hour's drive. He would be very pleased if she would agree to come with him.

'I'll have to think about it.'

'Don't think,' he said impatiently. 'Just say yes.'

'All right – yes.' She could always change her mind.

He put his hands on her shoulders and looked into her face, then he leant forward and kissed first one cheek and then the other.

'Thank you for this evening,' he said and went back into his long red car and roared off round the corner.

She stood on the pavement, abstracted and bemused, watching the red tail lights dwindling. When they had disappeared, she blinked and touched first one cheek and then the other. This is getting ridiculous, she told herself.

Holly, bicycling back from Giorgio's, was passed by Maximo Tonelli's red Ferrari. He had someone with him, she observed, as he went flashing by, but could not tell if the head was male or female. The car turned into the next street. When Holly reached it, she stopped and looked along. She saw Tonelli helping a woman out of the car. The woman was Anna.

Holly thought she would faint from the shock. Jesus Christ, it *couldn't* be Anna; she'd got to be hallucinating. Giorgio must be putting something in his tomato ketchup. But it *was* Anna; even though it was dark, Holly recognized her by her height and by the way she stood and by the set of her head. Anna always looked perfectly balanced; she never listed to one side or another or stood on one foot with the other parked behind it, as Holly herself liked to do. She watched while Tonelli took Anna by the shoulders and kissed first one cheek and then the other. *What did Anna think she was doing?* Holly almost cried out aloud. Surely Anna hadn't gone over into the enemy camp? Of all the people that Holly had ever met, Anna was the straightest. Or had seemed to be.

Anna was now picking up her bag and walking off down the street, taking the way the Ferrari had gone. Holly waited, giving her time to round the corner and get home. Then she hoisted herself back up on to the bicycle seat and pedalled after her.

There were lights showing on the top and bottom floors of the Villa Neapolitana, and on the middle floor of Shangri-la. She saw Anna appear at her window, pause for a moment to look out – at the house across the street? – and then draw the curtain across. Evangeline's bedroom window was dark. Holly crept in and before going upstairs pushed a letter under her door.

Evangeline was up before Anna came down that morning. The rain of the night before had given way to bright sunshine; it looked like an ideal autumn day outside, sharp air, blue sky. A good day for a walk. And then she remembered her engagement at the Villa Neapolitana – it would be the first treat of the day.

She listened. The house was quiet. Both Anna and Holly must have been late home; she had heard neither of them come in. She pulled on her woollen dressing gown and stooping carefully, hearing her knees scrunch as she went down, she plugged in the electric fire. Then she saw the letter.

Another painful bend, and she had it in her fingers. She recognized Holly's impetuous handwriting. Slitting open the envelope, she took out a sheet of lined, pink paper.

'PP's joint,' Holly had headed the page. 'Sorry about the paper but I got it from Janice who is writing to Michael Jackson. She likes pink, and lines, apart from MJ.

'I have just started on Anna K. Just. I haven't got past the first sentence.'

Evangeline thought of that sentence: *All happy families resemble one another, every unhappy family is unhappy after its own fashion.* It had made her pause, too, when she had read it the first time, and consider her own family. She would not have said that her childhood had been unhappy, not in the way that

78

Holly's had obviously been, but they had been a family divided: she had been happy with George, unhappy with her parents who had seemed to have no liking for children. They had had them, no doubt, because it was expected of them for the continuation of the line, and they were probably inept when it came to contraception. Her mother and father had moved into separate rooms when Evangeline was eight.

She recalled then the quotation underneath the title of *Anna Karenina*. *'Vengeance is Mine, I will repay.'* Had that given Holly pause for thought, too? Holly seldom spoke of her family, shrugged off questions. I had no mother, she had said once; I appeared from under a stone when I was fourteen – before that I didn't exist.

Evangeline went back to the letter. 'By the way, as regards taking the lolly – I am *NOT* going to and nothing you will say will make me. I wouldn't take his money if he paid me, ha, ha! I want to stay in Shangri-la. Must go – pizzas are calling. Love Holly X.'

A domestic servant, female, in black and white, and speaking limited English, opened the door. Evangeline was expected. 'Come,' said the woman, smiling broadly. Evangeline entered the pink marble hall. It was strange after so many years of staring at the house, and conjecturing, to be inside. It was familiar, yet different, of course; the terrazzo floor gleamed with cleanliness and the walls were the peppermint green colour of which the Tonellis seemed to be so fond and covered with gilt-framed pictures of the Virgin and Virgin with child. They looked like copies of the Italian masters. Evangeline recognized a Bellini. And there was the Filippo Lippi madonna with plump child and two knowing angels. She went closer to take a better look. Not a bad copy at all. A very nice pensive face on the Virgin. Next to it was Masaccio's madonna and child with St Anne enthroned behind them and gold haloes all round. Evangeline moved along. Ah yes, unmistakably Parmigianino's Madonna of the Long Neck. The baby was also fairly elongated, and emaciated, compared with the other plump bambinos frolicking on virginal knees.

'I choose all of this myself,' said Sophia, who had entered

through a side door. 'Maximo – my husband – he says do what you want. So I do. He take care of business, I look after house. You like my Virgins?'

'Very much. I find them most interesting.'

'I love the Virgin. This one is my favourite.' She laid a finger on the frame of the Lippi. 'Is she not *bellissima?*' Sophia smiled beatifically. 'You are Catholic?'

Evangeline confessed not. Though, at nineteen she had flirted with the idea. 'Flirted?' 'Toyed,' explained Evangeline. 'I was tempted but when it came to the point of commitment I found that I couldn't go through with it.' Sophia commiserated, saying it was best to be born Catholic, and they moved to a sitting room furnished with a Louis XIV reproduction suite in pink brocade and small walnut tables with curved legs. Four more Virgins, in varying moods, kept watch from the walls which, again, were green. Signora Tonelli was fond of pink and green? Evangeline observed.

'My favourite colours. But not in every room, you understand. Some rooms blue; the kitchen red, white and green, like the flag. You want to come and see?'

Evangeline did, very much, and she must take note of every detail so that she would be able to satisfy Holly's curiosity. They set off on a tour, Sophia giving a commentary, explaining how, when and from where everything had come. The dark walnut dining room table, which could be extended to twenty feet, as Sophia demonstrated, and the twenty high-backed chairs had been shipped by Antonio from Turin, the red Turkey carpets from Istanbul, the kitchen units from Harrods, the four-poster bed with pink brocade curtains from Naples. 'I bring this as my bridal bed. It was very good!' Sophia slapped her hip and laughed. It was infectious laughter and Evangeline laughed, too.

Sophia's mother's room was blue-grey and the lady herself was garbed in black from head to toe. She did not get out of her deep armchair. She looked so old and shrivelled, like a prune, that Evangeline thought, My goodness, do *I* seem as old as that? She could not believe it. She exchanged a few words with the mother in Italian.

'Do they feed you?' demanded the old woman, her voice

surprisingly loud and fierce. 'They don't feed me. They starve me. My daughter is no good. Look at me – I am skin and bone.' What she said was partially true. She extended witch-like fingers for examination.

'You lie, Mother!' screamed Sophia. 'You are a nasty old woman. You eat like a wolf-hound. Guzzle, guzzle, all day long!' Then she said to Evangeline, more quietly, 'She is going loop-the-loop.' And she twirled her finger round. 'Though she has always been bad-tempered.'

The old woman was not invited to join them for coffee (so that *had* just been a pretext) which was served in Sophia's sitting room by the domestic. They had Milanese cake covered with icing sugar to accompany the coffee.

'This is extremely pleasant,' said Evangeline. She felt as if she were back in Italy. Even the sun added to the illusion. They spoke in a mixture of English and Italian and she allowed Sophia to lead the conversation, or rather did not attempt to divert her from her favourite topics, which were the Virgin and shopping, especially shopping at Harrods. Evangeline recalled having often seen the dark green van with the gold lettering in the street.

'They deliver everywhere,' said Sophia. 'Come let me show you some of my things.'

She opened cupboards to reveal shelf-fuls of fine china – tea sets, dinner sets, coffee sets, gold-rimmed, patterned, plain, lustrous – all unused, as far as Evangeline could tell.

'You should remember they deliver.'

'I have everything I need now.'

Sophia nodded. 'That must be true – at your age. You have no family, Miss Hudson?' None close, Evangeline admitted. 'That is very sad,' said Sophia. There was nothing better than the family. What would she do without hers? Holy Mother of God, the very thought appalled her! She looked at a Virgin for reassurance. 'It is not good to be alone, Miss Hudson.'

'I'm not alone. I have Anna – Miss Pemberton – who is very kind to me and the young girl Holly upstairs.'

'But you don't live *with* them? You should be in some place where you can be looked after in a proper way. What if you are to fall and break your leg? My mother had a nasty break in her thigh, never the same again. Can hardly walk. She cannot come down the steps. I know that my husband suggest to you a sheltered house but I tell you of something better. A friend of mine – very good friend – has a very nice nursing home, very nice. I would love to live there myself. How I would love it! All private rooms, nice bathrooms – '

'From Harrods?' Evangeline interrupted.

'I am not sure, I ask, but very very nice. Coloured suites, mixer taps. The food is very good – Italian, not British. Most people in this home are Italian but you would be welcome, Miss Hudson, and you would practise to speak Italian since you say that is what you would like. I take you to see this home, I take you in my car, this afternoon. We go at two. I have the appointment.'

'How kind. But I'm afraid I always have a nap at two.'

'At three then!' cried Sophia.

Evangeline was sorry to have to disappoint her but she said she really could not go. She would enjoy the outing and the home sounded jolly but she would be wasting Signora Tonelli's time and her friend's. 'Shangri-la is my home. I don't suppose you would like to leave The Cedars?'

'If I am old and alone then I would. It is a lovely place this home, I am truly sorry that I am not going to live there myself when I am old . . .' Sophia enthused for a further ten minutes but when she realized that Evangeline would not be moved her smile was replaced by a scowl. A pity, thought Evangeline, for she liked the woman and would have enjoyed continuing the association.

Sophia stood up. 'Miss Hudson, that house' – she pointed across the street – 'belongs to my husband. He paid much money for it. It is his. It is not right that you should stay there.'

Evangeline, realizing that Sophia could not cope with the idea of the King's wishes being thwarted, apologized again and fumbling for her stick, eased herself out of the Louis XIV chair. Sophia's stout body was bristling with annoyance and for a moment Evangeline wondered if she might not come hurtling towards her and strike the stick from her hand.

Sophia opened the door and she and Evangeline made their way out into the hall just as Claudio was coming down the stairs. His mother, forgetting her wrath, went smiling to greet him.

'Claudio!' Her face shone, as when she had contemplated Lippi's Virgin. She reached up to kiss him first on one cheek, then on the other. He was smiling, too. 'How are you today? Are you tired? You are a little dark beneath the eyes. You do not sleep enough. You work too hard. Miss Hudson, this is my son, Claudio.' She spoke with much pride.

'Delighted to meet you.' Evangeline proffered a hand and Claudio put out his long slim one to take it. He looked into her face and smiled. He had a delightful smile. He was different from his brothers, more finely built, taller, more sensitive looking. She asked about his restaurant and he said that she must come, one evening. Then she drew back, saying that she must go, for she had observed that Sophia did not like her monopolizing the young man's attention.

'Thank you for the coffee, Signora Tonelli. It has been a most agreeable visit. And I would be delighted if you would take tea with me one afternoon in return?'

Anna was sandpapering the front door of Shangri-la; tomorrow, she planned to start painting. Getting up that morning, feeling full of extra energy, in spite of the late night and wine consumed, she had decided that she must tackle some of the blackspots of the house, the more reachable ones, at any rate. The roof, and such like, would naturally have to be left to the Tonellis, who would surely see to that rather than let it fall in. She would get Holly to give her a hand with the garden, to help clear some of the worst of the jungle and cut back the branches from outside Evangeline's windows.

When she had come downstairs to see Evangeline, she had found a note on the hall table. 'Gone to take coffee with the Queen. I presume the King will be in the counting house.' As Anna sandpapered, she kept an eye on the front door of the Villa Neapolitana and when she saw it open watched Evangeline closely to see if she would need help. But she seemed to be walking fairly well, taking her time. Half-way down the drive of the Villa Neapolitana, she paused and raised her stick towards the top floor of Shangri-la. A moment later

Holly came bounding down.

'What *has* Evvie been up to?'

'I'm sure she's about to tell us.'

Holly ran to meet Evangeline and to give her her arm. They all went into the house and Evangeline began to tell her story.

'Lucky thing!' said Holly. 'I'd give anything to see inside.' Then she remembered Mary-Lou whom Giorgio had said was desperate for visitors. She might just take her up on her invitation, after all.

'Yes, I enjoyed it thoroughly,' declared Evangeline. 'But I wonder when the Tonellis are going to stop pussyfooting around?'

In the late afternoon they each received a visit from Roberto Tonelli. He had come to collect the rent, which was due, and to give them notice that it was to be doubled, as from the beginning of the following month.

'Doubled?' said Evangeline. 'Do you realize how much the old age pension is, young man? How would you like to manage on it?'

She had an alternative, he said; she had been offered help. He did not sit down, although invited. '*We* have to pay the upkeep on this house.'

'You have yet to spend a penny on it,' she said tartly. 'And remember this – you knew when you bought the house that there were sitting tenants in it! We were not sprung upon you. Oh yes, I'm sure I know what you thought – we'll get rid of those three women easily enough! It wasn't very smart of you, was it? You made the mistake of thinking that everyone is ready to fall into patterns of your making.'

He did not reply but laid on the table the written notice of the rent increase. Evangeline tore it up.

Anna was teaching a pupil and came to the door of her studio to speak to him. They stood on the cold landing. 'I suppose you have taken legal advice?'

'Of course. And we are advised that we are well within our limits to double the rents. They have been ridiculously low.

You occupy three apartments here, plus kitchen and bathroom, that's correct, isn't it?'

Anna did not argue, she took the notice and returned to her pupil. She suspected that what he had said was true and they were going to have to try to meet the increases.

Holly said to Roberto, 'I remember the rent man coming round when I was a kid. He wore a grubby raincoat and he carried a tattered book with a greasy red cover in his pocket. He had sweets in his pocket, too, and he tried to give us kids the sweets and when we came near him he'd slip his hands round our bums. We used to call him Dirty Dick.'

'You've got a big lip on you.'

Roberto prowled around Holly's room with his hands in his pockets and the white raincoat bunched out behind. She wondered if he wore the raincoat in bed. She didn't want to think about him in bed. She didn't even like him gawping at her posters with that smirky look on his kisser; it made her feel he was looking into some private part of her.

'If you had any brains at all you'd take that grand while you've got the chance and get shot of here.'

'You think everybody's for sale, don't you?'

'Well, aren't they?' He turned back to her. 'It's just a case of the price. You'd go for a hundred grand, wouldn't you? Don't tell me you'd pass that up! Not that we're offering that. A thousand's much too much as it is for a little alley cat like you!'

She flew at him, nails outstretched, and lunged for his face. He caught her by the wrists and held her, half lifting her off her feet. She struggled, tried to kick, and he delivered a fast kick instead to her ankle, making her gasp and fold over.

'You bastard! I'll – '

'You'll what? Report me to the police. I'm acting in self-defence. You'd have taken my eyes out if I hadn't. Maybe we should go down to the police station? I wonder if they've got anything on you? Might be interesting to find out.' The smirk was spreading across his face again, like a bad stain. 'You wouldn't like that, would you? Maybe you do have something to hide? Have I got you worried, eh? Been on the game, have

85

you? I wouldn't be a bit surprised.' She couldn't speak at all now. Her chest felt as if someone had put a clamp round it. 'So what were you up to before you came here?'

She tried to spit in his face, found she did not have enough saliva in her mouth.

'I'll let you go if you promise to behave yourself?' Suddenly, he released her wrists and pushed her away from him and she went reeling against the wooden horse sending it rocking.

Her wrists were on fire with the pain, as was her ankle, and her back, where it had struck the hard horse. She could feel bruises beginning to swell up. Her skin was pale and marked easily. She wanted to curl up into a ball on the floor and howl. But she wasn't going to let him see that he'd left his marks on her. She put her arms behind her back, linking the fingers of both hands loosely together for comfort, and bit down hard on her bottom lip to steady herself. He put his back to her.

He went to inspect the other three rooms on her floor that were standing empty. She followed as far as her own doorway and stood leaning against the jamb watching him.

'They're good-sized rooms. Double rooms. We could put another six up on this floor alone.'

'Six what? Gorillas?' She'd found her voice again though it sounded cracked.

'Waiters, dear. *Male* waiters. You know – *men*. Ever heard of them? We're always short of accommodation for our waiters.'

He went off down the stairs, his hands back in his trouser pockets, whistling.

'Asshole,' she said, after he'd gone. But her hands were still shaking when she lit a cigarette.

SIX

Holly spent an hour agonising over what to wear for her date with Simon. Did he exist – or had she dreamed him up? She'd just have to go to the Odeon at eight and find out. She spread her entire wardrobe across her bedroom floor and picked her way through it, rejecting everything that came to hand. He looked the kind of boy who would probably like girls in Laura Ashley dresses. Trouble was she didn't have any Laura Ashley dresses. Trouble was she didn't have any dresses. She had only one skirt, a short black leather one. She put that on with her long black boots and prowled up and down feeling like Dick Whittington, then she yanked them off again and took a break while she caught up with the goings on of Vronsky and Anna K. Anna was going to make a fool of herself over that guy, she could see that coming a mile off. Still, it didn't mean she should stick with that boring jerk of a husband, did it? Just so that she could be safe. There was the kid though . . .

In the end Holly read for too long and had a frenzied rush to get ready; she threw on jeans and a scarlet T-shirt bearing the one black word YALE on its chest, slapped on some eye make-up, stuck gel on her hair and pedalled downtown. Half-way there the chain came off and she got oil all over her hands trying to persuade it to go back on again. It was ancient, like the bicycle itself, and the ratchets kept slipping. She cursed and kicked the back tyre which looked squidgy. She would have to abandon the damned thing. Padlocking it to a lamp-post (even though it was unlikely anyone would consider stealing it), she set off at a run.

She arrived at the Odeon twenty-five minutes late, with a stitch in her side. Simon was there, though he looked as if he had been just about to go. He was wearing grey flannel

87

trousers and a sports jacket and polished shoes. Holy Toledo! Holly looked down at her oil-stained T-shirt and mud-spattered trainers. Gasping for breath, she launched into an apology.

'That's all right,' he said, rather stiffly.

She rattled on for another five minutes about the antiquity of her grandmother's bicycle. 'She used to ride it when she was a student in Cambridge.'

'I'm going to Cambridge next year.'

At least he was speaking to her. Encouraged, she asked if he had forgiven her and he smiled that angelic smile which made her heart crumble. He really was beautiful. The film had started, he said, and he didn't think it was worth going in now. Would she like a cup of coffee?

Scrubbing her hands in the café toilet, Holly wondered how much a Laura Ashley dress would cost. Once upon a time she'd just have gone into a store and nicked one but she'd given all that up since coming to live at Shangri-la. She'd used to reckon that if it was a big store they wouldn't miss it, not the profit, that is, since they were probably doing more than all right, and she hadn't had enough money to buy decent clothes. They were rich, she was poor. Evangeline agreed that that wasn't fair but said you couldn't base your own moral principles on the commercial values of the market place. Better not to covet what you can't afford, in Evangeline's opinion; that way you'll help keep up your self-esteem. And that was more important than dresses. Holly had come to the conclusion that Evangeline might be right. Not that it stopped her from doing a bit of coveting from time to time.

Over their capuccinos, Simon produced a few details about himself: he'd left school in the summer (boarding school) and was having a year out before going up to Cambridge, to King's, to read economics. 'What college did your grand-mother go to?' he asked. 'Girton,' said Holly. He looked at the slogan on her tee-shirt. 'My aunt went to Yale. She thought it was terrific.' (She was being careful about her diction and trying to match her accent to his.)

And then it was her turn to make some revelations. He was looking at her expectantly. She told him she lived with her aunt and grandmother and that she was also having a year out before she went to university, which was why she was working in the pizza joint. 'I wanted to get some experience. My grandmother thought it would be good for me to see how the other half lives.' She hadn't yet decided which university to choose. 'I might go to the States. Yale or the University of Kentucky.' She shrugged. 'It depends.'

They drank three capuccinos. He seemed uncertain as to what else to propose until, finally, Holly said her stomach was swimming for its life and if she put any more liquid into it it would hold its arms up in the air and go under. 'It would be drowning not waving. Do you like Stevie Smith?'

'Never heard of him.'

'It's a she. Have you read *Anna Karenina?*'

He had not and she couldn't help feeling disappointed for a moment as she'd been looking forward to discussing Anna and Vronsky with him but then she reckoned she couldn't expect him to be perfect in every department – she wasn't herself, after all. He added that he had once started *War and Peace* but he didn't like long books. Or novels much at all. He preferred non-fiction. He said he found it difficult to get interested in made-up people. Then he asked if she would like to go for a drive.

In his pocket he had the keys to a brand new Jaguar parked round the corner. 'Gee!' Holly whistled and leant over to look at her reflection in the bonnet. It was his father's car, he explained. His parents were on holiday in Bali.

They went for a spin – as Simon called it – down the motorway. He had soon eased the car up to a hundred, a hundred-and-five. It purred along. Holly lay back enjoying the speed and the smell of the new leather though she noticed that Simon looked rather nervous and kept bobbing his head about looking in the mirror. And he was gripping the steering wheel with clenched fists. It might be better not to risk getting picked up by the cops, she suggested, especially since it was his father's car, and with him being away in Bali, too. It might spoil his holiday if he were to come back and find Simon had got a speeding ticket. Simon let the speedometer needle fall back immediately. He had just been trying to impress her, she thought and smiled to herself. *He* wanted to impress *her!*

On the way back into town he cleared his throat and asked in a gruff voice if she would like to come home with him. 'Sure,' she said. She was dying to see where he lived. He drove to an outlying suburb and turned into an estate of large, new, detached houses, with double and triple garages. Caravans and boats stood on driveways. It was what the estate agents call 'executive-style' housing, though Holly was not aware of that. Simon lived in a split-level, five-bedroomed house, with garage and games room underneath.

'What about a game?' She lifted a table tennis bat and faced down the table. She began to weave about from the waist as she'd seen them do on television.

'Let's go upstairs,' he said and took her hand.

The house was warm. She couldn't help commenting on it as the door closed behind them and the heat engulfed them. Of course she was used to Shangri-la with its nippy corridors and draughts blowing in under the doors. (Not that she minded about details like that.) Simon flicked on lights set low on walls and tables. Rugs lay scattered on the shining parquet floors. The living area was open-plan and glassed from floor to wall at the garden end. There seemed to be a patio and shrubs outside.

'That's where we barbecue,' he said, pulling a cord and immediately velvet drapes swished across to exclude the night. It was like being on a movie set. She could be Rita Hayworth. Well, maybe not in these jeans. She'd have to get herself something slinky to wear.

The chesterfield suite was made of soft pale blue leather which sighed when she pushed her hand down into it. It must have cost a bomb. She'd never seen such soft, supple, leather. Everything in the room amazed her. At one end there was an arrangement that looked just like a real cocktail bar, with bottles of spirits and wine stacked on the shelves behind and four high stools ranged in front of it. Fancy having your own bar! she thought but did not say, for she didn't want him to think she wasn't used to people having bars in their sitting rooms. Against another wall stood a shelving unit containing a vase of flowers (artificial, but deceptive until you touched them), a Readers' Digest dictionary and a Readers' Digest atlas, four books on golf, six on cookery in different countries, a Toby jug, a Japanese bowl filled with pot pourri and several copies of *Vogue* and *Harper's Bazaar*. She wondered if Simon's mother got herself kitted out to look like the women posturing on the front covers. There were family photographs standing on top of a white, half-sized grand piano. Simon's parents on their wedding day, flanked by a battalion of flowery bridesmaids and men in duck-tails holding grey toppers. His father looked constipated, his mother had a silly smile on her face. Then there was Simon as a baby, easily recognizable: the same china blue eyes gazing sunnily out on the world. Another baby, female: you could tell by the pink embroidery on her smock. 'My sister Jocelyn. She's away at school.' An up-to-date photograph of each: Simon in a blazer holding a silver cup – 'For fencing.' – and Jocelyn in a hard black hat seated on a pony holding a rosette. 'She's mad about horses.'

'Are you a happy family?' asked Holly.

Simon looked startled. 'I suppose so. I've never really thought about it. We don't have any terrible rows or anything.'

'Do your parents love one another?' As soon as she'd said it, Holly realized that it was not the kind of question you asked in this kind of house. Quickly, she began to admire the house. 'I've never been inside one like this before. We live in an old one, you see, mid-nineteenth century. It's been in our family for generations.'

Simon didn't seem to be particularly interested in her lineage. He hung around in the middle of the room with his arms dangling, looking preoccupied. Then he asked if she would like a drink and went behind the bar as if relieved to have something to do. Holly chose Campari because she liked the colour. Simon drank brandy. Holly didn't care for the taste of the Campari but persevered. They got a little drunk.

'Would you like to see the rest of the house?'

They went hand-in-hand to stare in at sumptuous bathrooms, one with a jacuzzi bath, the other with a sauna (Holly's bath at Shangri-la stood on curved black legs and was green

91

with verdigris under the taps), at Jocelyn's walls studded with pony pictures, at the oyster-satined parental bedroom, and ended up in Simon's room where Holly felt more at ease amongst the model cars and aeroplanes and mobiles and stacks of books and records. She poked around; he stood in the centre of the room again, his hands hanging loose.

Then he pounced. He grabbed her by the shoulders, in the manner of a rugby tackle, and whirling her round, kissed her, inexpertly, banging his teeth against hers. He was panting hard, like a steam engine waiting in the station ready for the whistle to blow. His move did not come to her as a surprise. She moved in closer to him, put her hands round his neck and caressed the back of his thick fair hair and then, smiling, she stretched up on to her toes and kissed him. This time it was better and they stayed glued together, mouth to mouth, until Simon, who had been shuffling his feet, again perhaps in the way he was accustomed to do in a scrum at rugby, manœuvered her round until he had brought her to the side of the bed. They dropped down on top of it.

They undressed one another, flinging clothes in all directions, so that the room looked as if it had been hit by a whirlwind. Naked, they crawled under the downie and clasped each other tightly. The feeling of skin on skin was good, thought Holly. 'Gosh,' said Simon, who was trembling violently. His eyes looked as if they were about to go into orbit. Bright spots of colour burned in his cheeks. They kissed again and Holly ran her foot up the inside of his leg.

Then, 'Just a minute' he said, embarrassed, and stretching out an arm, keeping hold of her with the other, he opened the drawer of the bedside table and brought out a packet of condoms. His ears were scarlet. Holly wanted to giggle. She imagined him going into a chemist, asking for them, not looking the chemist in the face, and she imagined his father giving him a lecture on Aids, telling him, Watch what kind of girl you pick up, don't pick up just any kind of girl, make sure you pick up a girl from the right background. A girl whose grandmother went to Girton. And whose aunt went to Yale. But his father was in Bali now, wearing a grass skirt perhaps and doing the hula-hula under a palm tree. He would not be thinking about his son.

Simon must have practised putting on a condom but he had some trouble with it and she had to help him and they laughed so much they rolled off the bed on to the floor. He struggled to get up but she said, Lie there, what's wrong with the floor, and climbed on top of him. He didn't know what to do – she had suspected he was a virgin – so she had to show him. It was over in a minute. 'Is that all?' he asked. 'For now,' she said. 'Let's do it again,' he said. He was already rising up. They did it five times before they fell asleep – in bed – exhausted.

In the morning she was wakened by him rolling on top of her. 'You're marvellous,' he cried, riding her like a rocking horse. When he collapsed on to her chest, crushing her ribs, knocking the breath out of her, he said, 'I love you, Holly.' She wanted to say, 'I love you, too, Simon', but found the words difficult to say. No one had told her before that he loved her. She held him close to her, not caring if she could hardly breathe, not caring if he flattened her ribs to pancakes, wanting never to get up, wanting to stay in this warm bed with the sun pouring through the window lighting up the room, striking the little silver aeroplanes and the delicate mobiles which shivered in the draught. 'I like your room,' she said. 'I *love* it.'

'We'll have to get up now though, I'm afraid.' He sighed, pushed back the quilt. Mrs Maple, the cleaning lady, came at nine, and Holly would have to be away by then. 'Like Cinderella,' she said, mock-mournfully, not liking it all the same. And underneath a nasty thought stirred: now that he had got what he wanted, did he want to get rid of her? Could he *really* love her?

Couldn't they have a bath in the jacuzzi first? she asked. Last night he had said that they would but now he was in a hurry, was leaping from the bed and preparing to sprint for the shower. 'There isn't time. You go over to the other bathroom. Be quick now!' He was much more decisive this morning, was no longer playing the part of the dangling man. 'Make sure you clean up after you,' he called over his shoulder. 'So that Mrs Maple won't suspect.'

Sod Mrs Maple, thought Holly, as she trailed naked along the deep-piled cream carpet to the bathroom. She hoped the woman would come early and see her. 'And who are you then?' 'I'm Simon's fiancée. Didn't you know? He's crazy about me. We're getting married at Christmas and we're going to go to Bali for our honeyed honeymoon.'

She stayed so long under the shower using the different shampoos and hair conditions and body gels that Simon came to yank her out. Laughing, water running off her, she tried to grab hold of him, but he danced out of her way protesting she would soak him and he'd have to change his clothes again and there wasn't time and they'd have to mop up the floor which was in a heck of a mess and the windows were steamed up and they'd have to change the sheet on his bed. When he'd pulled off one of the condoms, it had spattered all over the bed, making them go into hysterics at the time.

After they'd sorted his bed, he rumpled it again with his hand – 'Mrs Maple would think it funny if I'd made it myself' – and then he looked at the dirty, bundled-up sheet. 'What am I going to do with that? I can't put it in the laundry basket. Can you take it home and wash it?' He rammed it into a plastic bag.

'Mrs Maple must be a dragon.'

'She can't keep her mouth shut, that's the trouble.'

Holly took the sheet; it would mean that he would have to see her again to get it back. Otherwise, she'd have told him to take it to the launderette himself.

It was seven minutes to nine – there was no time for breakfast. She had hoped to have fresh orange juice made from the juicer and fresh coffee made from coffee beans ground up in the wall-mounted grinder and to have sat side by side at the breakfast bar with their knees touching and their elbows bumping.

'Quick, Holly, quick, for goodness sake!' He was swinging the car keys in one hand and ruffling up the back of his hair with the other.

She got into the passenger seat.

'Would you like me to lie on the floor?' she asked, sarcastically.

'Good idea,' he said and threw a scratchy tartan rug over her head. They hurtled backwards out of the drive, the Jaguar's tyres squealing. Her head struck some blunt edge; the glove compartment, perhaps. They hadn't washed up their Campari and brandy glasses, she remembered, with great satisfaction; that would give Mrs Maple something to wonder about. When they'd swept round the first corner, she couldn't resist poking her head out of its covering to take a gander at the street and saw two women who looked like Mrs Maples trudging past with their headscarves tied round their chins and their shopping bags in their hands. One of them looked up at that moment and her eyes widened with astonishment. The sticky lady herself, thought Holly, and clutched the door handle as they took another bend.

'You should join the New York cops,' she said through an opening in the tartan rug.

'You can come up now,' said Simon, settling his back against the seat and easing his grip of the wheel.

'Thanks a lot.'

He turned his head to smile at her. 'Sorry about the rush but it could have been awkward, you know, if Mrs Maple had walked in.'

'And caught us naked on the floor together?'

He blushed.

Perhaps he'd better drop her round the corner from her own house, she suggested, as she didn't particularly want her grandmother and aunt to see him. They didn't like her to spend the night out with boys. 'Not that I've ever done it before,' she added hastily. But first he should drive down the street and she would point out her house so that he would know where she lived. They turned into it.

'O.K., slow up – that's it on the right.'

'The Cedars.' Simon read the name on the gate. 'Looks quite a house.' A gardener was mowing the front lawn.

'It's not bad,' she said off-handedly and smiled. It was at least twice, if not three times as big as his house, and who knows, it might even have a cocktail bar in its sitting room?

He stopped round the corner and she got out. He passed the plastic bag over.

'I'll bring it to *Pavarotti's*.'

'Come here a minute,' he said and she bent down and he kissed her through the open car window and she felt her knees begin to tremble all over again. Silly little fool that she was! Just as silly as Anna K. Simon drew back. 'I guess I'd better go.'

'Guess you'd better. Mrs Maple might think someone's stolen you and ring the police.'

He flushed a little, then said, 'See you later,' and drove off.

Swinging the plastic carrier bag in her hand, Holly went home to her own bed to recover from the night.

Anna was still working on the front door when Maximo Tonelli arrived with Mr Ponti the builder.

'Mr Ponti is just going to look the place over, see what needs doing and give me an estimate.'

Anna said nothing and resumed sanding, which she did with renewed vigour. Manual work in the fresh air was a good way of releasing pent-up feelings. Exactly what those feelings were composed of she had not allowed herself to contemplate; she knew only that they were complex and that the sense of equilibrium which she tried to maintain in her life had temporarily deserted her.

The two men went inside, to Dorothea's old apartments. They left the doors open. Anna, suspending her sanding, heard snatches of conversation which seemed to suggest that Dorothea's sitting room was to be converted to a gaming room but that the main one would be upstairs, at the front. Her own sitting room!

While the builder was surveying the outside of the house, Tonelli came back to speak to her. 'You don't have to do that. I'll be getting the outside painted. I see you've been working in the garden, too. But that's a waste of time really as I'm going to bring in gardeners to landscape it.'

'You mean for the casino?'

She gave the door an extra hard scuff and her hand slipped. She winced and lifted it to her mouth. A large jagged splinter had jabbed right into the palm.

'Let me see.' He took her hand between both of his, before

she could object. He pursed his lips. 'It's a nasty looking splinter. We'd better see if we can get it out for you.'

'It's all right, I'll manage.' She withdrew her hand and went inside. He followed her upstairs.

The hand was her right one and the splinter lay deeply embedded. When she tried to poke a needle in with her left hand she drew blood.

'Let me!' he said.

He positioned her arm firmly between his own arm and his side, holding her captive. They stood in her bathroom leaning against the sink. He frowned as he bent his head and applied himself to his task. The needle probed gently. 'Am I hurting?' 'No.' 'I may have to, a little.' 'That's all right.' She was conscious of the heat of his body and of his smell. The needle pierced her. She jumped. He held her wrist firmly. 'Just another second, it's coming. I've got it! Good girl. Have you got any Dettol?' He took the bottle from the medicine cabinet and daubed her wound with disinfectant. 'I told you you shouldn't have been doing that, didn't I?'

'Thank you.' She screwed the top back on the Dettol. He took the bottle from her and replaced it in the cabinet.

'Are we going to go to the opera together?'

'How can we go?' she exploded. 'When you are planning to take over our house – '

He cut in. He said he was sorry, he knew it must be very painful for her and Miss Hudson, but what was he to do? 'I can't maintain this house as it exists at present. It's not commercially viable, I've told you before, Anna.'

'Perhaps you shouldn't have bought it, then.'

'But I *have* bought it. I didn't realize you would all care about it so much. I thought you might be glad to go to better accommodation.'

'So you've found out you were wrong. For once you've miscalculated. You thought you could squeeze us out, didn't you?' She edged away from him, round the other side of the wash basin; they had been standing much too close. 'You've raised our rent but we'll find that, even if we have to eat less. We won't go. And Holly has turned down your offer. *We are*

97

not for sale! You'd better get that into your head. And as long as we stay you won't get permission to change the house into a casino.'

'Let's not quarrel. I don't want to quarrel with you.'

'I don't see how we can avoid it.'

'Look at me, Anna. Are you afraid to look at me?' he asked softly.

She did not look at him. 'I think you should go.'

'We had a good evening together, did we not?'

'I still think you should go.'

'What about the opera?'

She shook her head and then, suddenly, and unusually for her, allowed herself to get really angry: 'Apart from the fact that you *happen* to be married – how could I sit and watch an opera with you when your son Roberto came here and manhandled Holly? Do you know that he grabbed her by the arm and left huge bruises on her wrist and on her leg where he kicked her? Your son is a bully!'

Maximo became angry, too. 'I shall speak to Roberto. I won't have him treating a woman like that! But are you going to hold me responsible for the sins of my son?'

Yes, she said, she was. 'You reared him, didn't you?'

Holly called in on Evangeline on her way to the launderette to see if she had any washing. 'A few bits and pieces, dear. That would be kind of you.' Holly gathered them up in another plastic carrier.

She looked to see what Evangeline was reading. *'Pride and Prejudice.* Don't you ever get tired of reading the same things?'

'When you've not got much time left you don't want to waste it reading books you might not enjoy.'

'Don't keep saying that!' said Holly fiercely. 'You'll live to be a hundred, I know you will.'

Evangeline smiled. 'Don't worry, Holly-Berry, I'll be here for a while yet. I like life, you know. And how are you getting on with *Anna Karenina?*' Holly had volume two on top of her dirty washing. 'You've read part one already? You eat books, child!' They launched into a long discussion about Anna and Vronsky and the power of love until Holly, noticing the time, sighed and said she supposed she'd better go and tangle with the soap suds.

From the doorway, she looked back. 'What do you think about love, Evvie? Do you think it can overcome – well, differences between people and things?'

'Of course, dear. If it's the right kind of love. If it's true.'

How could you know if love was true or not? Holly asked herself as she trudged up to the main road with the two bags. The launderette was next door to Giorgio's chip shop, which was closed at this hour of the afternoon. It looked cold and dead without the frying going on and people bustling. Giorgio would be having his afternoon nap – he slept between lunch and evening opening.

After a run-in with the dragon in charge of the launderette who had hysterics if you dropped as much as a teaspoonful of soap powder on her none-too-clean floor, Holly settled down with Tolstoy in front of the glass window behind which Simon's sheet tumbled in close embrace with her knickers and T-shirts and Evangeline's flannel nightgowns. 'The brilliant victory won by Aleksei Aleksandrovitch in the assembly of the 17th of August had unfavourable results,' she read and sighed with pleasure. She wished she'd lived in nineteenth-century Russia. Not as a peasant, of course.

When the washing came to rest and the light clicked off, she got up to open the door. 'Oh no!' she moaned, sinking down on to her haunches. Her red T-shirt had run and made pink smudges all over Simon's pale blue sheet. It was a good one, too; it wasn't even as if it was fraying at the edges or wearing thin in the middle, like her sheets. All two of them. She'd bought them second-hand to start with, at a stall in the market.

'Get a move on,' said the dragon. 'There's other people waiting and they haven't got all day even if you have.'

'Belt up,' said Holly under her breath. 'Frustrated sex life, that's your trouble.'

'What did you say, miss?'

'I said you must be having too much sex,' said Holly loudly and raised a laugh from the line of people waiting on the benches. The dragon turned purple in the face and slithered off into the nether regions. Maybe not slain, but definitely wounded.

Holly dragged the tangled clothes out of the machine and carried them to the drier. The sheet reminded her of those potato paintings they used to do at primary school ten thousand years ago, when they'd cut potatoes in half and rubbed them in paint and then daubed them on bits of paper. She'd never thought much of the activity, even then. What was she going to do with the damned sheet? Simon would be in a tizzy when he saw it. Plainly, neither he nor the fiercesome Mrs Maple could be allowed to set eyes on it. Life was growing more complicated by the hour. And then there was Evangeline's bicycle languishing against a lamp-post half-way downtown.

With the clean but mottled laundry in the bags, she went in pursuit of the bicycle and having reclaimed it, pushed it into the centre of town where she priced sheets of the same quality as Simon's and was greatly taken aback by the price. She told the assistant she'd think it over. She then went into a clothes shop and tried on three dresses. The fitting room was a communal one. She put on a short, emerald green dress with a flouncy hem, ideal for dancing the cha-cha-cha in, if she would ever have an occasion to do the cha-cha-cha. She couldn't see Simon dancing Latin American style with a rose between his teeth. As she turned to look at her back she recognized the girl in the mirror next to her who was wriggling into a red satin dress. It was backless and its neckline plunged almost to her waist.

'What do you think?' asked Mary-Lou Tonelli.

On her way back from her afternoon walk Evangeline was overtaken by a young man – a very young man, a boy really – carrying a beaten-up suitcase held together with thick twine and what looked like a rolled-up sleeping bag under his arm. He was wearing a short grubby raincoat and shoes that needed heeling. He was tall and gangling thin and black-haired. He turned in at the gate of Shangri-la.

Evangeline tried to hasten a little, whilst still taking care. A slip on the crooked path and a broken femur had started poor

100

Dorothea's descent into the extremities of old age. The boy was now on the doorstep and appeared to have a key in his hand with which he was attempting to open the door. Evangeline hailed him.

'Can I help you?'

He stared blankly back at her. Then she understood. She repeated her question in Italian and his face, which had been rigid with misery, melted into a smile and he said, gratefully, *'Per favor. Grazie.'*

He had recently arrived from the small fishing village at the foot of the cliff on the Bay of Sorrento whence the Tonelli dynasty had sprung, though he himself was not a Tonelli but some distant relation, by marriage. He had come to work in Giorgio's fish and chip shop and was to lodge in a room on the top floor of the women's house. Roberto had given him the key, and his instructions. His name was Carlo.

Evangeline took him into her room and fed him macaroon biscuits and coffee and quizzed him gently. It was a big chance for him to come here, he said, but he was sad to have left his family and he was cold for his shoes leaked and his coat was thin and he had not known the wind would be so cold. His parents had been sad, too, when he had left and his mother had wept but had told him to go, such opportunities might not come twice in life. 'Look at Maximo Tonelli,' she had said. 'One day you might be a great man like him and then you come back here in a big red Ferrari and take your poor mother for a drive down the coast to Amalfi and the tourist buses and the cars will pull in against the cliff wall to let us go by.'

'It is fine to have dreams,' said Evangeline.

She rang the bell for Anna who came down and was introduced and then escorted Carlo up to the top floor. He stumbled as he climbed the marble staircase. He had been travelling for two days by bus, train and boat. Anna took him into a room which contained a bare, stained mattress and a hard chair. There were neither curtains nor rugs for the previous tenant had taken them with her. Anna explained that the rooms were normally rented unfurnished; each tenant provided her own fittings. He looked dazed. She then showed him the bathroom and kitchen, rooms he would have to share with Holly. 'A girl?' He sounded both alarmed and excited. But he would have to supply his own food, Anna stressed: he would not be able to eat Holly's. In the cupboard there was a packet of cornflakes, half a stale loaf, a tin of beans and a tin of tomato soup. 'Not for you,' stressed Anna. 'They belong to Holly.' She suspected he would live off fish and chips and fried chicken. She left him and went back down to Evangeline.

They debated whether they should give the boy one or two things to help make his life more comfortable – it was not his fault, after all, that he had been sent here to act as a pawn in the game – but they came to the conclusion, somewhat reluctantly, that they had better not. If they were to be too helpful it might encourage Roberto to fill the place with lost young boys newly arrived from Italy. They really ought to be freezing Carlo out, rather than making him welcome. And Holly would be furious when she found that her territory had been invaded.

SEVEN

'It was great running into you like that,' said Mary-Lou.

They were sitting, she and Holly, on her blue nylon fur settee under her midnight-blue, gold-starred ceiling, drinking coffee and eating cream meringues which they'd purchased on the way back from town. Holly had pushed Evangeline's bicycle and Mary-Lou had pushed the pram. The plump-jowled baby, plugged at the mouth with a dummytit, now swung to and fro in a canvas sling suspended from a hook in the starry ceiling, looking so much like Giorgio that Holly almost expected to see her wave a fish fryer in her hand.

'I get dead bored at times on my own so I do,' said Mary-Lou, flicking meringue crumbs off her fuzzy pink jumper. 'If Giorgio's not at the shop he's sleeping. And does he stink of frying when he comes home! I think he should branch out into something else. When we got engaged he promised me he would, said he wasn't going to spend the rest of his life in a chip shop. Men! They'll say anything to get what they want from you. Now if Giorgio only had some of Roberto's go! Roberto's always got something new on the boil.'

'Like casinos?'

'Well, it'd be a heck of a lot more exciting than a bleeding chip shop, wouldn't it? I think it'd be great, it'd bring a bit of glamour to the street instead of all those old people's homes. They give me the creeps so they do, just even to see them through the window shuffling along with their zimmers. Give me a casino any day with big limos stopping in the street and people getting out in slinky dresses and fur coats.'

'Las Vegas, eat your heart out!'

'Roberto says you've got to think big. He's promised me a job.'

103

'As a croupier? I can just see you leaning across the table with a long stick – hey, you could wear your red dress and let your boobs hang out! – and hauling in the chips when the wheel's done turning.'

Mary-Lou's face lit up: she could see it, too. 'Or else I might be a kind of hostess that looks after the customers – you know, sits with them, has a few drinks and chats them up. Roberto says I've got hostess potential.'

'Roberto seems to say a lot of things. Does he give the orders round here?'

'No, not really. Not yet, at any rate. I mean the old man's still – '

'The King?'

'Yeah, I suppose you could say that. He and Roberto argue sometimes and the old man doesn't like it. You see, Roberto wants to bulldoze that old place down across the road – '

'You mean *our* house?' Holly felt deeply shocked, as if a bulldozer had run over her chest.

'I don't know what you want to hang on in that old dump for. If I was you I'd take their offer and clear out. They'll get what they want in the end, anyway, you can take it from me. They always do, one way or another.'

'They might be in for a shock this time,' said Holly, then gloomily fell to contemplating the golden swirls on the carpet. They were easy words to say. But she didn't have a very good track record when it came to getting what *she* wanted. How did they do it, these people? Was it just money? Ruthlessness, too, she supposed. Yes, a real lack of ruth must help you get on in life.

'Roberto wants to start the casino from scratch – have it custom-built, as he calls it – rather than trying to make it fit inside the existing house. And he'd have a health club on the top floor; gym, saunas, massage, everything. But his father says Shangri-la must stay, he likes looking at it from across the street. He says it's part of the history of the street. A bit barmy if you ask me.'

Mary-Lou chattered on and Alexis, who was beginning to emit a pungent smell, oscillated, reminding Holly of Simon's mobiles and thus of Simon himself. Would he come to

104

Pavarotti's tonight? She wanted to talk about him to someone, *needed* to, for by talking she would make him seem more real. When Mary-Lou paused to light their cigarettes with her heavy gold table lighter, Holly took the chance to change the conversation and bring in Simon's name.

'So you've got a fella? I wondered if you did.'

Holly gave a detailed account of Simon and Simon's house.

'Sounds as if they're well-heeled. You should stick in there. That's the kind of house I'd fancy – a brand new one all to myself instead of having to share this big heap with the rest of them. There's no privacy here, let me tell you, my mother-in-law could walk through that door right now without so much as knocking. In fact, it's a wonder she's not been up. She'll have seen me bringing you in – nothing goes past *her*. Don't ever live with their mothers, take my advice! Giorgio's mother thinks her sons are angels and should be waited on as if they were gods and all that crap. She's never got over her Giorgio marrying a girl who wasn't an Itie. Talk about being racist! I could report her to that board that hauls you over the coals if you say anything against darkies.'

'It's a wonder she didn't try to stop him?'

'Oh, she did. But I was five months gone with Alexis.'

And she'd be anti-abortion, observed Holly. Mary-Lou said she was, too; she was Catholic. If she hadn't been she didn't think the Tonellis would have gone for it; they'd have tried to buy her off. They'd had a half-hearted go as it was. Sometimes she wondered if she should just have let them do it but Giorgio had been dead keen to get married. 'He was crazy about me.'

Holly eyed a gold cross on the side wall. 'Do you go to church?'

'Of course. I was brought up to it, wasn't I? It's a good thing, you know, Holly, it makes you feel you're being looked after. It's, well – it's comforting.'

'Like having a dummytit in your mouth to suck?' Mary-Lou looked offended and Holly, having no wish to be rude to her, added quickly, 'I was only joking. I can see that it must be comforting and there's times you need to be comforted, aren't there? I'd like the bit about being able to confess your sins.'

'What sins have you got to confess? Screwing Simon?'

105

'I don't think that's much of a sin.'

'Is he good in bed?'

Holly laughed but revealed nothing. Even though she didn't even know if she'd ever see Simon again she meant to be loyal to him.

'Giorgio's no great shakes, let me tell you!' Mary-Lou moved closer to Holly on the settee. 'He lies on me like a ton of bricks huffing and puffing then he rolls on to his back and starts snoring.'

'He's nice, though, Georgie. I like him.'

'You don't fancy him, do you?'

'Not in that way. I just like talking to him. You can talk to men, too, can't you? Anyway, I've got a fella of my own. He's the jealous type, he'd kill me if I as much as looked at another guy.'

'Will I tell you a secret?' Mary-Lou lowered her voice. 'Hey, this is great having another girl to yack to again! Roberto – you won't tell?' Holly licked her finger and made a vague sign of the cross over her chest. 'Roberto is one hell of a lover.'

'Do you mean you get in the sack with him? In this house?'

'Maybe not the sack. But this settee's kind of nice.' Mary-Lou rubbed the blue nylon fur with the flat of her hand, splaying out her fingers. Her eyes had a slightly glazed look. She ran the tip of her tongue round her top lip and smiled at Holly. 'In fact, it's very nice. It's a real turn on.'

'But what if his mother were to come in?'

'That makes it even more exciting, don't you see? We put a chair against the door and if we hear her trying the handle and calling my name we keep dead quiet. Roberto puts his hand over my mouth to stop me laughing. One day the dummytit fell out of Alexis's mouth and she started squalling and just about gave the game away.' Mary-Lou doubled up and clutched her stomach. 'We had to put a spurt on and then Roberto hid inside the cupboard while I went to speak to his mother. There was I with no knickers on holding my skirt together at the side. Talk about a laugh!'

While Mary-Lou was laughing, the Neapolitan queen, as if she had been awaiting her cue in the wings, made an entrance. She stopped in the doorway for a second, arms akimbo, to survey the scene, then made straight for the baby's legs and catching hold of them, stopped them revolving.

'This child is absolutely stinking,' she declared. 'To the heights of heaven!' And she glanced upward as if for confirmation.

'I changed her only ten minutes ago, didn't I, Holly?' said Mary-Lou indignantly.

Signora Tonelli disentangled her granddaughter's legs from the canvas swing and scooped her up into her arms. She removed the dummy and pressing the baby's face to her shoulder, rocked her to and fro, crooning softly. 'Poor little bambino! She won't be able to shut her mouth if you keep that thing stuck in it! She will have a mouth like one of those mints with a hole. *Viene con la nonna, cara,*' she said and went stamping out of the room, setting the glass ornaments on top of the sideboard a-jingling.

'See what I mean!' said Mary-Lou. 'Bloody cow! What a nerve, taking my kid off without as much as a by-your-leave! And she didn't even say hello to you. Talk about bad manners! Like I tell you – never live with their mothers.'

Holly thought about Simon's mother at intervals throughout the evening in *Pavarotti's* – every time they had a lull. She drew up an identikit picture of her in her head: lacquered blond hair with not a single strand out of place, blue eyes like Simon's, a honey-coloured tan, scarlet lips parted in a silly smile, scarlet nails, spotless white trousers, and a shirt tied together at the waist to show off her brown midriff. She wouldn't look her age, certainly not. She'd have had her face lifted and she'd exercise for an hour every morning like Nancy Reagan.

'Did you know Nancy Reagan exercises for an hour every morning?' she asked Janice. 'I expect Jane Fonda does, too.'

'I'm going on a diet, starting tomorrow, no, honest I am, I mean it this time, my mum and me together, grapefruit and bananas.'

'Why don't you buy yourself a Nancy Reagan exercise bike and kid on you're cycling to Biarritz?'

'Why Biarritz?'

'Sounds like a nice place to cycle to.'

The door opened and Holly jumped. But it wasn't Simon, *again*. Where the hell was he? It was half-past ten.

'Looks like lover boy isn't coming,' said Janice.

'Looks like it was a one-night stand,' said Jackie and Holly threw at him the remains of a pizza that someone had left on her plate. He ducked and it hit the wall making a smear.

'Better get that cleaned up before Mr P shows up,' said Steve.

Simon came in just after eleven while Holly was in the toilet having a cigarette. When she went back through, there he was sitting at a table smiling at her. And when she saw him she felt as if she had always known he would be there. Why had she let herself go through hell doubting it? She brought him a capuccino with extra chocolate on top.

'What about the sheet?' he asked, sounding sheepish.

She said she hadn't had a chance to get to the launderette yet.

'Never mind. Maybe you'll be able to go tomorrow? Will I wait for you tonight? Do you want to come back to my place?'

He made a habit of coming in around eleven o'clock every evening and then, when she finished work, she went home with him and stayed the night, getting up in the morning in time to be gone before the arrival of Mrs Maple. Mrs Maple had missed the sheet and had counted the contents of the laundry cupboard several times over, whilst muttering to herself and scratching her head. She couldn't understand it and she hoped Simon's mother wouldn't think *she'd* taken it. Simon said he was sure not. Holly eventually owned up about the pink stains and she and Simon, who were at that point drinking sweet martini (from Simon's father's bar) and eating chocolate-backed digestive biscuits (normally reserved for Mrs Maple's morning coffee) in Simon's bed, laughed out-rageously, so much so that they spilt martini on the clean sheets and Holly had to take them to the launderette the next day. This time she put them in on their own and they emerged as good as new.

Holly longed to meet Mrs Maple but Simon sobered at the thought.

'Perhaps I'll meet her sometime.'

'Yes, perhaps.'

'I haven't seen much of you recently, Holly-Berry,' said Evangeline.

'I know, Evvie, I'm sorry – '

'I'm not complaining,' said Evangeline, though she knew that she was, much as she disliked the idea of being a complainer. It was something she had to guard against, now that her life was limited and she sat most of the day in her room reading or listening to the radio. She listened also for the sound of Anna's and Holly's feet in the hall. Sometimes they passed by. It was understandable, she told herself; they were still in the thick of life, had other things to do. She did not like the small jab of resentment that pierced her when they did not come in. She loved their visits so much: they punctuated her day, helped orchestrate it. They were her main treats.

Anna had gone yesterday to London and would be away for three nights. Last night Evangeline had lain alone in the house knowing that there was no one to call if she needed help except for the young boy Carlo who, Holly reported, slept the sleep of the dead when he returned from his stint at Giorgio's. No amount of racket Holly made disturbed him. He was proving to be of little trouble, for when he was not at work he was asleep. He did no cooking and he took a bath once a week.

Anna had been anxious before she left. 'You're sure you'll be all right?' 'Why shouldn't I be?' Anna had brought the telephone with its long cord from the hall in to Evangeline's bedroom. They ought to get jacks in the different rooms, she said. It was crazy to have one phone in a house this size, but that would cost money and she didn't suppose their landlords would pay for it. 'We'll manage,' said Evangeline. They always had.

And last night Holly had not been in the house, either.

'What are you up to these days?'

Holly blushed.

'Have you got a young man?'

Holly nodded.

'Is he nice?'

'He's gorgeous, Evvie, you've no idea!' Now that the flood

109

gates had been opened, Holly talked for an hour about Simon. 'I can't believe it – he's so wholesome, do you know what I mean? He's whole, that's what it is. He hasn't got any problems. Nearly everyone's got problems – Janice is always moaning about how she looks, Steve's wife's bugging him because she wants a cottage in the country and she hates him working nights, Jackie's life is zero when he isn't making pizzas. He's like a lump of dough waiting for someone to make him into something. Now Simon – he's like the sun, round and shining.'

'Will you bring him to meet me sometime?'

'I might.' Holly became guarded. 'I'll have to see.'

Evangeline pressed no further. They reverted to their favourite topic: books. Holly had been fed up that Anna Karenina had had to throw herself under a train in the end. 'Why can't there ever be happy endings unless it's a soppy romance?' It was difficult, said Evangeline; she was by no means a pessimist – Holly knew that – yet when she'd been writing, her novels had inevitably had less than happy endings. 'Perhaps writers are afraid of not being taken seriously if they make the ending happy, at least contemporary writers are. In previous times they haven't been so cowed. All of Jane Austen's novels end on fortuitous notes.'

'Do you think that sometimes endings in life can be happy, too?'

'Of course! If what you're talking about is a relationship between two people. You know that Dorothea and I had many happy years together. The fact that she ended in that awful home hasn't changed that.' Evangeline's eyes went past Holly and she withdrew into her own private recollections.

Holly thought about the romances she'd been reading since meeting Simon – Mills and Boon and Barbara Cartland. She'd been reading two or three a day. She borrowed them from Janice who had them lined up in her bedroom by the yard. She didn't discuss them with Janice afterwards – what was there to discuss? – but tossed one aside and plunged into the next. She had been seeking clues. What was it that the women had that enabled them to overcome the difficulties that lay between them and the men they fell in love with? Faith, hope, intelli-

110

gence, experience, beauty? Hope, she concluded, was the commonest common factor. Most of them weren't too intelligent in her opinion. And too much experience seemed to be a drawback. As for beauty, well they weren't presented as real ravers but they weren't too far out, either. None had club feet or wore pebbled glasses or lived in houses with damp walls and outside loos. Thieves, prostitutes and murderers weren't featured. Nothing too extreme. You had to fall within a 'normal' range for that kind of love. At the end of her binge she had felt depressed and soggy in the head.

'I need something to read, Evvie,' she said.

'What shall we give you?' Evangeline went to the bookshelves. 'I think maybe it's time for a Dostoevsky. What about *The Brothers Karamazov*?'

'What's it about?'

'Crime and punishment, I suppose, if I have to give a quick answer.'

'Crime and punishment? I don't know if I could handle that, not right now. Do you think crimes *are* always punished in the end, Evvie? Even when you seem to be getting away with it? Mary-Lou says they are unless you confess to a priest.'

'It's difficult to know. All sorts of scoundrels appear to get off but who can tell?' Evangeline took the book from the shelf. 'It's really the way that he portrays humanity that is important.' She passed it into Holly's hands.

'Another two-volume job,' observed Holly. 'Nine hundred pages. I'll take something else as well.' She liked to be involved in more than one book at a time, to allow for her fluctuating moods. Sometimes she couldn't stand these dense Russian novels full of melodramatic goings on; at others, she was transported.

Evangeline gave her the collected short stories of Katherine Mansfield.

The telephone rang, and Evangeline answered it.

'Anna! Yes, I'm fine, dear. I had a good night, thank you. And how are you? How is London?'

When she replaced the receiver she said, 'It's a fine sunny day in London, Anna says.'

'I hate London,' said Holly vehemently and before

111

Evangeline could ask why, took Katherine Mansfield and Dostoevsky and went upstairs to begin reading about the fortunes of the Karamazov family, and when she realized what the theme was, became hooked.

The gallery was already full of people holding glasses of wine and talking, their backs to the pictures – the usual thing. Anna slid round the fringes of the gathering and began to work her way along the walls. He's becoming stale, she thought, there's no longer any development in his work, he's going over old ground and that's beginning to look parched, in need of moisture and fertilizer. Perhaps his comfortable life has taken the edge off, has encouraged him to become complacent, or perhaps she was just thinking that in order to comfort herself for her own lack of security. There was always the argument that lack of commercial pressure left one free to experiment more. But that had certainly not been the case with Julian. On her walk here through the streets, still warm after a day of autumn sunshine, she had been thinking that it was time she revamped her own mime programme, took some new ideas on board. It was easy once one had found a reasonably successful line to go on following it.

She was able to go about unaccosted, unlike most of the people here who appeared to use such occasions for meeting up with old friends and acquaintances. *Clarinda! Matthew! Darling!* The cries rang out, lips scuffed cheeks taking care not to leave vampire marks in carmen, scarlet, fuschia. She herself knew almost no one and had not the kind of face that others thought they ought to know. She did not look like Someone.

As she watched, a red dot was placed beside a painting of apples and pears in a blue bowl. It was called 'The Blue Bowl'. On her bedroom wall she had a similar one of which she was very fond and she felt a little hurt to think that someone else would have this blue bowl filled with fruit on his wall. They had been given the bowl as a wedding present, she and Julian, but when they had parted and had undergone the inevitable dividing up of the spoils, she had said, even though the bowl had been given to them by her friend Beryl, that he had better take it. 'It's part of your painting history. And I suppose you might just want to use it again.' Though she had hoped not. An unreasonable hope, of course. It had turned out that Julian retained most of their decorative objects and she the kitchen utensils and cutlery and odds and ends of crockery. They'd had no furniture worth taking; they'd been poor throughout their short marriage. Struggling artists, as they used to call themselves, laughing. But, in fact, it had not been funny – two people (artists) at home all day in a cramped flat with insufficient elbow room. They had ended up jabbing one another sharply in the sides.

Lack of furniture had been no problem for Julian: his second wife Celia had a fully furnished house in a London square. She had a private income, inherited from her deceased husband, and an interest in art. Ideal for Julian, as one of Julian's friends said. It was when Celia had bought a painting of Julian's that they had met. She had commissioned him to do another, a large one, for her downstairs hall. That had started the chain of events leading to Julian's and Anna's separation. No, that's not strictly true, Anna reminded herself, as she moved along to the next painting, of a vase of lilies (she recognized the vase); the seeds were sown long before, right from the start of their marriage. She and Julian had never managed to establish a way of living that was satisfactory to them both. When they had broken up, they had said they should never have married, but remained lovers. They had known great delight together. But during the long, trapped days of living in the cramped flat, unable ever to be alone, hearing the sound of his footsteps on the other side of the thin wall, his cough, his swearing, when his work was going badly, unable to work herself, unable even to think clearly, Anna had come almost to hate him. They had argued about the respective importance of their different art forms. 'Of course painting is more important than mime!' he had shouted. 'It's creative, for a start, whereas mime is only interpretative.' Well, O.K., she had conceded, maybe that was true in absolute terms, but it didn't take into account the needs of individuals. 'My work matters to me! And it's not as if you're Rembrandt!' 'I always knew you didn't think much of my work! An artist needs someone to believe in him.' From the moment that he said that she knew he would find someone who would.

On bad days she would give up, leave the premises to him, and go out and walk for miles, along the streets and the embankment, through the green oases of the city. In parks, where people paused to sit and read a newspaper or picnic or woo one another or feed the pigeons, she lingered, having subjects to observe. And then her inner turmoil would subside, for a while. Beryl said that she should never have married, she was too obviously a loner. Was it true or not? Anna had not been able to decide. Perhaps what she had now at Shangri-la suited her best. And that was under threat.

Julian, catching her eye through a gap in the crowd, waved and mouthed something which she could not catch. She waved back. He hadn't changed much over the years; he hadn't gone grey or run to fat which, once, she had thought he might have done. His blond hair had receded only slightly and he still retained his boyish air. Celia was keen on fitness, as well as art; they belonged to a health club, drank freshly squeezed carrot juice, were careful about food additives and counted their weekly units of alcohol. Celia was ten years older than Julian. Anna could see no sign of Celia but it would be easy for even her, with her striking clothes – often scarlet and black – to be lost in the crowd. Anna liked Celia; she was more discerning and more intelligent than she appeared, and very warm-hearted. She and Julian had a good marriage, sound, based on ground rules which neither transgressed. Each got what they wanted. I am not good enough at compromising, thought Anna; that may be the drawback to my being suited to marriage, perhaps more than liking my own company. She knew that some people thought her to be a flexible, perhaps even rather docile person, but that was not so. If it were, she would have found a way to establish a *modus vivendi* with Julian. She had wanted to live life in the way that suited her. Even when her mother became too frail to cope alone Anna had insisted that she come to live with her, and not the other way round.

Anna was relieved to find that she liked two of Julian's paintings: one of a woman in a red dressing gown (not Celia)

114

and the other of a child with an outsize ball in a park. She would be able to enthuse over these without feeling hypocritical. Like most of those present, she would not speak the whole truth, but that would be neither expected nor welcomed. At this stage in the business of preparing for and setting up an exhibition, Julian would be in need of reassurance.

Having completed the circuit of the gallery (which was not large), she withdrew to a spot near the door from where she could view the previewers. She had seen them all before – the Know All, the Admirer (usually young, female, trailing in Julian's wake), the Gusher, the Niggard who would never gush over anything, The Critic (trying to look benign), the Pink Waistcoat and Spotted Bow tie who never missed an opening and was talking now about one that he had been to at lunchtime, the Trillers (mostly female, alas). And then there were the Yuppies, though perhaps not as many as she'd seen on previous occasions. Perhaps, thought Anna, I might do a skit entitled PREVIEW. She could still not see Celia. They couldn't have split up, could they? No, she didn't believe that.

Gradually the glasses of red and white wine vanished from the white-clothed table, and the room thinned out. Julian reached her. They kissed each other on the cheek.

'I'm so glad you came, Anna dear. What do you think?'

She told him. He was well enough pleased. He said her opinion was important to him.

She asked after Celia and he told her that she'd gone to a health farm in Malta for a week. 'It was the only booking she could get – she was in need of a break so I told her to go. Will you have dinner with me, Anna?'

'Are you sure?' She looked vaguely round at the handful of people left, thinking there might be someone influential with whom he perhaps might wish to dine. But it seemed not for he said he was absolutely sure, he had kept himself free hoping that she would be here. A quiet, relaxed evening was what he needed. That was the context in which people saw her, thought Anna, even Julian with whom she had not lived quietly; a not altogether flattering light to be seen in since we would all like to think of ourselves as being stimulating, if not exciting at times. That was her appeal, too, for Tonelli, she thought; she provided a contrast to his demanding, busy business life and vociferous family. Damn Tonelli! She had not come here to think about him. She had come here *not* to think about him. It was true; she was prepared to admit it now to herself.

Julian went to say goodbye to the remaining guests and Anna thought a youngish woman with streaming blue-black hair – the Admirer – looked disappointed when Julian thanked her, with his usual charm, for coming, and escorted her to the door. She looked surlily back at Anna. On the doorstep the girl and Julian spoke for a few minutes, she gesticulating and hunching her shoulders and speaking torrentially; he replying calmly, but firmly. Had he slept with her? Probably. He was an attractive man, easily liked by women, and within their set of rules he and Celia allowed one another a few sexual adventures, as long as that was all they were. But neither, Anna felt sure, wished to rock the boat. She could never have accepted a marriage on those terms. They had once discussed it, she and Julian, in the first year that they were together and she had said, 'I would always be faithful to you and would require you to be the same, as long as we are together.' She had thought that if two people loved one another they should be faithful to one another. She didn't care if it was an unfashionable view to hold; that was how she felt. 'You are a little Puritan, aren't you, Anna?' he had said teasingly but added that he agreed and would be mad with jealousy if he thought another man would ever touch her. Now she wondered if he always had been faithful to her during their marriage. She wondered, too, if he had asked her to have dinner tonight so that he could escape from the girl with the blue-black hair who was proving difficult to dislodge. Finally, with a toss of her splendid mane, she swept across the street into the path of oncoming cars and taxis which swerved and honked. Nothing hit her. Probably nothing ever would.

Julian came back, making a face, saying she was a bit of a pest that young lady, she would keep ringing him up at odd hours demanding to see him and sometimes she kept a vigil outside his house.

'Like Gwen John and Rodin,' said Anna and he was not

displeased by the parallel.

They went to a small, discreetly lit, expensive French restaurant, reminiscent of the one she had gone to with Tonelli. She concentrated on Julian, asked what he had been doing – apart from preparing for the exhibition – what his plans were now . . . was he going to have a break from painting . . . did he and Celia intend to travel over the winter? They had gone to Arizona last year. He had liked the light. He did not ask what her plans were; he assumed her life to be uneventful. And he couldn't understand how she could put up with trailing from town to town, from one grotty hall to another.

'It's been a lovely evening,' he said, when he'd laid his credit card on the saucer for the waiter to carry away. 'It's really helped me to unwind. Will you come back for a nightcap?'

Anna had been in his house before on several occasions. It was unostentatiously but not cheaply furnished; most of the fitments had come from Heals or Harrods. They sat on the settee in Celia's off-white drawing room and drank brandy out of exquisite balloon goblets and when Julian ran his fingers up Anna's arm and said he had never ceased to find her attractive she smiled and allowed him to slide his other arm around her. She had known he was going to make a pass at her. Knowing it, she had come. They kissed.

'It's a pity we couldn't make it together,' he said. 'Let's go to bed, for old times' sake.'

'Celia?'

'She wouldn't mind.'

Anna queried that. She thought Celia might not consider her to be simply a sexual adventure.

'Still the same old Anna! Does it make you feel any better if I tell you that Celia has a masseur in Malta whom she's very fond of?'

Anna went to bed with him; the die had been cast when she agreed to come back for a nightcap – or perhaps even before. They used the spare room bed, she would not lie in Celia's. Not that I am so very moral, she thought, as she undressed; he is no longer my husband, and, anyway, I am using him, deliberately. They slid into the cool sheets and they made love,

117

or, more accurately, had sex together, displaying affection, without any sparks being struck. It was like an extension of the pleasant evening at the restaurant. He seemed happy enough; he leant on his elbow and smiled down on her and said a part of him had never ceased to regret the passing of their marriage and she would always be special to him. 'There's something to be said for polygamy. Now you and Celia together would have made an ideal pair of wives for me – a *ménage à trois!* I've often fancied it.'

'Perhaps Celia and I might not.'

'You like one another, don't you? Our marriage ended too soon, Anna. We didn't give it enough of a chance.'

But she could not agree, although did not say so: the marriage had ended when it should.

'I do value your friendship, Julian,' she said.

'Is there no other man in your life?'

She shook her head.

'You are very self-contained, Anna.'

'Not *so* very,' she said and went to take a shower. And under the shower she thought that that was the last time she would ever have sex with Julian. For her, it had been a mistake; it had solved nothing and would make her reluctant to come to his next show in case he thought a precedent had been set. They had twice before made love since their break-up but both occasions had been a long time ago, when they had come together through spontaneous, combustible desire. For a year or two after that she had stayed away from London and for several years had felt the tug of desire when she had seen him. But she had been careful not to be alone with him. And now, as she raised her face to the refreshing stream of water, she realized that all passion between them was truly spent. He had become too smooth, and too bland, for her taste.

'Stay the night if you like,' he said, when she came back to the bedroom.

'No, I'd better get back. Beryl will wonder what's happened to me if she gets up in the morning and finds I'm not there. And it's too late now to ring.' Beryl had never married or lived with a man and had her set routines of bedtimes and bedtime drinks and hot-water bottles. Her life was time-

118

tabled into evening classes and outings to the theatre and cinema and the South Downs on Sundays and meals with women friends. When Anna came to stay she lectured her on widening her range of interests.

Julian called a mini cab.

They kissed warmly.

'Let me know when you're next in town,' he said, as he saw her into the car.

She went back to the sofa in Beryl's flat to dream, disturbingly, annoyingly, of being hurtled round the Amalfi coast in a long red capsule.

EIGHT

'*Buon giorno,*' said Evangeline.

'*Buon giorno,*' said the youth, setting his suitcase down by his feet and flexing his right wrist as if it had been overtaxed. He had possibly walked from Roberto Tonelli's office downtown. Evangeline supposed that Roberto might not even have given him his bus fare.

The youth's arrival, like Carlo's, had coincided with the termination of her afternoon outing. She leant on her stick and addressed him, again in his own tongue. Was he coming to lodge at Shangri-la? Had he been told to take a room on the top floor? Where was he to work and what was his name?

He was called Stefano and he was due to start work at Claudio's restaurant that evening. No, he had not been a waiter before though had worked at a bar outside Sorrento. Many tourists came to this bar. He could speak English and German, but when Evangeline tried him in English he looked confused. He swaggered a little, was older than Carlo, and might not prove to be as little trouble in the house.

He was not pleased with the bare mattress on the floor of his room and came down to tell Evangeline so. At home he had a proper bed, with a rug beside it and a chair and a cupboard for his clothes and curtains at the window. As he spoke, Evangeline saw a simple room, sparsely furnished, bare boards warmed by sun, rag rug woven by an old woman in black sitting on a chair on the pavement, window standing open letting in the balmy sea air, flimsy curtains eddying in the draught. She had spent several weeks in such a room when she was little older than this boy; it had been her first taste of freedom, of travelling alone, of not being subjected to other people's demands, of shaping each day to her own satisfaction,

120

and it had been her first taste, too, of the south, of a different culture, of Italy. The simple room had been for her a symbol of freedom; for this boy, a cage – even though he now praised it – from which he had wished to escape and venture forth. Well, it was only natural. And her own room was no longer simple but full of the odds and ends of a lifetime. But since that first time in Italy she had lived in either one or two rooms, never more. Her mother had allowed her to go alone to Italy, thinking her to be staying with a 'suitable' family, but being only marginally interested in her daughter's affairs she had not pressed for details. The boy's mother would be much more interested in his welfare and where and how he slept. He was saying so now. She would not be happy if she were to see him sleeping in such a room, she would be very angry. He expressed her anger for him, volubly. And who would do his washing? he demanded.

'There is a launderette on the main road. I'm sure the lady there will show you what to do. *I* am not the housekeeper here, you know. If you have any complaints you should make them to Mr Roberto Tonelli. He appears to be acting as general factotum for the house.'

Stefano turned away, scowling, and slouched back upstairs. He would not be so foolhardy as to think that he could complain to Roberto Tonelli without paying for it.

The next day there was a row on the top floor. Holly came home to find Stefano sitting in *her* room, eating a bowl of *her* cornflakes, watching *her* television.

'Out!' she screamed. 'Go!' She pointed to the door.

He did not move. He went on munching cornflakes and watching the screen. Humphrey Bogart sauntered across in his belted raincoat and trilby hat and when Holly saw what she was missing she was even more enraged.

'This is *my* room. Do you understand?' She strode over to the television and snapped it off. 'Out!'

He slid down into the chair and putting one leg over the arm, swung the foot to and fro. There was a hole in the sole of his shoe, she noticed, and he wore no socks.

She marched downstairs and asked Evangeline to tell her the Italian for 'Get out, at once, you bastard! You are trespassing.

121

I'll call the police.' She then went back up the stairs to repeat what she could remember. He had turned the television back on and she had to shout. *'Polizie! Subito!'* she repeated, when he still made no move. She must learn Italian – Evangeline said it was a beautiful language and Holly supposed it could be when you didn't have to use it to yell at an oaf who was sitting in your chair leering at you, defying you to evict him. She must get Evvie to teach her, and she could practise on Giorgio. She had seen Giorgio that afternoon. He had come in when she'd been drinking coffee with Mary-Lou and had said, 'I'm glad you two are getting on so well.' He'd swung the baby round and round in the canvas contraption and she'd chortled and let the dummy fall out of her mouth. Mary-Lou had had to pick it up and wipe it and she'd given poor old Georgie stick for exciting Alexis. Holly wished she had Giorgio here now. Not that he was much good at exerting himself, but he could at least speak fluent Italian.

She went towards the door, saying, 'All right – *polizie* it is!' At that, Stefano got to his feet, taking his time, and leaving the cornflake bowl upside down on the floor. He swaggered past her. She resisted the impulse to deposit a sharp kick on his shins and cursed the fact that women should have been made physically weaker than men. That was the cause of half the trouble between the sexes; if only they were better matched in strength then men would behave differently to women. They'd have to. They wouldn't get away with rape and assault. Anna said the theory was that men were trying to assert power when they intimidated and assaulted women. But why should they need to when they *were* physically stronger? That was what Holly couldn't understand. Not all men were macho, of course, trying to pretend they were cave men dragging you by the hair. Giorgio was not. Simon was not. Holly smiled at the thought of Simon. He treated her so considerately. He wanted to please her, to make her happy. He was crazy about her, he had told her that he was.

Anna went to have a word with Stefano. He was lying on his mattress reading a soft porn magazine. He might not be able to read English but he could understand the pictures. He had the magazine opened at the centre spread. When he looked up at her his eyes widened in recognition. She recognized him, too. He had worked at the bar where she used to take her nightcap when she was on holiday on the Sorrento coast.

He sat up. He grinned. 'Ah yes, I know you! You liked Eduardo?'

She did not respond to that comment, she told him that he must stay out of Holly's room. 'It is private, do you understand?'

'Eduardo has a sweet tongue. I think you find it sweet, no?'

'Please remember what I said,' she said tartly and left him.

'I send Eduardo your love,' he called after her. 'I tell him to come!'

After that he did stay out of Holly's room but continued to eat her food. She brought her stores in to her sitting-room and Steve came round and put padlocks on the outside of her sitting and bedroom doors. When she was out she locked them and when she was in she pushed furniture against the doors. Stefano used the pots and dishes in the communal kitchen and did not wash them, he left greasy rings on the bath, hairs in the wash basin and didn't flush the lavatory. Anna told Holly to come down and use her kitchen and bathroom and leave Stefano to stew in his own mess. The next time Anna was working in the garden and saw Roberto come out of his garage she ran across the road to intercept him and inform him that his tenant Stefano was reducing the top floor to a slum.

'You can't expect boys to be domesticated, Miss Pemberton.'

'But I'm afraid I do. This is the late twentieth century. And this is not rural Italy.' That jab went home, she was pleased to see. 'Who is supposed to clean up after these boys when they haven't got their mothers with them? Not us, I have to tell you!'

Roberto shrugged. 'The house is a slum, anyway. It needs to be demolished.'

Two days later, Giovanni arrived. He was also a waiter in Claudio's restaurant, had been in this country for some time, spoke passable English, was not rude, but was noisy when he came back at night, which was usually between one and two in

123

the morning. He sang and whistled and the sound echoed in the marble hall. His feet clattered on the floor. Sometimes he brought back his friend Pietro and they drank and played records until three or four o'clock. He had been assigned to one of the rooms on Anna's floor and told to share her kitchen and bathroom, but she looked him in the eye and said no, he could not share with her, he could join his friends upstairs. He pouted, did not insist, but when she was in bed – if not asleep – he used the rooms. They were not locked. He cooked food for Pietro using her ingredients, also used her soap and toilet paper, washed his hair with her shampoo and left black curly hairs in the bath.

The women conferred in Evangeline's room.

'They could move in another dozen,' said Holly gloomily.

'They could,' agreed Evangeline. 'They probably have an endless stream.'

And I may come to recognize them all, thought Anna: bar boys and hotel waiters and motor bike riders, all from Tonelli territory. There appeared to be an inexhaustable supply.

Giovanni's friend, Pietro, took up permanent residence. Every night now, coming home from work together, the two young men called loudly to one another as if separated by the length of a football pitch. Their laughter filled the stairwell. Stefano came back drunk once or twice and vomited half way up the stairs. Carlo wept with homesickness on his bare mattress.

'Something will have to be done,' said Anna.

She decided to make an appeal to Claudio. She chose her time carefully, about an hour before the restaurant opened, when Claudio would be there but not yet too busy.

Giovanni opened the outside door and raised an eyebrow when he saw Anna. 'We are not open yet,' he said. She said she wished to speak to Claudio. He hesitated, she stood her ground, repeating her request and then he conducted her up the stairs to the office. Claudio was sitting at a desk doing what looked like his accounts. Giovanni hovered but on being asked to go by Claudio, withdrew. Anna explained her business quickly.

Claudio apologized, shrugging, holding out his hands. He

124

had a thin, mobile face. 'It's difficult – they're young and boisterous. They finish work late, they don't realize they are disturbing people.' But he would speak to them and try to make them realize. He looked unhappy. According to Holly, who received her information from Mary-Lou, he played no part in the family's political affairs and stayed out of them as far as possible. 'I will do what I can, Miss Pemberton.' He rose and shook hands with her.

She went back down the stairs through the restaurant, passing the line of waiters whose eyes followed her. They must have guessed the reason for her visit. They did not look perturbed. Stefano was smiling and smacking the side of his leg with a serviette. Anna felt sure that Roberto would have instructed them to make nuisances of themselves.

As she reached the door, it opened to admit Maximo Tonelli. They stood face to face.

'Anna! What are you doing here?'

'I have come to complain about the waiters,' she said loudly. 'Their habits in the house are disgusting and they make as much noise as they can coming home in the middle of the night. They are making our lives a misery. Not that I suppose you care about that! I daresay it pleases you. Well, we shall stand our ground. We shall not be so easily intimidated by your bully boy of a son Roberto!'

'It does not please me at all,' he said quietly. 'Come and have a drink with me and we will talk about it.'

There was nothing to talk about, she said, and at that moment the door opened again, at Maximo's back, and he stood aside to let his son Roberto enter.

'I was just telling your father that we will not be bullied by you and those young boys you're using as pawns,' said Anna. 'And now, if you will excuse me?' The men allowed her to pass. Maximo was frowning, she saw. Roberto gave her a little bow.

Walking away, she felt the adrenalin surge through her body. She could have delivered a longer and more vitriolic attack had she wished. She fancied she had disturbed Tonelli senior. Though had she really? She could not be sure. She could not read this man.

For a few days the male tenants of Shangri-la were quieter coming home, though when they closed the front door, they still disturbed Evangeline who slept lightly. 'Shh!' she'd hear them say – Giovanni or Pietro, anyway. Stefano would not lower his voice. The King himself had spoken to them, apparently (the news came, again, *gratis* from Mary-Lou) and he and Roberto had had a row. Roberto had said that he was in charge of tenanting the house, *he* was the rent collector in the family and should be allowed to conduct his business in his own way. His father had told him that *he* was still the Boss and that he would not have the women treated in such a way. Roberto had seethed, Mary-Lou reported, and had paced up and down his room, which was directly over her head, making the ceiling shiver and little Alexis in her canvas sling shoogle and burp and the golden chandelier jingle furiously. Mary-Lou had trembled for the fate of her chandelier, having spent much time and trouble trying to acquire it. Such chandeliers were not easily to be found.

Gradually, as is the way, the waters forgot and became their usual, noisy selves again.

Holly and Simon spent thirteen peaceful, happy nights together. They laughed on the stairs of Simon's house, slammed the front door shut behind them. No one reproached them. There was no one to reproach them. Holly counted the nights as they slid past as if she were threading beads on a string, feeling each one smooth and round and whole beneath her fingers. They slipped easily on to the string and she held them close, holding, too, the knowledge that they could not be taken away from her.

On the morning after the thirteenth night, they slept in. They had drunk too much of Simon's father's cherry brandy before coming to bed. They awoke, blearily, disorientated, to hear the thud of a door shutting below. Heavy footsteps followed. Simon frowned, scratched his head. Then he streaked out of bed.

'Mrs Maple!' he cried. His hair stood on end and he looked wild-eyed, unlike his usual well-regulated self. Holly laughed

126

and snuggled under the quilt. She had been avid for the sight of the sticky Mrs M for a while and reckoned it was about time she was rewarded. 'It's not funny,' said Simon. 'We'll have to get you out of here.' He was searching for his clothes.

'We left them downstairs,' said Holly and began to giggle.

They had undressed in the sitting room and sat on the soft white rug playing records, drinking cherry brandy and eating cold pizza, and making love. It had reminded Holly of the picture of a French painting in one of Anna's art books – when they were reclining on the rug eating and drinking, except that in the picture the men had been dressed and the women not. (She'd asked Anna why that was and Anna had said perhaps it was more erotic? Holly couldn't make up her mind about that.) 'Something about lunch on the grass,' she'd said to Simon but he hadn't heard of it. He hadn't done art at school, he said. She had seemed to remember that one of the women had a ribbon round her neck – or was that another picture of a nude? Holly had wished she wasn't so ignorant, though had not said so to Simon. She had taken the lace out of one of his training shoes and tied it round her throat. 'Is that sexy?' she'd said. 'Really sexy,' he'd said and jumped on her.

She touched her neck: the lace was still there.

'Good God!' Simon stood, stark naked, in the centre of the floor, looking like the picture of Michelangelo's David in one of Evangeline's guides to Florence.

'Let's go to Florence, Simon.'

'*What?*'

'Florence, Italy. Everyone's been to Italy but me. I'm learning to speak Italian. Or we could go to Santa Fé, if you'd like,' she went on, speaking rapidly. 'Or St Louis.' She shot up in the bed like a jack-in-the-box. '*Meet me in St Louis Louis, meet me at the fair . . .*'

'Be quiet, for goodness sake, Holly! Don't you realize – this isn't funny! She'll *hear* you.'

They could hear her. She seemed to be banging pots and pans or dustbin lids. Like the women in Belfast, said Holly, when the soldiers were coming round to search; she'd seen them on the television news.

'I'm not interested in the women in Belfast! It's all right for

127

you – *I'm* the one who's going to have to face her.'

Holly saw reflected in his eyes – his china blue eyes, a little streaked with blood this morning – the vision of their clothes as they lay spreadeagled around the sitting-room floor: their jeans and T-shirts and socks and shoes, his Y-fronts and her black lace knickers which had cost nearly half of last week's pay packet. A quick blink, and the image was replaced by one of a female dragon expelling fire through tunnel-like nostrils.

'I'll face her if you like.'

'Don't be silly.'

He was pulling on another T-shirt and another pair of jeans. He stubbed his toe and cursed. He yanked a comb through his hair.

The roar of a vacuum cleaner started up below: a low, growling, angry sound. Holly wondered if it might not be Mrs M herself.

'It'll be O.K., Simon. Just play it cool. Go in and pick up the clothes and don't say a word. *It's not what you do, it's the way that you do it,*' she sang softly. 'You've got to have style, my grandmother says.'

Simon looked anything but cool. She was not even sure that he'd heard her; he was breathing hard, as if he had come back from a jog, or had just made love to her. His face was bright pink. He heaved his chest up and down, then went determinedly down to face the dragon. Holly wrapped a towel round her waist and followed him as far as the landing. The downstairs being open-plan, voices travelled freely. One voice did. The vacuum cleaner was killed abruptly and expired on a high-pitched whine. Simon said not a word, as Holly had suggested.

'I must say I am *very* surprised at you, Master Simon. *Very* surprised! It gave me quite a turn it did coming in here this morning to find all *that*! I never would have thought it of you. I always thought you were such a *nice* boy. I was saying to my Harold only yesterday, if all the boys could be as nice mannered and clean as that young Simon Simmons we'd have nothing to worry about. We could walk the streets unmolested. And what are your parents going to think? Poor things, and them away enjoying themselves in the South Seas.

128

It was to be the holiday of a lifetime so it was – that's what your poor mother said to me. A second honeymoon: those were her very words.'

Holly had to stuff the end of the towel in her mouth to stop herself laughing. Craning over the banister rail, she managed, at last, to get a proper look at the fire-breathing, sticky-mouthed monster, the fabled Mrs M: a small, squat, aproned woman with a squarish head ridged with pink plastic rollers. Her feet were planted wide apart in the fluffy greyish-yellow slippers which she kept under a shelf in the laundry room.

'Whoever she is she must be a right little tramp. Taking her clothes off in the *sitting* room!'

Simon came slinking up the stairs, head down, ears scarlet, clothes bundled under his arm. Mrs Maple moved further into Holly's line of vision and looked up, her neck creased so that her head could drop back. Her eyes bulged as they met Holly's. Half-way up the stairs Simon dropped Holly's knickers then, bending to retrieve them, he lost a T-shirt and a shoe. Holly exploded like a firework going off and dropped the towel.

'Slut,' hissed Mrs Maple.

Simon pushed Holly inside the room and threw the clothes on to the floor in a heap.

'Get dressed, quickly, for God's sake!'

'It's not my fault.' When he didn't answer, she said, 'It's not, is it?'

'No, of course not.'

'You're a big boy now, Simon. You don't have to care about her.'

'Don't tell me what I don't have to do!'

'And don't you stand there glaring at me as if it *was* all my fault!'

They had their first row.

Holly finished dressing.

'Would you like me to jump out the window so that I don't have to walk past The Dragon? I wonder if this is the Year of the Dragon? I seem to be coming across them everywhere.'

'Come on!' He grabbed her hand and towed her out of the room, down the stairs, through the dining area, towards the front door.

129

Mrs Maple was standing in the hall, strategically placed, with a cigarette in her hand. She blew short belches of smoke into the air above her head and narrowed her eyes to take stock of Holly. 'I was right, weren't I? Where did you pick *her* up?'

Holly made a lunge towards her but Simon, with a vice-like grip on her wrist, hauled her away.

'You're a foul-mouthed old bitch!' Holly yelled over her shoulder. 'I've seen your kind before – by the ton! Bloody hypocrite!'

They didn't speak in the car. When Simon stopped in the usual place, round the corner from her street, Holly said, 'You *are* annoyed with me, aren't you? It's not fair!'

'I'm not. I would just rather it hadn't happened.' He kept his hands on the steering wheel and stared down into the centre of it. 'When my parents left me on my own in the house they asked me not to bring people in or have wild parties or anything like that. They said they'd trust me.'

'Give Sticky Face a tenner and ask her not to say anything.'

Now she had shocked him. She had said it as a joke – well, half as a joke, anyway.

'That would be bribery,' he said.

'And corruption. Yes, I know. I guess you don't like the idea of getting your hands dirty. It's not a perfect world, is it?' she said, self-mockingly and swung open the door. 'Will I see you tonight?'

'I'll come to *Pavarotti's*.'

She was on edge all evening, broke a cup and dropped a twelve-inch pizza, cheese side down. 'Talk about a cat on hot bricks,' said Jackie, tossing another round of dough up into the air. 'Waiting for your tom to arrive?'

'You're not pregnant, are you?' asked Janice, when she and Holly went to the toilet together for a smoke.

'No, I'm not,' snapped Holly and almost wished she were so that she would have a bit of Simon inside her, but there wouldn't be any chance of that for he'd taken his father's advice seriously and bought in a huge stock of condoms. (You must have bought the shop out, she'd said to him, and he'd blushed. She loved it when he blushed.) What was she think-

130

ing? she thought, appalled. She couldn't stand small, squally, snot-nosed kids. She'd had enough of them; the last thing she wanted was one of her own. Janice was forever drooling on about her sister's baby, talked of having three herself, maybe even four, two boys and two girls, and spent much time musing on possible names, like Jason and Troy and Crystal.

Simon came in at ten, earlier than usual. Holly's heart did a double flip; that was what it felt like. She put her hand over the place to calm it. What an idiot she'd been to think he wouldn't come! She should have trusted him. That was one of her problems: not being able to trust. She went to him at once, sat down in the booth opposite, slid her hand across the table and took his.

'I'm sorry, Simon, I didn't mean to tease you this morning or laugh at you. I wasn't really laughing *at* you – it was just, well, it was kinda funny, though I guess it wasn't for you, having to face old Sticky Face.'

'It's all right.' He squeezed her hand then released it and picked up the menu which he studied even though he must have been able to recite it backwards. 'I won't be able to take you home tonight, I'm afraid. You see, my parents are due back in the morning, early, and I have to go to the airport to meet them.'

He didn't order anything and left after ten minutes. Holly went with him to the door.

'Will I see you tomorrow?' she asked, despising herself for asking, unable to resist.

'I'll try to get away. It'll depend.'

'On whether your daddy'll let you out?' He pushed open the door and walked off. She called after him, 'I'm sorry, Simon, I didn't mean it.' He didn't look back.

'The party's over,' quavered Jackie, violently off-key.

Holly threw another pizza at him, a freshly cooked one, hot from the oven, just as Mr Pavarotti arrived for his evening visit. This pizza hit Jackie full in the face making him yell. He stood there with gobs of cheese and tomato paste sticking to his nose and jowls and Janice had to cover her face with her apron to stop herself from laughing out loud. Mr Pavarotti sacked Holly on the spot, said he'd had enough of her fiery

131

temper. She told him he could stuff his lousy pizzas and his lousy job up his rear end. Then she took off the ghastly orange uniform for the last time, flushed *Pavarotti's Pizza* hat down the lavatory, sprang on to Evangeline's bike and cycled round the town, pedalling furiously in and out of traffic to the honking of horns and the mouthing of drivers behind car windows. She went flying through red lights; passed groups of people straggling along the pavement on their way in and out of pubs and clubs; passed four booted youths having a three-to-one fight with the one in the middle going down down down; passed a girl in a mini mini skirt and black fishnet tights leaning against a wall; passed a policeman on foot who yelled, 'Hey you!'; missed hitting two drunk men; rang her bell at a mad, bad, barking dog; swerved around cars parked this way and that; streaked through the quiet streets, lifting her feet on downhill runs and holding her legs out to form a wide Vee. Wheeeeeeee! Not a jubilant whee, but a whee, nevertheless. She spurred on her steed as it bumped and thumped beneath her. No streamlined vehicle this, like the low-slung, silver racer that Simon rode. When he was not gripping the wheel of his father's car. At the thought of Simon's father, Holly slowed, and stopped at a stop sign.

She took the turning to the right, to the estate where Simon lived. No light showed in his bedroom but the window was open at the top. He liked to sleep with the window open, he always had, ever since he was a baby when his mother tucked him up and read him bedtime stories about Jemima Puddleduck and Little Tom Kitten. (He still had the books.) Holly stood beneath the window. 'Simon,' she said softly, knowing he could not hear. She wanted to roar his name aloud. But she had her pride: so she told herself.

That night she wrote a letter telling him she loved him, that she had meant no harm when she'd said what she had and he couldn't hold that against her, could he, not for ever and ever, till death did them part? People sometimes said things that later they regretted. Not everyone could be like Edith Piaf singing *'Je ne regrette rien'* on Anna's record player. Holly put the phone number of Shangri-la at the top of the letter for it had occurred to her that Simon might call at the Neapolitan Villa and be met by the blank look of the Neapolitan maid.

She took the letter round to Janice's house in the morning and asked her to give it to Simon if he came in to *Pavarotti's*. *When* he came in. 'He'll come, I'm sure he will.' She might do better to forget him, said Janice's mother; when a boy was finished with a girl there was no point in her running after him. 'I'm not running, Mrs Binkie!' Janice's mother made them mugs of instant coffee which she set on coasters (white with gold rims) newly purchased from the shoppers' catalogue lying open on the kitchen table. Mrs Binkie was an agent for a mail order firm. 'There's some lovely pyjamas, Holly, real nice shades, hundred per cent polyester. Wouldn't you fancy a pair of the lemon? They'd go with your hair.'

'Nothing goes with my hair.'

'Now you mustn't put yourself down. I'm always telling our Janice that. If you don't think a lot of yourself nobody else will, that's what I say.' Holly, in a stupor from the heat of the room, watched Janice's mother turning the pages of the catalogue with hands rough and red from years of early morning office cleaning, the square fingers tipped with chipped, frosted pink varnish. 'Here's some nice frilly knicks,' said Mrs Binkie, 'dead cheap at the price.'

'I'm broke. I'll have to go and sign on.'

'Cheer up, luv. Have a marshmallow. Janice's favourite's – aren't they, Jan? I expect you'll get another job, Holly. Smart girl like you.'

'Selling hamburgers. If I'm lucky. *Lucky!*'

In the evening, Holly thought of her letter lying in Janice's orange pocket while Janice shuffled up and down the café with her tray, bending over the tables creasing the envelope. By the time Simon got it, it would look as if a dog had chewed it and he'd smile as he straightened it out and he'd think that looks like a Holly letter!

At midnight, Holly phoned *Pavarotti's*. Jackie answered, putting on his American accent, which he liked to do on the telephone.

'Oh, it's you, doll! By the way, I've forgiven you for

133

throwing that pizza at me even though I shouldn't. But you know me – far too good for my own good.' He laughed. 'How're you doing, anyway? We've got a new gal in your place. She's quite a chick. Yeah, she's something else all right! She's got a real sassy walk – you know, wiggles her ass a lot. Wouldn't mind getting a bit of it in my hand. Reckon I could go for her. I'll let you know how I make out. Hey, did I ever tell you that I went to Disneyworld?'

'I don't care if you went to the moon.'

'You what?'

'Just let me speak to Janice.'

'You're wasting your time. Lover boy's not been in. He was just playing with you, I'm telling you! You take it from Jackie!'

Holly wrote another letter, in her very best handwriting, having bought the most expensive unlined pale blue writing paper that she could find, and sent it to Simon's house. 'Please reply,' she said, 'even if you don't want to see me again. I need to know. I can't stand not knowing.'

From her window she watched for the postman and at the first sight of him approaching their stretch of street, ran down. For five mornings in a row she dashed to meet him and fell back, dejected. She talked it over with Mary-Lou who, although of the opinion that Holly should forget him and find someone else who would appreciate her more and give her a better time, suggested she phone his house. 'That way you'll have to get an answer. Ring from here.'

Holly palmed her hands off on her jeans and dialled the number which she had already looked up in the directory and knew by heart. A woman answered – not Mrs Maple. This woman had a pleasant, friendly voice. A motherly voice. Holly could imagine it reading *The Tale of Tom Kitten*. She asked if she could speak to Simon.

'I'm sorry, he's away at present.'

'When will he be back?'

'Not for six months, I'm afraid.'

'*Six months?*'

'Yes, he's gone to spend six months on his uncle's sheep farm in Australia. Who's speaking, by the way?'

'Nobody,' said Holly and dropped the receiver. No body. She was body-less. She ought to be able to float up in the air. All the way across the world to Australia and hover over Simon's uncle's sheep farm and watch the sheep running and Simon running. He didn't go off there at six days' notice, that's for sure, said Mary-Lou, that must have been planned ages ago. 'The bastard, he must have kept it from you deliberately.'

'Can you see me?' Holly asked Evangeline, when she went back across the road. 'Do I exist?'

'You seem to. Yes, I would say you do. What's been happening to you? Has your beautiful boy deserted you?'

'He cheated me! He wasn't straight with me!'

'Why don't you tell me about it?' When Holly had, Evangeline said, 'He should have told you, of course, right from the beginning, that he would be going away, but I suppose he was a bit of a coward. It doesn't mean that he didn't love you when you were together.'

'I *hate* cowards,' said Holly. 'I *hate* them *hate* them *hate* them.'

'We are all cowards, at times.'

'Oh, I didn't really expect it would last, anyway, Evvie.' Holly sighed. 'I'd be kidding myself if I said I did. It was like having a lovely dream when you're all warm and cosy and you try not to wake 'cos you don't want to lose it. Nothing good ever lasts for me. I ought to know that by this time.'

NINE

They started their celebration with a bottle of champagne. Bollinger 1966. Anna eased off the cork with a satisfying plop. Wine foamed from the smoking bottle into the wide-brimmed glasses which Holly held.

'Happy birthday, Evangeline! Here's to your eighty-sixth year!'

'Many *many* happy returns, Evvie!'

Holly and Anna raised their glasses. Evangeline drank, too.

'Good year, '66. Dotti's brother Cedric knew how to pick them. It was a pity his son didn't inherit his taste. Cedric would never have sold us to the Neapolitans. I'm sure, too, that Cedric would have wished us to drink up his wine. It might not belong to us legally but it certainly does morally.'

Anna and Holly had carried the remaining wine up from the cellar – now reduced to a mere dozen bottles – and locked it away in a cupboard in Anna's room. Roberto had been poking around Dorothea's apartments with a large black notebook in his hand and a gold pen tucked behind his ear; making an inventory, presumably. They had made sure that they had beaten him to the cellar. The thought of Dorothea's vintage champagne going glugging down the throats of their enemies had sent the two women scurrying underground at once. Anyway, the Tonellis had their own champagne and were drinking it tonight, to celebrate the thirtieth wedding anniversary of the King and Queen.

Caterers had been coming and going all day at the Villa Neapolitana. A florist's van had drawn up and disgorged enough flowers to cover the drive had they been laid end to end. Only the legs of the two men could be seen as they carried the enormous bouquets in to the house. To begin with the

136

women had wondered if Sophia's mother might have died. Holly had gone across the road to visit Mary-Lou and brought back a full report.

They were having two hundred guests at the party, a butler, and ten maids in black dresses and white aprons. The house smelt of flowers and floor polish; champagne was cooling in buckets; long, white-robed tables were festooned with smoked salmon and caviar, roasts of honeyed ham and beef and a suckling pig, guinea fowl and ducks, dishes of tomato and mozzarella cheese, small potatoes dressed with chives and garlic, salads beyond Holly's describing, baskets of fruit, bowls of dessert, platters of cheese. Sophia had been marching up and down between the tables calling out instructions, stabbing her index finger in the direction of anything which was not fully to her liking. The colours were amazing, said Holly; she'd just stood and gaped. And there was an enormous square white cake with thirty scarlet candles arranged in the shape of a heart and Maximo and Sophia written in silver writing.

Mary-Lou had bought a semi-topless, long, gold lamé dress for the occasion, and gold brocade shoes with five inch heels.

'She can hardly walk, between the shoes and the dress. It's skin tight round the hips.'

'Then she'll just have to slink,' said Anna and mimed Mary-Lou inching her way across the room, jutting out her hip bones, with her neck stretched back. Then she lurched over on one ankle and clutched her hips, her eyes wide with horror – the dress had split! She made Evangeline and Holly laugh. They were in Anna's room; she had prepared Evangeline's birthday feast and set the table prettily with wedgewood blue serviettes and candles to match set in silver candlesticks.

From where she stood by the window, glass in hand, poised to go to the kitchen to attend to her cooking, she could watch the guests arriving at the Villa Neapolitana. Long limousines were sliding into the street. Car doors were slamming. Men in black ties called out to one another. Women in long gowns hugged fur stoles close to keep the wind from their shoulders. The King himself came to the door to greet the chosen. They brought gifts: packages wrapped in silver and gold, of many

137

shapes and sizes. Anna saw the gleam of Maximo Tonelli's white shirt as he stood under the outside light that shone above the door. His right hand shot forward to grasp the hands of the men and his left went to their shoulders. He embraced the women, first one cheek and then the other. The presents were passed to the butler who stood behind the King, in his shadow. Music could be heard.

Anna put down her glass. 'The scene at the court of the Neapolitan King!' she announced, with a bow. 'Enter the Crown Prince!' She drew herself up, slightly curled her lip, tossed back her head, then strode across the room with her shoulders up and her fists clenched, letting her eyes swivel to right and left.

Her audience clapped and Holly cried, 'Now Giorgio!'

Anna slowed, allowed her head to sink down into her neck and her shoulders to droop. She smiled and nodded and smiled and nodded.

'Poor Georgie,' said Holly. 'He's so sweet. He's all pudding and pie.'

'And what about the King himself?' asked Evangeline.

Anna hesitated for a moment as if she might smile and refuse with a shake of the head. Then, staying quite still, she let her eyelids slide slowly half way down over her eyes. She looked at Holly and Evangeline levelly, piercingly.

'Bravo!' cried Evangeline.

Anna turned, drew the curtains across the window and went to the kitchen.

'I finished *The Brothers Karamazov*,' said Holly.

'And?'

'You know when Dmitri hits the old guy Gregory and thinks he's killed him and he's all racked with guilt? Well, then he finds out Gregory isn't dead after all and he's over the moon with relief.'

'That's understandable.'

'Yes. But was he guilty or not? He'd whacked him over the head so it was just luck that he didn't kill him, wasn't it?'

'True. But he didn't *mean* to kill him. Intention plays a large determining factor in the defining of guilt.'

'I suppose.' Holly frowned, but had a look on her face that

138

suggested she was thinking of something else. Evangeline could not quite follow her mood. Holly had spoken a lot to her about this book while she was reading it, about killing parents and about guilt. She was staring now into the bottom of her glass.

'Old man Karamazov deserved to buy it though, didn't he?'

'Perhaps, but if we were all to go round doing in immoral people the world would be strewn with corpses. And we would have their blood on our hands, which I would find objectionable.'

'Yeah, you're right.' Holly sounded gloomy. 'Why do they say parricide is the worst kind of murder?'

'Perhaps because it's like killing a part of yourself? Are you thinking Roberto might be considering killing the King?' asked Evangeline, with a little smile.

'No, I wasn't thinking about the Tonellis at all.'

Evangeline had not thought that she was. She pressed no further, having always made a point not to dig too deeply into Holly's past. It was up to her to tell what she wished to tell. They – she and Anna – had accepted her as she had come to them, arriving on a cold winter's afternoon clutching a torn piece of newspaper and asking if this was the place where there was a room going. She'd looked a bit like a wounded sparrow, even carried one shoulder higher than the other as if it had sustained a hurt. She'd looked ready, too, to bring her hand up across her face for protection and when she'd turned away they had glimpsed a lurid bruise on the side of her neck. They had not asked where she had come from, or for references. They had known she would have none, anyway. During the first weeks of her stay in the house she had talked to no one, had run up and down the stairs without looking to left or right. Gradually, the shoulder had dropped and the look of mistrust in her eyes diminished and she paused to speak when spoken to, and as time moved on she had started to talk, and to ask questions. They found that she loved to talk. About everything except her own past. Do you remember how quiet you were when you first came, Holly? they would ask, and laugh.

'Evvie?' Evangeline's head jerked up and she saw Holly's

face in close up, beside hers. The girl was bending over her.
'Were you asleep?'

'Certainly not, Holly-Berry! Would I sleep on my
birthday?'

Anna carried in the first course and they went to the table.
Evangeline kept the mohair stole which Anna had bought for
her birthday round her shoulders. It was a soft moss green.
Holly had given her a book on Venice published in 1904, with
a hundred colour illustrations by one Mortimer Menpes, and
the text by wife or sister, Dorothy. She had found it in a
jumble sale on her travels round the town. And had been so
exhilarated by the find that she had not been able to wait for
Evangeline's birthday and had had to present it to her straight
away. Together, they had pored over the pictures (a trifle
garish) of the Grand Canal and the Palazzo Pisani and the
Salute at Sunset and Evangeline had said that perhaps she
might manage one more trip to Venice, if Holly would come
along and help her. 'Of course I'd come! When I get a job I'll
start saving.' Holly was spending much time roaming the
streets on Evangeline's old bicycle looking for work – so far
without success – and rummaging round second-hand shops.
She was restless. Anna and Evangeline were aware of her
restlessness even within the house.

'Are you warm enough, Evangeline?' asked Anna. 'Shall I
turn up the fire?'

'I'm fine, dear. Just perfect.'

The weather had turned colder, the corridors and downstairs hall were freezing when they emerged from their
warmer rooms. The four male tenants grumbled and hunched
their shoulders inside their thin jackets. Holly sat in her room
wrapped in blankets unable to satisfy the electric meter which
gobbled up her coins. She had had to allow Evangeline and
Anna to help with her rent money, for the dragging of feet that
went on at the Department of Social Security meant that it
would take some weeks before her rent allowance would
come through, even though she haunted the place daily, like
many others, and ranted at the unfortunate clerks behind the
counters. And the Rent Man would not wait.

They spent a happy evening for Evangeline's eighty-fifth

birthday, with lots of wine and food – watercress soup, rack of lamb, lemon mousse and a birthday cake (coffee and walnut, Evangeline's favourite), on top of which one silver candle glittered. The talk flowed back and forth, three-cornered, about food and wine and Italy and America and the theatre and mime.

'I love watching you, Anna,' said Holly, whose earlier, blacker mood had given way to a lighter, more effervescent one. 'You change *so* much.'

'She loses herself,' said Evangeline and Anna smiled.

'I wish I could do that,' said Holly.

'Lose yourself? Or learn mime?'

'Both.'

'I'll teach you, if you like? Just for fun. I think you might be good. It's all to do with communication, sending signals. Body talk.'

'But I'm not quiet like you are. And I can't stay still.'

'You could learn to stay stiller. If you wanted to.'

Holly considered. 'Yes, I guess I wouldn't mind. I sometimes feel I'm all over the place, do you know?'

They smiled.

It was time for Evangeline to go downstairs. Anna and Holly helped her to her feet.

'Our next celebration will be for your eighteenth birthday, Holly. It's Christmas Eve, isn't it? I can understand why you were called Holly.'

Holly blushed. 'I think I've drunk rather a lot,' she said, putting the back of her hand against her cheek.

'Mime deals with essence,' said Anna. 'It seeks to create a minimum of movement. It is rooted in the ground – earthed, if you like – whereas dance is weightless and belongs in the air.'

'I would like to be rooted,' said Holly, regarding her reflection in the mirrored wall, twisting this way and that and pouting at herself. She was wearing an old black leotard of Anna's which was too long in the body. She took up the slack and crumpled it between her hand.

'Be still!' commanded Anna. 'See if you can.'

'I twitch.'

141

'Don't move a muscle. Concentrate! You're frozen. Solid. Like a stone statue. Feel how heavy you are – you couldn't lift yourself off the ground even if you wanted to. Now run! On you go, round the room! Now freeze! Hold it! O.K., you can relax. Let's do some warm-up exercises.'

They lay down on their backs, pulled their knees up to their chests and rolled from side to side. Holly giggled. This was good fun, she said. It was a long time since she'd done physical exercises of any kind, not since she was at school, and that was yonks ago.

'You'd think you were Methuselah,' said Anna, coming up into sitting position with her legs crossed. 'And don't talk so much.'

'Funny idea really, me doing mime. I always used to be called Rattlemouth.'

They exercised for half an hour after which they experimented a little, moving first in slow motion, all their actions flowing through from one into the other, and then in staccato rhythm, with hands, arms, legs, working in quick succession as if jerked by strings.

'This is like being a robot.'

'Right. And the slow movement is like being in a trance or a dream.'

'Except that my dreams don't usually go in slow motion. They're mad and hectic. Like somebody winding a film through too fast, you know?' Holly rotated her wrist, at speed.

'You see – you mimed that! And you kept your head still.'

Holly was happy that afternoon and seemed more relaxed than she had been for some time. That was why they were so surprised when she took off the next day.

'I'm going away for a bit. Don't worry about me. Love Holly X.'

The note, written on the expensive pale blue paper purchased for Simon's letter, was addressed to both Evangeline and Anna and had been left on the small table in the downstairs hall where they put mail and notes for one another. Holly must have gone early, whilst they still slept, must have crept

142

quietly down the stairs, eased the heavy door shut behind her, tiptoed down the drive and walked off along the dark street. Evangeline had heard nothing.

It was Anna who found the note when she came down in the morning to see Evangeline. They read it two or three times, turning the page over seeking other clues, but there were none. Anna went up to Holly's room and found nothing missing other than the large, sausage-like drawstring bag which she'd been carrying when she'd arrived at Shangri-la.

'She's probably only taken a change of clothes,' said Anna uneasily. They felt uneasy. Had Holly disappeared back to whence she'd come? Would they ever see her again?

'I don't think she'd go to London,' said Evangeline. 'She always said she hated the place.'

'That might not stop her going there.'

Anna was due to set off that afternoon on a mini tour – three nights away – and was now worried about leaving Evangeline alone.

'Of course you must go! I shall be absolutely fine on my own. Besides, I shan't be totally alone, shall I? Not with our four Italian waiters in the house!'

'Fat lot of use they are! When they're not out they're asleep or making such a racket that they'd never hear if you were to shout.'

But Anna was also concerned about leaving Evangeline *with* the four boys. Carlo was harmless, and Giovanni and Pietro seemed simply to be noisy, but Stefano bothered her. What if he were to try to take advantage of Evangeline? Evangeline might not have much in the way of possessions but she did have more than Stefano. But what could she do? She couldn't cancel her engagements at this late stage. For a moment she felt annoyed with Holly for taking off at such a time, leaving Evangeline without cover. She had known Anna was going away. But Holly was young, after all, and should really not be expected to take on such burdens. Anna suspected, anyway, that on the point of flight, Holly had totally forgotten.

After much thought, Anna went to Giovanni's room and asked if he would keep an eye on Miss Hudson while she was away.

'Si, Signora. Certo!' He stood in his doorway, yawning, dressed in a crumpled nightshirt. Behind him, the room resembled a jumble sale in progress: clothes, towels, tins, bottles were strewn randomly about. 'She is a very fine lady, Signora Hudson. I watch out for her like my grandmother.'

Anna thanked him. 'If you could just knock on her door when you get up? Ask if she's all right? I'll leave the telephone number of her doctor on the hall table and also a list of numbers where you can reach me.'

'Si, signora.'

Packing to go, Anna was full of misgivings. She was not at all certain that Giovanni had taken in everything she had said, that he would remember when he did surface in the mornings, or rather, early afternoons. Evangeline was getting steadily less steady on her feet. What if she were to fall and lie on the floor until she came back in three days' time? But she couldn't really think that way. If she did, she wouldn't be able to lead her own life at all. And Evangeline was determined that she should.

'Anna,' she had said, 'if you start to cancel your engagements on my account than I shall *have* to move out into that sheltered housing that the King is so keen to push me in to.'

Holly sat in a motorway café drinking a cup of tea and eating one of the sandwiches that she'd made before leaving home. *Home*. The word burned in her head as if it had been put there by a branding iron. She could almost smell it scorching. The image of Shangri-la with its curlicued rooftop and pink brick walls and jungly green garden was fading and another beginning to firm up, to swim into focus like a negative settling in solution. This picture was black and grey; she could see no colour in it at all. She pushed it to the back of her mind, not ready yet to face it.

She lit a cigarette, leaving only one in the packet, and looked round the café, assessing the possibilities. The place was half full, mostly of men – men on their own, truck drivers, business men, sales reps. They were eating breakfast, smoking, yawning, rubbing their eyes, reading newspapers. This was not a holiday season. She'd got a lift here in a private car.

144

She preferred trucks, the bigger the better, the further they were going the better, even though she might not be going all that far with them. But she liked to hear the talk. Last month when I was in Belgrade . . . Milan . . . Strasbourg . . . She'd often fancied the idea of being a truck driver herself but there weren't many women on the road, not long haul drivers, not yet at least. It was time there were, she said to the men, who said she wouldn't be strong enough to handle a heavy load. She planned to do some weight training. And she'd have to learn to drive something other than Evvie's bicycle!

The other advantage of a ride in a truck was that you had the width of the engine between you and the driver. Her lift this morning had managed to run his hand up her leg while he was changing gear. 'Sorry,' he'd said falsely and eyed her to see if he was on to something. He'd soon found he wasn't. Keep your hands on the wheel, Buddy! she'd told him and parked her legs right up against the passenger door. And she'd fingered the scissors in her right hand pocket and the drum of ground pepper in her left. She hadn't liked the look of him when he'd stopped: ferrety eyes, toothbrush moustache, smell of sweat, a naked rubber doll swinging on the back window. But at six in the morning on the outskirts of town there hadn't been a lot of choice and she'd been desperate to get on to the motorway. So she'd got in, reckoning she could handle him, anyway. He was no macho giant with tattooed forearms. The seats were covered with fake leopard skin. 'Just drop me at the first service station on the motorway,' she told him. 'No need for that, love. I'm going further.' A lift of the chin, and a little smile into the driving mirror. Her lip curled as she saw the smile. The toothbrush moustache was stroked with the edge of a nicotined finger. Fortyish, he was. Travelled in ladies underwear, so he said. That's what half of them said; it was supposed to excite you. 'Oh yeah?' Holly yawned. 'Got a nice line in black satin knickers.' 'Spare me,' she said, wishing she could close her eyes and doze off, but daren't. 'I'm not interested in your samples.'

When the service station signs came up he said, 'You don't really want to be dropped off, do you, dear? Not when we're just getting to know one another.' She said that if he didn't

145

stop she'd wave her red scarf out of the window and set off her rape alarm. 'I'm well prepared. And I've got a pair of sharp scissors in my pocket.'

Cursing, he pulled the car into the side road. 'Don't worry, I wouldn't touch you with a barge pole. Scrawny bird like you! I can pick up better off the street corner any day.'

'God knows what else you'd pick up with it.' She'd dragged her bag out of the back seat and slammed the door.

Creep! she thought, as she stubbed out her cigarette in the service station ashtray. Still, he'd got her here even if she had had to listen to a saga of the women he'd fucked, or thought he had, or wished he had. In a few minutes she'd walk round to the lorry park and try to pick a decent looking driver. She liked sitting in motorway cafés watching the people come and go, knowing they were all on journeys. She watched how they lifted the cups to their mouths, how they held their heads, folded their newspapers. Watch, Anna had told her, and try to stay still. She thought of Anna coming downstairs to find her note on the table, reading it to Evvie, discussing it. She knew they would be worried and she didn't like doing that to them but she'd had no choice. After a turbulent night she'd awakened from an especially vivid dream where she'd been pursued by headless monsters through snow drifts (Siberia?) which had suddenly started to smoke and in a flash had turned into raging fires and she'd known this was the time to start her own journey, even if it was into hell.

When she went outside the drizzle, which earlier had misted the surrounding countryside, had cleared. The service station seemed to stand in the middle of nowhere, surrounded by flat, sodden fields. The tarmac in the lorry park gleamed wetly. A dozen or so trucks were parked. The tankers weren't allowed to pick up hitchers. Holly walked past these, saw a driver adjusting his load of timber, pulling on the ropes, securing them. He probably wasn't a long hauler but he had a fresh open face and he smiled as Holly approached. O.K., he said, he'd give her a lift, even though he didn't often, for you had to be careful with hitchers, even the girls, some of whom could turn nasty. He'd had one woman who'd taken off all her clothes and wouldn't put them back on again. There they were driving down the motorway with her starkers on the seat beside him and everybody looking at them and the other drivers flashing their lights. He could laugh about it now, but not then. Even when he'd stopped to put her out she wouldn't get dressed and she'd stood on the edge of the road plumb naked and waving her arms and yelling 'Rape!' He'd never taken off so fast in his life.

'I promise I won't take my clothes off,' said Holly and clambered up into the cab.

His name was Dick and he had a wife and a one-year-old kid whom he adored and whose photographs he had pasted to the dashboard. He hated being away from home so much. Liked the driving all right and being on the road, wouldn't want to work in a plant eight-to-four being ridden by a gaffer, not any more, but he didn't look forward to Monday mornings and saying see you in a day, or two, or sometimes three. 'But you can't have everything, can you?' 'Seems not.' Holly told him a little about herself, not much. 'I'm going home to see my family. Haven't seen them for a while. I've been living with my aunt and grandmother.'

She enjoyed the ride. She loved being on the road, sitting high up, watching the lozenge-shaped trucks whiz past, and the rounded tankers, and the streamlined cars exceeding the speed limit. Dick travelled at moderate speed. He was a moderate man. Today, that was good for her. At lunchtime he turned off the motorway to an old lorry driver-style caff with steamed up windows and a smell of bacon and egg where the men all seemed to know one another and the two cheerful women behind the counter. It was a cosy place unlike the chrome and formica one where she'd eaten breakfast.

Dick insisted on buying her a hot meal. Sizzling hot sausages, bacon cooked to the right crispness, fried eggs that weren't greasy, a stack of hot buttered toast and a large pot of strong tea. Holly had been prepared to have a cup of tea and eat the rest of her sandwiches.

'You look as if you could do with a bit of fattening up,' said Dick. 'You look like my sister. She's skinny, too.' Holly wished she had a brother like Dick.

She was sorry when the time came to say goodbye and she

had to leave his warm cabin and jump down into the cold. He passed out her bag and she took it into her arms. They had stopped at another service station. She stood looking up at him longing to climb back up and go. Go, man, go, *anywhere!* Dick, she was about to say, let me come with you, when he put his head out of the cab window and said, 'Take care then, kid!'

'I will.' She took a step back, still clutching her sausage bag to her chest. 'Thanks, Dick! See you again maybe.'

'I'll look out for you. Cheers!' He honked his horn.

She waved him off, then turned in to the service station. What she needed now was a lift that would take her off the motorway to her own town. It was only six miles away.

Her own town? She hadn't thought of it as that for more than three years. She had done her best not to think about it at all. She had never expected to come back.

TEN

Anna checked in at her hotel, a one-star affair which was not custom-built but had been converted from an old dwelling house, reminiscent of some of the ones in their own street. A bulbous glass front had been tacked on which added to the air of general makeshiftness. The letter 't' was dark in the red neon 'hotel' sign, leaving an anagram for hole. Anna wondered that the proprietors did not see it for themselves and make an effort to find a new 't'. The armchairs grouped round the television set in the lounge were of mock leather, with splits revealing the stuffing beneath; the one in Anna's room was covered with slippery, mustard nylon cloth. She had a room with a view (of the sea, which was out, almost at the horizon) but the wardrobe had been so arranged that one could not see the window from the bed. The bathroom was at the far end of the corridor. She hated such places but must bear with them. They were cheap.

After she'd unpacked her case she went for a walk along the promenade, almost deserted on a late afternoon in early winter, except for a few elderly people who walked dogs and stopped now and then to gaze expressionlessly across the mud flats to where the sea met the sky. Beware Mud on Beach, the notice said. The light was dwindling fast and soon the tract to Anna's left, losing its last vestiges of colour, became a vast nothingness; to her right, on the other side of the ornamental gardens, the lights of cars winked as they sped homeward.

There were lights in the small theatre at the end of the prom. The poster on the door said: *Anna Pemberton in Mime.*

The manager, a cheerful young man called Bob, was in the box office. 'We've got a good house for you, Anna – almost full!' In this small seaside town, out of season, any event was a major event. Its inhabitants filed out to lectures on flower arranging, Indian cookery, Cannibalism in New Guinea.

Anna and Bob went over the evening's arrangements together. Everything was in order, as it always was. She had come here on a number of occasions, would recognize many in the audience who, afterwards, would come forward to talk to her. There were two or three elderly widowers who were very attentive and jostled one another to reach her first. Her fan club, Bob called them. It was all very comfortable. Perhaps too comfortable? She ought to be trying to push out her boundaries. She ought to be trying to set up tours abroad. Mime was appreciated much more in many other countries than here. But how could she leave Evangeline? Did she use her as an excuse? That was what Beryl said. 'Before Evangeline there was Dorothea, and before Dorothea there was your mother. You seem to like taking burdens on yourself, Anna.' The inference was that if she were free, like Beryl, the world could be her oyster.

Bob told Anna he'd got a new job, starting after Christmas, in a bigger theatre in a bigger town. So, if she came next year, he would not be here. And the theatre he was going to would be unlikely to be interested in booking her, she knew; it was too large for such esoteric entertainment.

They went out and had a half pint and a sandwich in a pub and then he drove her to the hotel to pick up her suitcase. While she was there she made a quick phone call to Evangeline. 'I'm doing fine, dear,' Evangeline said, as Anna had known she would. 'Don't worry about me. Good luck for tonight! Wish I could be there. No word from Holly, by the way.'

Anna put her room key and the front door key of the hotel in her bag; the hotel's Reception closed down at eleven and sometimes, after the show, she and Bob would go out for a meal together, usually Chinese. There wasn't much else on offer in the town.

She had a pleasant little dressing room at the theatre, warm, well lit, with a clear, uncracked mirror. She did her warming-up exercises, spread out her towel and laid on it her items of make-up. Spreading out the towel gave her the feeling of

150

creating her own space. As she began to apply the make-up she felt the quickening of excitement that she experienced when she was about to go out and face an audience. It was not an excitement Beryl could feel going to her office – the same office now for twenty years – in the City. Beryl grumbled about it all the time; for her it was a means to an end, providing the money to finance her numerous activities. Anna shuddered at the thought of Beryl's life, as no doubt Beryl shuddered at the thought of hers.

'Five minutes,' said Bob, looking in. 'Looks like every seat will be taken.' He raised his thumb.

The auditorium was an attractive shape, not too deep, with an apron stage which suited her solo performance well, and it held a hundred people. The atmosphere was intimate. The applause began as soon as she came in from the wings.

Seated in the middle of the front row was Maximo Tonelli. She experienced no sense of surprise when she saw him; it was as if she had been expecting him to be there. She felt his eyes beaming straight at her, like two stabbing searchlights. He was smiling and he held his hands high while he clapped.

She bowed. The house quietened. She turned over the first of the cards displayed at the side of the stage: A WINDY DAY ON THE PROMENADE.

She lost her hat, chased it high and low, pounced on it with her foot, wagged her finger at it, lifted her foot, lost the hat again, finally seized it and pulled it firmly down on to her head, then roped it into position with yards of string and tied it in a large bow under her chin. She clutched her skirts which were blowing up. She walked a small dog, tugging it behind her, staggering every now and then as a large swirl of wind from the sea buffeted her. She walked a large dog who towed her behind him. The audience's laughter was sweet in her ears.

From start to finish, the evening went well and, afterwards, her small band of admirers detached itself from the rest of the audience and she stepped down to meet them. You were marvellous, Miss Pemberton. Better than ever. Superb. The honeyed words flowed around her, pleasing her. There was one man on the edge of the group whom she did not recognize, a stranger to the town; an American, she judged. When the others had trickled off, saying see you next year, wish you could come more often, he came forward to introduce himself.

'Ralston Cummings,' he said, producing a card. East Coast, she thought. She was right; he was from Boston. 'I enjoyed your show very much, Miss Pemberton.' He had heard about her, had come especially to see her – though not from America. He laughed. He was on holiday in the area, visiting relatives. Did she ever tour abroad? he asked. Would she be interested in coming to New England?

By now, Maximo had risen from his seat and had come to stand nearby, within listening distance. He stood in an attitude which signalled that he was waiting to claim Miss Pemberton once she was free of her professional entanglements.

'I could well be,' said Anna. 'I have toured in the States but that was some years ago.'

'Could we go some place and discuss it? Say over a drink or a meal?'

Maximo moved up into the front line. 'Maximo Tonelli,' he said, giving the American his hand. 'Miss Pemberton and I are just about to go and have dinner together.'

'Perhaps Mr Cummings might join us?' said Anna boldly. 'I would like to discuss the possibility of a New England tour with him.'

Maximo took the set back to his plans well. He inclined his head politely. 'Of course. Please be my guest, Mr Cummings. I've booked a table in a country hotel outside town.'

'Are you sure? I wouldn't want to barge in.'

'It would be a pleasure, Mr Cummings,' said Maximo, keeping his eyes fixed on Anna.

Evangeline dined by the fire off the remains of her birthday feast – Anna had put it in the fridge in the downstairs kitchen before she left – and drank a glass of claret. The telephone was on the shelf beside her chair, and with it were Anna's phone numbers for the three nights she would be away. Anna had thought of everything. Evangeline smiled. She had been pleased to receive her call earlier and whilst she ate had thought of her playing in the little theatre beside the sea. She admired

Anna, the way she picked up her suitcase and set off for dark towns and ill-lit halls and gallantly faced her audiences. At least, as a writer, she had been able to stay inside her own room, concealed from her readership, although it appeared that, nowadays, writers were expected to go trooping all over the place like circus performers giving one woman (or man) shows, reading aloud, answering questions, revealing their inner secrets and details of their domestic lives, promoting their wares like the sellers of unpatented medicines and miracle cures had done in previous times. Roll up, roll up, get your marvellous potions here! Guaranteed to cure anything from a Hangover to the Love Sick Blues.

Thinking of love sick blues reminded her of Holly, not that it needed that to bring her back into her mind for she had scarcely been out of it all day. She had not phoned. When the phone had rung earlier, Evangeline's hand had trembled as she reached for the receiver. It had been Anna, which had not been a disappointment, but if it had been Holly it would have been a relief as well as a pleasure.

'Have you forgotten us, Holly-Berry?' said Evangeline softly, into the room.

Her meal finished, she placed the dirty dishes on a tray and shuffling slowly, taking each step cautiously, she set off for the kitchen. She couldn't let dirty dishes collect for three days. Anna said the boys' mess in the upstairs' kitchens was attracting mice; they might have to think of getting a cat, otherwise the house could become vermin-infested. They wouldn't put it past Roberto to introduce a rat or two into the house himself. How long was this siege going to go on! Holly had heard from Mary-Lou that Roberto was getting more and more impatient, and accusing his father of getting soft in his old age. Old age! The King was only in his late fifties, nearly thirty years younger than she was.

As Evangeline reached the door, the telephone began to ring. It was Holly, she was sure it was. She turned too quickly, lost her grip of the tray, tried to retrieve it, failed, and losing her balance, keeled over and went crashing down to the floor, on top of the fallen, broken crockery, her left leg bent beneath her. The phone went on ringing, and ringing. The wine glass rolled across the floor, leaving a red snail's trail behind it as it released its last dregs. It came to rest against the leg of a chair, unharmed.

Eventually the phone stopped ringing.

Holly replaced the receiver and scooped her rejected ten pence piece out of the slot. She frowned, tapped the coin against the back wall of the phone box. She stared at the graffiti etched into it. Four letter words. Drawings. Done with knives, from the look of them. Where could Evvie be? In the kitchen perhaps, or the bathroom. Though she'd let the phone ring and ring, to give her plenty of time to reach it. She'd try again in a minute. She leant against the shelf, feeling suddenly tired.

Behind her, the door opened, letting in a rush of cold, damp air, and a boy with a quiff of orange hair and fingers studded with thick, heavy rings said, 'You gonna be in there all night?'

She relinquished the booth to him and his mate who had a white face and wore black leather. They'd been prowling up and down outside for the last ten minutes, making faces at her and thumbing their noses. She'd kept turning her back on them and they'd kept moving round with her and flicking their finger nails against the glass. This was the first kiosk she'd found, after trying five others, that was working.

The boys hadn't gone in to make a call; they were shooting speed. Holly walked briskly off, her bag looped over her left shoulder, the fingers of her right hand curled round the scissors in her pocket. This was no area to hang about in. She knew; she had lived here for fourteen years.

She passed grilled, padlocked shops, two empty ones boarded up, the pub which spilled light and noise across the half-dark street. A number of the street lights were out of commission. Stoned by kids, more than likely. She'd done her share in her time.

She passed three men making for the pub, two black kids with their hair so tightly braided that she wondered it didn't hurt, three dogs dancing on their hind legs snarling and barking, a woman in a headscarf, hurrying.

She passed two tower blocks, grey by day or night, but less harsh looking by night with their lighted windows making irregular, geometric patterns. She had once had a friend called Eileen who'd lived on the top floor of one of them. They used to stand on the balcony with the wind whipping round them and they'd lean over the rail and gaze out across the world. Mind you don't bleeding fall and kill yourselves, Eileen's mum would yell at them from within. That's the world out there, they'd say, ignoring Eileen's mum. On clear days they could see the distant hills, purplish-blue, tempting. Let's start running, see if we can get there, Holly had suggested. Don't be daft, was what Eileen said. Eileen had got knocked up when she was thirteen and had been sent away to a relative somewhere. She'd said she'd write, but she hadn't. Holly had gone up two or three times to ask how she was getting on. Eileen's mum hadn't opened the door. The last time Holly called she'd stuck a note through the letter box and it wasn't long after that that she'd taken off herself.

She passed a line of straggly looking sticks, trees, so-called, though they had never properly taken, set along the edge of a stretch of scrubby grassland that had never properly grown. Their green belt!

She came to a block of flats, only five storeys high, but stretching out in a vast wide arc like an embrasure. Communal balconies ran along each floor. Decks, they were called. When she was small she used to imagine she was on a ship and when she looked down that she could see the Atlantic Ocean. New York next stop! Hang on to your hat and you'll soon see the Statue of Liberty coming up, folks!

She stopped in front of the building and looked up. Many of the windows were boarded over. Graffiti was rampant: Everybody Was Here, the IRA, the National Front, Killers, Terrors, the Indecipherables. This was the hell block in the estate (not that the others resembled the Kingdom of Heaven); the pits, which no one in their right mind wanted, where people with few points, people who hadn't had the wit to put their names on a housing list, the unemployed, the feckless, the violent, the irresponsible, the mentally – and physically – unstable were housed.

She entered one of the bottom stairwells and immediately the stench – of urine, excrement, cat, mould – hit her and she

155

took a step backward. The stair was murky; the dark shadows might conceal anything from human or animal turds to a rat or a man crouching, waiting. She took a deep breath, put one hand over her nose, keeping the other in her pocket, and charged. Like a kamikaze. This was how she'd always come home at nights.

She'd reached the first deck safely. She was panting slightly. Out of training! There seemed to be no one about though it was always difficult to be sure. She moved into the next section of stairway and then was on the second deck. *Their* deck.

Moving quickly and quietly on the balls of her feet, she travelled along the walkway. From behind some doors came the sound of music, voices, television sets turned up high. She heard car tyres screeching and the crackle of gunfire. Bang bang you're dead! Other doors were dark and silent. As she drew closer to their own, she slowed. Her heart was banging away as if she were still running up stairs and she felt sickness at the base of her throat.

Then she halted, abruptly. Their flat was boarded up! Planks of rough plywood had been nailed across the window frames. Someone had written FUCK YOU in red spray paint. The frosted glass panel on the front door was broken.

Peering through the jagged hole, Holly looked into darkness. She thought she heard a soft scratching sound. It might be mice, or cockroaches scuttling. Without their regular dose of kill powder they would be swarming, over the draining board, in the sink, up and down the grease-yellowed gas cooker, clambering over one another's backs, ugly and determined. A shiver ran up Holly's spine and made her head twitch. And the fungus would be growing high on the bathroom wall.

She pressed the bell which hadn't worked for years, rattled the letter-box flap. It was a waste of time; nothing but cockroaches and vermin could possibly be living in there.

Was this the beginning of the end? wondered Evangeline, as she lay with her cheek against the rough pile of the carpet, staring muzzily at a shard of white china which stuck up like a

156

spike a few inches in front of her face. It was part of a cup, she had decided. It had taken a few minutes to decide. But she had not had a stroke, thank God, she knew she had not; she had simply fallen and probably broken her left leg which felt numb beneath her. Simply! Breaking a limb was often the way it started. And to crawl across the room, whose length stretched away into infinity, reach for the telephone, ring for help, would be a task of the most immense difficulty. It was impossible. When she tried to move, she blacked out.

All evening, she had moved in and out of consciousness. Surfacing into pain, she had once or twice let herself sink back down again. In those spells she had dreamt of drowning; the waters had been calm and peaceful, not at all turbulent or threatening, and turquoise blue, like the colour of the Aegean Sea in which she and Dottie had swum, cutting gently through the limpid surface causing little ripples of white to eddy round them, or diving down into the strange, magical underwater world where nothing was set or concrete. She marvelled at the mobility of her body, then. In the dream she had seen Dottie who had appeared to be floating on her back, beyond her reach. Was this also a portent? she wondered. Perhaps; perhaps not. She had dreamt regularly of Dottie since her death, which was not really to be wondered at.

It would be easy to let oneself sink right down and not come struggling up to the surface again, gulping for air. Might it not even be best? But she was not ready yet to go. She could not go without knowing about Holly. So, from time to time, she had shifted her head a little, into a more comfortable position, had eased her right arm up so that she could move her wrist and flex her stiff fingers. It seemed essential to move something. She was getting steadily colder. The coal fire had dwindled and died and the electric one, whose orange coil she could just see out of the corner of her eye, was too far away to give her warmth. She thought of Holly and of Anna. She recited snatches of Shakespeare inside her head. Once, she could have recalled whole speeches and sonnets, but did not complain about that now snatches would do. *Shall I compare thee to a summer's day? Thou art more lovely and more temperate.* She had recited that to Dottie one day in high summer, lying in a

157

meadow in south-west France, smelling the canteloupe ripening in an adjoining field, and they had laughed. They had not been overly sentimental with one another. Evangeline tried to smile, winced instead.

Out in the hall, the grandmother clock struck twelve. She had been waiting for that. Like Cinderella! To be turned into a pumpkin at this moment might not be all that bad for pumpkins were soft and boneless and would never have to lie in such a tortured position. She had always loved the sound of the clock; its mellifluous notes made her feel she was not alone in the house, and, tonight, it was giving her hope. Each time it chimed, she thought, another quarter of an hour gone, another half-hour, an hour. The striking of the hours were the highlights; they lifted her spirit. I have made it to nine o'clock, ten, eleven. And now midnight, and a new day! The clock sang through her body. If only she could hold on until the boys came home. Then she would shout for help. Shout? Well, whisper maybe. She had tried out her voice. *Help!* The noise she had made had been pathetically feeble. You've got to do better than that, Hudson, they'll never hear you behind a bus ticket! She had had another go and managed to do better, slightly. But the boys made so much noise, banging and clattering and talking, that she was aware that they might not hear her. What else could she do?

The spiky piece of china shimmered before her. If she could reach that, she might try to throw it at the door to which she lay close. Inch by inch, centimetre by centimetre, she moved her hand towards it. After some minutes her fingers made contact, curled round and began on the long labour of dragging and pulling until the shard was in position. Ammunition ready! The effort had exhausted her. She dozed off again.

Her eyelids jerked open with the thud of the outside door. Footsteps rang out on the terrazzo floor.

'Help!' Her voice wavered, seemed hardly to rise up her throat. Her fingers grasped the piece of china. The feet were going up the staircase, quickly, beating out a loud tattoo, which, soon, too soon, became quieter and quieter. And had now died away. She strained her ears to hear. A door closed distantly, somewhere at the top of the huge, echoing house. Silence. Complete and utter. Her fingers relaxed their grip. There was blood on her hands. She wanted to howl. God, how she wished she *could* howl. Like a wounded lioness bellowing in the middle of a wide open plain so that all the beasts of the field could not fail to hear and come running to lick her. Fat lot of good that is, howling *inside*, Hudson! And self-pity will get you nowhere, which was made plain to you from an early age. Her nanny had been full to bursting of such aphorisms. *Discontent is want of self-reliance; it is infirmity of will.* Her nanny had not taught her that one, not having read Emerson, but she would have agreed with it.

And then the outside door opened again, and closed. Feet advanced across the hall floor. Making a supreme effort, summoning all her will, Evangeline raised her head and yelled. The sound might not have emerged as a yell but it was sufficient in volume to stop the feet in their tracks. 'Help,' she said again, less strongly. She tried to pick up the shard but did not have the strength.

The door was opened, cautiously, and Carlo's startled face peered round.

'Fetch Signora Tonelli,' said Evangeline and fell back into oblivion.

Wakening to see a pale gold velvet chair standing on a pale gold carpet, yellow roses on a mantlepiece, a bowl of fruit on a gleaming mahogany table, Anna knew that she was not in her one-star hole with its ugly wardrobe and candlewick bedspread smirched with burn marks and stinking of stale tobacco smoke. This room smelt sweet, and luxurious, and the sheets were of pure linen. She moved her leg and encountering another warm one, rolled over on to her back.

Maximo turned too, at the same moment, and threw his arm across her. His arm felt heavy, but reassuringly, protectively so. They stared into one another's eyes.

'*Buon giorno,*' she said.

He smiled, drew her closer to him. His chest was covered with a mat of dark, curly hair, tinged only at the throat with silver. She liked the feel of it against her skin, wanted to rub against it as a cat might. She liked the stockiness of his body, and his smell. He stroked her hair. For such a heavy, solid man, his touch was exceptionally gentle, and sent shivers of desire through her. He would probably dance well, too, would be light on his feet. She would like to dance with him.

'You slept well?'

'Very.'

She'd slept deeply, and contentedly, and had been aware that she was smiling as she'd drifted down into unconsciousness. And she had known that when she awoke she would not feel any regrets. This time she might sing with Piaf.

She stretched, feeling the length of his body against hers. They were about the same height.

They made love again, and that was how it felt to her – they were making love, as well as fulfilling their bodily needs. There was warmth and passion between them, and tenderness, too.

'Anna, Anna,' he murmured, as they subsided. 'I love you.' He said it in Italian.

'You are a most unsuitable lover, you know.'

The night before, facing him across the great width of the king-size bed, she had said, 'I am not going to leave Shangri-la.'

'I am not going to bed with you to try to persuade you to leave Shangri-la. There is only one reason – and that is because I want you. Desire you. *Very* much. And you?'

'I want you, too.'

'So why should we not have what we both want?'

There were many reasons, as he well knew, but he did not want her to spell them out. Nor did she wish to do so. At that moment they seemed irrelevant, anyway.

Over dinner, Anna and Ralston Cummings had clinched a deal; she was to go to New England in the spring, he would work out an itinerary and be in touch when he returned to the States. He would have been happy to linger over coffee and brandy but as midnight came and went and the dining room emptied, Maximo asked if he would excuse them. 'Anna has had a long day. I think it is time I got her to bed.' Mr Ralston jumped up, full of apologies. He had had no idea it was so late. Maximo asked the head waiter to call a taxi.

'Would you be accompanying Anna on her trip to the States, Maximo?'

'It's possible.'

They said goodnight, then Maximo put his hand under Anna's elbow and guided her up the stairs into a room filled with flowers. A bottle of champagne stood in a bucket of ice. The suitcase containing her props (and looking very shabby) had been placed beside the door. She could only laugh.

'You were very sure, weren't you?'

'Yes.' He had his thumbs on the champagne cork.

'I thought I was supposed to be tired?'

'And are you?'

She smiled and shook her head. The champagne cork hit the ceiling. She thought of Evangeline and hoped she slept peacefully.

They had not fallen asleep themselves until after two.

'Ten o'clock,' Maximo said now, consulting his watch. 'Time for breakfast.'

It was brought to them – freshly squeezed orange juice, excellent coffee, eggs poached to perfection, hot croissants. In the hotel where she had not slept breakfasts were standard: bacon, egg, sausage, one of each, and a half, wrinkled tomato, all set in a film of grease. How easy it would be to develop a taste for luxury, she thought, as she sat back against the fat frilly pillows and sipped the fragrant coffee. Every detail had been taken care of. There was a red rose lying on the tray. No one could hanker after greasy eggs and communal lavatories. They were good for neither the body nor the soul.

The bathroom was also luxuriously fitted out, with shower, bidet and a jacuzzi. Expensive shampoos, bath essences, soaps were supplied, and thick terry towelling bath robes. She could spend a week in this suite, eating fruit, drinking champagne, bathing in the jacuzzi.

They took a bath together, splashing one another with scented water, soaking the marble floor, and laughing.

'Tonight we are going to stay in a castle,' said Maximo.

'You will be the king of the castle!' *And I shall be queen, dilly-*

dilly, she sang in her head, and she thought, How foolish I am being, and how much I am enjoying it.

'I've arranged to be away from home for three days so I am going to accompany you on your tour.'

'How did you find out about it?'

He smiled.

'You have your ways!' She pushed her foot against his chest and he caught hold of her ankle. Bringing up her foot, he kissed the sole.

When they were dressing he said, 'I must arrange some Italian engagements for you, Anna. Would you like that – for us to go to Italy together?'

It would be bliss, she said and thought of walking through the streets of Florence in the early morning, gliding over the calm waters of the Grand Canal at sunset. She felt as if she were floating through a dream. She was not concerned about waking up.

It was midday by the time they left the hotel. They then drove to the one on the promenade with the hole in its sign. Maximo remained outside.

'We were wondering what had happened to you,' said the woman in Reception, stretching her neck to get a better look at the Ferrari. 'When the girl went up to do your room she said the bed hadn't been slept in. Meet an old friend, did you?'

Anna paid the bill and collected her belongings and they sped off down the coast road to the sound of *The Magic Flute*.

Suddenly, she remembered that she'd forgotten to phone Evangeline.

'You can do it when we arrive,' said Maximo.

'You've been amazingly lucky,' said the doctor. He was a youngish man, and looked tired. It was not surprising, thought Evangeline, who was feeling very tired herself; he'd been on duty in Casualty when she'd been brought in, and he appeared to be still on, even though it was now daytime. 'Lots of people your age lie three days at the back of the door before someone comes. Hypothermia, that's the killer. You were found just in time.'

She had a few cuts and bruises, very minor, considering,

162

and her left leg was fractured, just below the knee, but the break was not a bad one, the consultant had told her when he'd come by earlier on his rounds. She was to spend today recovering from her ordeal, getting her puff back, and tomorrow he'd pop her under and set the fracture. 'We'll have you discoing again in no time.'

The sister said they would need the name and address of her next of kin. Evangeline gave Anna's name, adding that she was away at present, on business, and would not be back until Friday.

'Is there nowhere we can reach her?'

'I don't think that should be necessary, do you, Sister? I mean, it's only a small operation, isn't it? Perhaps you could just put my neighbour Mrs Tonelli down in the meantime? I'll tell her how to reach my friend if she needs to.'

Sophia had ridden in with her in the ambulance. Evangeline had recovered consciousness after she'd been lifted on to the stretcher to see, wavering in front of her, the square head of Sophia, bound about with a black scarf which did not totally conceal her old-fashioned steel curlers. A red woollen dressing gown, firmly knotted at the waist, covered her body.

'I go in the ambulance,' she was telling the men. 'My son comes behind in the car to bring me home. My husband is not at home tonight, he is away doing business. He is a very busy man.'

She had talked to Evangeline throughout the short journey. 'You just relax, Miss Hudson, I look after you now. I was right, was I not? – I said you should be sheltered in your housing. Then this never happen. It is not good to be alone at your age. I said to you, "What if you break your leg?" And look what happens! It was like a prophecy, was it not?'

Giorgio was the son following behind. Evangeline glimpsed his face as she was carried horizontally under the arc lights and in through the swing doors of Casualty. She felt strangely distanced, then, as if it were not happening to her. Sophia stumped in behind her to see that justice was done. She had heard many tales of people being turned away through shortage of beds, doctors, nurses, porters, cleaners, lavatory paper. 'Any excuse! And you drive them for miles through the

163

night in ambulances. By the time they find a hospital with a bed they are dead.'

'It's all right, madam,' the young doctor said, preventing her from following the procession into the examination room. 'Your friend will be well looked after, I promise you.'

Sophia and Giorgio had waited, seated on high-backed chairs in the corridor, the former wide awake and passing comments to all who went by, the latter snoring softly, his head slumped on to his chest, until Evangeline was admitted to the ward. As she was wheeled past them, Sophia jumped up and said, 'I come tomorrow, Miss Hudson, and see what they are doing to you. I phone my husband's friend – he is a big consultant, he makes big noise in the hospital, he will take good care of you.'

'No need,' said Evangeline weakly. She put out her hand to take Sophia's. 'But you have been most kind, Signora Tonelli.'

At the afternoon visiting hour, Sophia arrived with Mary-Lou and Alexis. They were carrying flowers, grapes, bananas, a loaf of white Italian bread, a wedge of Cambazola cheese, a lump of chicken liver pâté, chocolates, and a bottle of grape juice. 'I know they give you bad food in these places. You need good food for strength.' Sophia sent Mary-Lou to find flower containers and water and set about rearranging Evangeline's locker, inside and out. Alexis sat in her pushchair sucking her dummytit and staring up at Evangeline in the high white bed.

Evangeline told Sophia about the piece of paper containing Anna's phone numbers. 'It's beside my bed. But there is no need to bother her,' she stressed. 'Not unless there is an emergency.'

'Don't worry, I take care of that.'

Mary-Lou returned with two tall thin vases.

'What use are they?' demanded her mother-in-law. 'They just about hold one rose each. I go and talk to Sister.'

'Mary-Lou,' said Evangeline, motioning to the girl to sit on the chair beside the bed. 'Holly didn't say anything to you about going away, did she?'

'Not a word. Why, has she taken off? She's been restless, mind you, ever since that Simple Simon gink gave her the heave. Out for what he could get, he was, if you ask me, right from the beginning. He wasn't going to be serious about a girl like Holly. Well, I mean she didn't come from the right side of the tracks, did she, not as far as he was concerned? Who does he think he is? I said to her. At least she can't have gone after him, can she – not all the way to Oz? Though you never know with Holly. She'd have a go at anything.'

'Did she ever tell you which tracks she did come from, Mary-Lou?'

'No, not Holly. Nothing that you could take serious like. One minute she'd say she was descended from a belted earl, whatever he is when he's at home, and the next, from Clarke Gable who met her mother when he was over here filming. Always said you were her granny though, but you're not, are you?'

'By adoption, yes, I think I would say that I was.' It was the first time that Evangeline had seen the relationship in that light, and she liked it. She felt a little stronger. 'If she phones you, Mary-Lou, by any chance, will you come and tell me? Or ring up and leave a message?'

Sister chased Evangeline's visitors away after fifteen minutes. She said, firmly, that the patient was looking tired and needed to rest. She drew the screens around her bed and took charge of the food.

'I don't suppose you feel like Cambazola and chocolate, do you, Miss Hudson?'

On returning to their street, Sophia went to Evangeline's room and found Anna's paper. Miss Pemberton should know what was going on, she had decided on the drive home. Any operation was a risk at eighty-five, as she'd said to Mary-Lou. She examined the numbers and dialled the one opposite Wednesday.

'The Bella Vista Hotel,' said a bored voice.

Sophia asked for Miss Pemberton and was told that she'd cancelled her booking and no, the receptionist didn't know where she was staying. 'I couldn't say, I'm sure. She just said she'd had a change of plans. The manager was furious, last-minute cancellation.'

Sophia replaced the receiver and looked round the room. There were dirty, broken dishes lying on the floor, newspapers in a higgledy-piggledy pile, months – years! – out of date, cold ashes in the fire. And books everywhere. On tables, chairs, window sills. Some lay open, some had pieces of paper stuck in them. What a terrible mess! Old people got into bad habits if they were left on their own. Her mother had started to hide lumps of cake in her handbags and drawers and every morning Sophia had to go around hunting them down.

In the kitchen, which was another mess, she found a large black garbage sack and set to to give Evangeline's room a good clean-up. She dumped in the bag newspapers, magazines, boxes of old postcards. Some were all yellow and faded and went back as far as 1920. *Mamma mia!* The dust made her sneeze and her hands were soon filthy. She worked on.

Maximo would be pleased if she could get Miss Hudson's rooms sorted out; that would be one lot less to clear when the builders were ready to move in. For Miss Hudson would not be coming back here from the hospital, that was for certain. She would need proper nursing. She would be lucky to get into even the sheltered housing now, with a lame leg – at her age fractures never mended completely – and she hadn't been all that steady on her feet to start with. She could go into the nursing home at the end of the street where Mrs Wilberforce had spent her last months. It would be handy for her friends visiting. And she herself would go, with nice things for her to eat, for were they not neighbours? She believed that you should love your neighbour as yourself. Of course she did! Had not Jesus son of Mary told them to? In the village where she'd lived as a girl all the neighbours had helped one another, especially at times of birth, sickness and death. It was funny that she'd never been in this house until last night. But they had not been Italian, and that had made a difference; and they had all been women, which had also made a difference, for it had not seemed natural or right to her that there should be no men in a house; and she had been busy with six children to bring up and Maximo to look after, and then there were the many relatives in other parts of the town and The Cedars was a big house to care for. A fine house. Such pride she felt in it! She glanced through the window at her home and knew that its paintwork would be gleaming and its windows shining. Unlike these ones! You'd think they were covered with grey gauze. She shook her head. And Miss Hudson was a woman from a high-born family, too, so Maximo said.

In the middle of her spring-clean, the telephone rang. She wiped her hands on a curtain – fit only for the rubbish tip, also – and picked up the reciever.

'Yes?'

'Evangeline?'

'No, it is Sophia Tonelli here. Who is that please?'

There was silence at the other end of the line for a moment and then the caller said, 'This is Anna Pemberton.'

ELEVEN

'That was Sophia,' said Anna, turning to Maximo.

'I gathered that it was.' He appeared unruffled.

'I had to give her this number. She asked where she could reach me.' Anna went to stand by the window. The day was shrinking. The deer which earlier they'd watched cropping the parkland were indistinguishable now from bushes and shrubs. Already, she thought, a shadow has come between us.

They had just come up from having afternoon tea in the drawing room. The last hotel had been luxurious; this one was sumptuous, and furnished with antiques which the owners had bought along with the castle.

'Evangeline has broken her leg. She is having it set tomorrow.'

'I gathered that, too.'

'I wonder if I shouldn't go back.'

'You can't cancel your performance now. You have to leave for the theatre in half an hour.'

'We could drive back afterwards.' They were about three hours from home, by Ferrari.

'What would be the point? What could you do? She's in hospital.' He came up behind her and put his hands on her shoulders. 'Do you want to go back?'

'Of course not.' She moved round into his arms and the shadow fled.

She phoned the hospital and they also said that there was no reason for her to come; Miss Hudson's condition was not particularly worrying, she seemed to have an amazingly strong constitution considering the trauma she'd been through, and the X-rays had shown a fairly straightforward break. Of course anything *could* go wrong at her age.

However . . . 'If you'd like to ring back late tomorrow afternoon? By then Miss Hudson should be out of the operating theatre.' Anna sent her love to Evangeline and rang off. She stared at the telephone, frowning.

'I wish I hadn't given this number to your wife. It was just that I was taken aback, I couldn't think – '

Don't worry, said Maximo; Sophia would not connect them. Anna did not ask if she knew where he was and he did not tell her that he had left a list of phone numbers, which included this one, with Roberto, in case it should be necessary for him to be contacted for business purposes. On the domestic front Maximo could always be confident that Sophia would cope without having to summon him.

After she'd found the flat boarded up, Holly wandered up and down the deck for a while, afraid to knock on a door and have someone come who would recognize her and say, 'Hey, I thought the police were looking for you!' In the end she had to risk it – she had to get information somehow. She tried the flat on the right and a West Indian man whom she'd never seen before answered her knock. He shook his head. The people next door had been gone when he'd come in and he had no idea where they'd moved to. She shifted up two doors, to the next flat which was showing a light. She had to knock three times before anything happened. Then the letter-box flap moved and an elderly voice asked, 'What are you wanting?' Holly spoke through the slit. The man said, 'They moved away a year or two back. Can't remember rightly. Good riddance to bad rubbish! Went to the Waterside Estate, I heard.' The flap dropped.

The Waterside Estate was on the other side of the river. It was considered a notch or two above this one and the council's policy had been to move families with children out of here and over there. To give them a better chance! Holly hadn't imagined that her family would ever have actually moved. So what to do now? It was too late and too dark to go roaming around the Waterside Estate asking people if they knew where the O'Malleys lived. But the first thing she had to do was to get out of this place.

169

As she sprinted along the deck a man whom she'd not noticed leaning against the wall called out, 'Want somethin', doll? I've got somethin' if you wan' it.' She raced on and went lunging down the stairs swinging her bag in front of her, striking the wall on either side. She felt fresh air coming up. Another leap downward, and she'd left the tunnel of hell behind her. In the archway, she paused to take stock. Two youths were throwing stones at a car not ten yards away. Clunk went the stones, clunk, and the boys hee-hawed. One turned and saw her.

Launching herself off the wall, she went running and didn't stop until she'd reached the main road. She stuck out her thumb. After an hour, when she was beginning to feel desperate, she got a ride from a plumber going home after an emergency call. He took her to the service station on the motorway. It stayed open all night.

She bought a cup of tea and took it to a booth in the far corner of the cafeteria. When she'd drunk it she pushed the cup aside, put her arms on the table, pillowed her head on them and slept until dawn, wakened then by a woman clearing tables around her.

Another cup of tea, and a bacon roll, and she was on her way again and by nine o'clock was on the Waterside Estate. A few late stragglers were going in through the school gates. She stopped and checked them over to see if she would recognize any of them. They'd always gone late to school, when they'd gone at all. I need you at home, their mother would say, especially to Holly, who was the eldest. Holly had had to look after the younger kids, do the shopping, take the washing to the launderette. When there was money to pay for it. She used to take the kids to the library, too, and sometimes there'd be a story-telling session for under-fives and she'd get half an hour's peace in which to read herself. Her mother had spent most of her days in bed, with or without a man, or sitting in front of the telly. In the evenings she went to the pub, with or without a man. The Attendance Officer must have been able to find his way to their flat blindfold, Holly thought, though she'd have been prepared to bet that he hated coming even in broad daylight with all his senses unimpaired. Once, he'd got pelted with rotten eggs from an upper deck. Most times her mother hadn't answered the door. People she expected to call, such as her sister or her current man, would shout through the letter box after they'd knocked. And all official-looking letters were thrown into the bin without being opened.

There were no tower blocks on this estate, or communal decks either. Flats were only four storeys high and some streets had the old-style traditional semi-detached houses, with two rooms down and two or three up. It was an estate in which many of the tenants had bought their own houses. You could tell which ones they were by the state of their gardens and the new paint on the front doors. Holly doubted if her family – whoever and whatever it consisted of these days – would have bought its own house. If it could buy enough food for the week it was doing well. She was pretty sure of another thing, too: no one in their old block would have bought their own flat, complete with cockroaches and nutcases creeping along the outside decks.

She came to a corner shop, of the kind that sold a bit of everything. A Pakistani man was putting tins of baked beans on a shelf. He turned to look at her. Did he know a family called O'Malley? she asked and saw at once that he did, by the look of mistrust on his face.

'One of the girls was in a minute ago. The one with the limp.' If Holly hurried she would catch her up. He told her which direction to go in.

Holly caught up with Sharon, her thirteen-year-old half-sister, in the next street, or almost did. She fell back as soon as she saw her up ahead and kept a few paces behind. Sharon listed, like a ship not properly keeled, going down heavily on the outside of her right foot. She'd been born with a twisted hip and their mother had never got round to taking her to the hospital to get it sorted. She was carrying a pint of milk in one hand and a loaf of bread under the other arm. Bought on tick, more than likely.

Sharon turned into a side street and went into the third house down on the left-hand side, a semi-detached, with a front garden full of litter and weeds.

Holly waited, then walked up the path and round the side to

the back door. She opened it and stepped inside.

Sharon was standing at the sink filling a kettle and her mother was sitting by the table in a dirty pink silk wrapper, yawning. A cigarette smoked from her right hand. For a moment the two within the kitchen froze, as if playing at statues, and then the older woman put the cigarette between her lips and took a long, slow drag. The jet of smoke she expelled reached almost to Holly.

'Look what the cat brought in,' she drawled. 'To what do we owe the honour?'

'I just came to see – '

'If I was still alive and kicking?' Her mother got up and came lurching over to stand in front of Holly. Her breath smelt of last night's drink. 'You bloody little bitch!' Bringing her hand up, she struck Holly across the face. The water overflowed from Sharon's kettle and shot down the side of the sink. Sharon wrenched the tap round quickly.

Holly stood her ground and even though her cheek stung did not allow herself to touch it. But she was no longer afraid of her mother. The realization had come in a single moment, when her mother had raised her hand to strike her. Holly stared back at the pouched, blood-shot eyes and the thin, puckered mouth with dried lipstick and dried spittle clogging the edges. She must only be thirty-five or six, her mother, but she looked at least fifty, and a used-up fifty at that. She looked years older than Anna, who was in her mid-forties.

'Don't ever do that again,' said Holly. 'If you do I'll knock you flat next time.'

'Oh, you're capable of it, don't I know it! Like to finish me off, would you?' But her mother backed off to the table and slumped down on the chair. 'I'm not well, but I don't suppose you give a damn about that.' She began to cough. She thumped her chest with her fist. 'Get that blasted tea made for God's sake, Sharon! I'm desperate for a cup.'

Sharon plugged in the kettle. Over her half-raised arm, she eyed Holly apprehensively.

Their mother crossed one leg over the other, showing that she had nothing on beneath the silk wrapper. 'It's a wonder you weren't frightened to come back. Aren't you worried I might set the cops on you?'

'No.'

'You ought to be. You could get put away for hitting your mother over the head with a shovel. And then running off leaving me lying for dead. If Sharon hadn't come back then I might have been a gonner, isn't that right, Shar?'

The girl did not answer. She spooned tea into a dented brown pot, spilling half of it on the floor.

'Watch what you're bloody doing! Tea doesn't grow on trees.'

'And what about what you did to me?' demanded Holly. '*You* could get put away for that.'

'Go on upstairs, Sharon,' said their mother sharply. 'Go on when I tell you and change Damian while you're at it. He'll be stinking by this time.'

So there was another baby. Well, that wasn't surprising. When Holly had left there were four kids and her mother had had two abortions and two miscarriages before that. She seemed incapable of following any kind of contraception. Half the time when she conceived she was drunk, anyway. Up any old back alley, her skirts round her waist, her head in dog shit, unable to remember the next morning whom she'd been with the night before. The identity of the father of only one of her children was known for certain – although she made various other claims regarding specific men, none of whom would acknowledge their paternity – and that child was Holly herself. Their mother had been married once, to Tim O'Malley, Holly's father. He'd taken off when Holly was two years old. She had a memory of a man with hair the colour of her own leaning over her cot, or thought she had. Her mother had kept no photographs of him. Right bugger he was, she used to say, when Holly asked her about him; always after the women. Holly had no way of knowing if that was true or not, any more than she could tell whether it was his defection that had driven her mother into the life that she led or whether her mother had taken to drink and other men beforehand and that was what had driven her father out. For years Holly used to nurse the idea that she would find him one day, but had abandoned that hope long ago.

The kettle's lid was rattling. Holly poured the hissing water into the teapot, then she rinsed out two cups (frazzled with cracks, harbouring God knows what kind of germs), rejecting the drying-up cloth which looked as if it had been used to wipe the floor, and poured the tea. Her mother watched her the whole time, through the hazy screen of cigarette smoke, her eyes narrowed. Holly leant against the wall to drink her tea.

'It's a wonder the kids haven't been taken away from you. Guess it's only because the social workers are overworked.'

'You'd better not be thinking of talking to them – I'm warning you, madam!'

'I might just talk to them. And you can't warn me about anything, not any more you can't.'

'Can't I? I've got friends, so just you watch it! I'd only need to say the word and you'd be sorry. The stupid social workers wouldn't believe a word you told them, anyway. The kids all know you hit me and left me for dead, they'd testify to that. As well as your Aunt Rita. She knows what you're like. A right bad lot!'

'The kids know about you too, though, don't they? Like men and booze and leaving them on their own. What do you do it for?' she cried and looked down into her mother's face. She wanted to take hold of her by the shoulders and shake her. And shake her. She dropped her arms. She didn't want to touch her. For a moment she thought her mother was going to speak to her – to *say* something – then the expression on her face changed and she took on that sly look again and she lifted the cigarette to her scummy mouth and she sucked in a lungful of hot smoke with a quick rasping sound. Holly walked past her, into the narrow hallway.

The house smelt, of everything that was obnoxious: of rotting and decay and gunge and unwashed clothes and unwashed bodies. It wouldn't have taken her mother long to reduce the place to a slum. Overhead, a baby – Damian presumably – wailed.

'Cindy?' Her mother had followed her into the hall.

Holly turned. 'I don't use that name any more. It's not *me*. I

174

hate that name – *Cindy* doll! That's what you'd have liked me to be, wouldn't you, for your fellas to play with?'

'What name do you use then?'

'That's my business. Just as where I live now's my business, too. You'll never know where it is, you'll never see it. It's a beautiful house, like a palace, with pink marble stairs and big wide windows that let in masses and masses of light. I've got a brand-new family.'

'Gawd, don't tell me somebody's adopted you! They can't have known what they were taking in if they did. Bloody wildcat like you! But why won't you tell us where this house is?' Her mother's voice had changed to a wheedle. 'I don't see why you should keep it from us. I'm your mother, after all, I've a right to know.'

'You've no rights, as far as I'm concerned.'

'You're a real hard bitch if ever there was one!'

Sharon appeared at the top of the stairs carrying the baby.

Her mother, looking upward, shouted, 'I thought I told you to stay up there.'

'He's hungry. He's needing his bottle.'

Sharon came on down. The baby wasn't attractive to look at; he had a narrow forehead and tiny eyes. Poor little sod, thought Holly. She had no desire to reach out and take him into her arms. Her half-brother. Her life had been full of halves before she'd taken off. And it wasn't true when they said blood was thicker than water. Not when it was bad blood, at any rate.

Sharon took Damian to the kitchen and holding him on one arm, reminding Holly of how she herself used to do, made up his bottle. Their mother refilled her cup from the teapot and sat down again at the table. She eyed Holly.

'Have you any money on you?'

'Sorry!' Holly reached out and took a cigarette from the packet on the draining board.

'You don't look as if you're living in a palace.'

'I put on my old clothes to come slumming in.'

'You always had a viper's tongue on you! Got that from your father.'

'What did you get from *your* father, Sharon?' asked Holly.

175

'Or don't you know? I don't expect you do. But I'm telling you something – as soon as you can, get your skates on and go, hell for leather, or she'll drag you down into her own filth.'

'You watch what you say!' Their mother half rose up from her seat, then dropped back as she saw the look on her eldest child's face.

'I mean it, Sharon,' said Holly. 'Do you know what she made me do?'

'Stop it, I tell you, you fucking bitch!'

'She made me have sex with one of her men. Just for the hell of it – so that they could have a good laugh. It got her all excited. I was about the same age as you. Maybe she's done it to you –'

Rising to her feet, their mother lifted her cup and flung the contents straight at Holly. Holly ducked and the hot tea hit Damian full in the face. He screamed. Sharon burst into tears.

'Throw cold water on him, Sharon,' yelled Holly. 'Quick!'

They doused him with handfuls of water from the cold tap and he screamed and screamed and their mother sat rocking herself over from the waist and moaning.

'Look what you've made me do! It's all your bleeding fault. What did you have to come back here for? Nobody wanted you!'

'I'll have to get a doctor,' said Holly. 'Or an ambulance to take him to hospital.'

'You'll call nobody,' said her mother, sitting up straight and forgetting to moan. 'He'll be all right in a minute. It's not as if the tea was boiling.'

'I'm going anyway.'

Holly tugged open the back door and without looking back, or heeding her mother's calls, went.

The first phone box she tried was out of order. Of course. She thought she'd go crazy, her head felt as if it was about to burst. She asked a man and he pointed her in the direction of the next kiosk. It was working.

She dialled 999 and asked for an ambulance, gave the name and address. She'd taken a note of that as she'd fled. 'Quick!' she said. 'There's a baby scalded.' Then she dialled 999 a second time and asked for police. 'There's a family that needs

176

help. The kids should be taken into care. The mother's a drunk and a nympho. Do something, *please!*' She put down the receiver. She was crying. God help her, what a state she was getting into! She wiped her eyes with the back of her arm and sniffed. Who's calling? the policeman had kept asking but she hadn't answered. And she wasn't going back to the house, she just couldn't. She'd done what she could. She'd left her bag behind but there was only a change of clothes in it and the Katherine Mansfield stories that Evangeline had lent her. She'd find another copy in a secondhand bookshop. The only thing she wanted to do now was to get home and tell Evangeline everything that had happened.

For the past day, ever since they'd wheeled her out of the room, Evangeline had had the sensation of drifting up and down through warm, limpid water. At times she was not sure whether she was unconscious, dreaming, or daydreaming; the states blurred and ran together. But when she opened her eyes and saw a white coverlet stretching out in front of her, then rising up into a great mound, and a nurse in a blue and white dress and a white starched cap standing at the end of the bed, she knew she must be awake. The scene was too sharply in focus to be a dream.

'I'm awake,' she said.

The nurse smiled. 'How're you feeling?'

Evangeline was not sure. She asked what the white hill was.

'That's a cage to protect your leg. You've had it set, under an anaesthetic. You remember going into the operating theatre, don't you? It all went splendidly.'

'So there's life in the old bones yet?'

'There certainly is.'

Looking beyond the bed, and the cheerful nurse, Evangeline saw that she was in a small room, and alone, and she was sufficiently wide awake to know that patients were usually moved into single rooms when they were seriously ill.

'Why am I here?'

'Mrs Tonelli asked for you to have a private room.'

'But I liked it in the ward!' She had liked watching the comings and goings of another world in action. A mini rage

177

rose inside her. How dare Sophia!

'The flowers are from the Tonellis.' The nurse stood aside so that Evangeline could see the bouquets massed along the window sill: carnations, roses, lilies, orchids.

'Looks like they were expecting a funeral.'

The nurse laughed and handed Evangeline a card. 'With very best wishes for your speedy recovery, from your neighbours, the Tonelli family.'

'The yellow roses on your locker are from someone else.'

This card said, 'From Anna with love. See you tomorrow.'

'She phoned not long ago, your friend Anna, and sent her love then, too.'

'No word from Holly?'

The nurse shook her head. 'Who is Holly?'

'My granddaughter.'

'I expect she'll ring later. Or perhaps she'll come in.'

As the girl came to resettle her and tidy up the bed clothes, they heard voices in the corridor outside, both female, one loud, with a marked Mediterranean accent, and the other quieter, but firm, trying to impose itself upon the former.

'Sophia,' said Evangeline.

'Sister,' said the nurse.

'Only five minutes then, Mrs Tonelli,' said Sister and the door opened.

Sophia entered. 'Ah, there you are, Miss Hudson! I tell them you are all alone, have no one to visit you but me, you have been deserted –'

'Not deserted,' said Evangeline weakly. 'Anna – Miss Pemberton – will be back tomorrow.'

'We talk on the telephone. I tell her no need to come back too soon, I look after you.' Sophia flopped down on to the chair beside the bed and opened her fur coat. 'Whew! It is warm in these places.' She picked up Anna's card from the locker and fanned herself.

Evangeline lay back, prepared to remain quiescent until Sophia's visit had passed, like a hurricane blowing over. Her energy was at a low ebb. Not surprising, of course, after the major shock her system had received, topped off by a general anaesthetic.

'You have to stay here for about a week,' said Sophia, 'and then you can go to a nursing home. I have booked you into the one at the end of our street. You will like that – it is not like going to a strange place.'

Evangeline opened her mouth to object but no sound emerged. How terrible it was to feel such weakness in the body, not to be able to express what her mind wished her to say. But Sophia would not have heard even if she had spoken aloud; she was intent on continuing herself.

'It is either that or a convalescent hospital for the geriatric. The nursing home is better, more like a home, with a sitting room and the television set, and it is easier for visiting. We can all come there. We walk down the street. And you are not to worry about the money for my Maximo will help you. He is very generous man. No, do not protest, Miss Hudson! We wish to be good Samaritans and you cannot go home, that is clear. How could you expect Miss Pemberton and the young girl Holly to look after you? You need to be nursed at night, someone to bring a bedpan. Miss Pemberton has to do this clowning all over the place – I cannot imagine such a quiet looking lady behaving like a clown – and Holly might not come back. Mary-Lou thinks she has gone to Australia.'

Lifts were slow that day. It had taken Holly four hours to travel sixty miles. Most of the drivers who said they'd have been willing to give her a lift were turning off the motorway before the next service station and the ones who were travelling long distance said they weren't allowed to pick up. She was starving. She had hardly any money, bought a chocolate bar and then was left with twenty pence. Two ten p's for the phone.

She put one in the slot and dialled the Shangri-la number. She'd dialled four times before that day, and each time no one had answered. The phone went on ringing and ringing and the noise of it in her ear said, There's no one here, no one here, no one here . . . When she hung up the receiver her money didn't drop down. She banged the meter box. Shit! How had that happened? Now she'd lost her ten pence.

This is not my day, Anna used sometimes to say, and so I

179

think I shall just lie low and let it pass over. It wasn't a bad idea, Holly considered, and only wished she could lie low, on a soft bed in a darkened room. She hadn't been to bed for a day and a half and at the rate she was going she'd end up spending another night on the road. She wanted to sleep and stop thinking.

She kept thinking about Evangeline and she kept thinking about Damian and Sharon and her mother. Both sets of thoughts brought ambulances and blue lights and shrieking sirens into her head. As she'd come out of the other telephone booth, the one on the Waterside Estate, an ambulance with its blue light gyrating had swished past her, closely followed by a police car. She'd run like hell and hadn't stopped till she'd crossed the river.

Anna and Maximo walked on a cliff top high above grey-green sea, with gulls wheeling and screeching overhead. They walked with their hands joined, swinging them gently between them. The turf was springy underfoot.

'It's a long time since I took time off like this,' said Maximo. 'Just to walk and smell good air. We must do it as often as we can.'

Anna smiled. He talked so confidently about what he wished or intended to do without considering the problems. His confidence was catching. He had not even been perturbed when Roberto had phoned the night before, to discuss a matter of business. It was a quarter to twelve when the phone had rung and they had been in bed. Maximo had kept his arm cradled round her while he spoke to Roberto. 'Sounds all right, go ahead and offer.' They had talked in rapid Italian but Anna had been able to follow most of it. Roberto had not asked where his father was or what he was doing.

'How are things at home?' Maximo asked at the end and Roberto appeared to say 'O.K.' and Anna had a vision of Sophia sitting amongst her Virgins with her hands on her lap. She and Maximo had not talked about Sophia. She knew that he would never leave his wife even though he talked, as he walked along the cliff top, about how he would like to live with her, Anna, on the island of Capri or Elba, or in a

180

mountain village in Tuscany, about how he would like to give up business and take time to live, just to walk like this and enjoy the sea and music and books. And she believed that he would like to do all those things, and with her. The images he conjured up made them turn inward towards one another and smile. His hand tightened round hers. But if he were to abandon Sophia he would cause a crack to run right through the middle of the family Tonelli and she understood that such a thing was inconceivable. He talked also about his family, about his daughters, and their families, and a little about Giorgio and Claudio. Of Roberto he did not speak at all.

'I cannot believe you have *no* family,' he said.

'Only Evangeline and Holly.' And one was ageing fast and the other had disappeared.

'You are so exposed.'

'But untramelled, too.'

'Is it worth it – the price you pay for your freedom?'

'Possibly not. Anyway, none of us are really *free*, are we? But it's how my life is and I have to dwell on the advantages, do I not?'

'Of course. As I do.'

Their hotel was in sight. She must go and change and get ready for tonight's performance. And tomorrow they would have to return to the world of Shangri-la and the Villa Neapolitana. But they still had a whole night ahead and tomorrow seemed a long way away.

A woman driving alone gave Holly a lift the rest of the way down the motorway. She was glad of the company. She was going home to visit her parents who were elderly. They were a worry, she said, their sight was failing but they didn't want to leave their home, they'd lived there for forty years. Sometimes they forgot to turn off the cooker and once they'd started a small fire in the kitchen but, mercifully, a neighbour had happened to come in and she'd thrown one of those fire blankets on it and doused the flames, just in the nick of time. Another minute, and the place would have gone up. Holly had a vision of Shangri-la going up, and then it subsided. The phone wouldn't have rung if the house had been burnt down.

181

'And I'm so far away. But what can you do? I can't give up my own life to see to them, can I? I mean, where would that leave me when they went?'

At some point Holly fell asleep and dreamt she was back in London. That was where she'd gone when she'd run away from home. In her dream she saw again the bridge she'd slept under, the stinking room, the men . . . She wakened, sweating, to see that they were approaching a town.

'London?'

'No, not London,' said the woman. 'This is where you live, isn't it? What's what you told me. I'll run you right in. I might as well. I'm not in that great a hurry.'

Holly blinked. The day had vanished, she saw with surprise, and the lights were lit. She felt disorientated as regards time and place. As she gave directions to the woman she was amazed that she could remember the layout of the town. But when they passed the launderette and Giorgio's chip shop she began to feel reassured. She saw Giorgio smocked in white moving behind the counter.

They turned into the street – *her* street. The trees looked beautiful standing stark and almost bare under the lights. 'This is where I live,' she said. And there was Shangri-la standing outlined against the night sky with its curlicued roof and tall chimneys. But it was dark. Not a light showed anywhere. Holly felt a queasiness at the pit of her stomach.

'This house,' she said.

'Big place, isn't it?'

'Thanks very much, it was very good of you,' said Holly and raced up the path, slipping and sliding on the gravel, and went into the house, making straight for Evangeline's sitting room. She clicked on the light switch.

She stared round the room with horror. The stacks of magazines and newspapers had gone, and the books had been tidied. Some stood in piles as if they were ready to be taken away. The carpet had lines on it that had been made by a vacuum cleaner. The window had been cleaned and the curtains were pulled right back and tucked out of the way, behind two pieces of furniture.

The bedroom had the same air about it: of a room

abandoned. The bed had been stripped, exposing the mattress. Evangeline's bedside table had been cleared, and dusted. There were no cups lying around, no glasses, no bottles of madeira or claret, no packets of cigarillos, no opened books. There was no sign of life.

Holly ran to the bathroom and vomited into the lavatory.

TWELVE

'I thought you were dead,' said Holly and laughed. 'Imagine!'
'And here I was all the time living in the lap of luxury!'
Evangeline waved her hand at the grapes and peaches on the
locker top and the flowers on the window sill – Tonelli gifts,
all of them.

Holly had not told her that her rooms had been cleared up,
she had simply said, 'I went in and I saw you had gone.' She
had then run across the road and Mary-Lou had told her what
had happened. Holly had been so relieved that she'd felt
winded and couldn't speak for a few minutes. She'd sat on
Mary-Lou's blue fur settee doubled over, clutching her
stomach, and the gold swirls on the carpet had appeared to
writhe like snakes around her feet. Mary-Lou had been kind,
had looked after her, given her food, run a warm bath scented
with jasmine for her, and put her to sleep in her spare
bedroom. In the morning Holly had got up, wearing Mary-
Lou's peach satin nightdress, and stood at the window of the
Villa Neapolitana and looked across the street at their own
house. The gutters were half falling off and there were slates
missing from the roof. But how she loved the place!

When she'd come downstairs on her way home, she'd met
Roberto and Sophia coming out of her sitting room.

'Ah, child, how are you?' asked Sophia. 'Mary-Lou said
you were in a bad state last night.'

'I'm fine now, thanks. Do you know when Anna – Miss
Pemberton – will be home?'

'Just a minute, I tell you. I have a piece of paper.' Sophia
disappeared back into her room.

'Are you going to see Miss Hudson today?' asked Roberto.
'My mother has arranged for her to go into the nursing home

184

along the street. She won't be able to live in Shangri-la any more.'

Holly was shocked. 'Her leg will mend,' she cried.

'But it will never be the same again, she is very old now. She can't live alone after this, you can't expect her to,' said Roberto impatiently.

'She's not alone. Anna and I will look after her.'

'You have to go out to work, don't you? Or do you intend to live off the dole for the rest of your life?'

Holly's opportunity to answer back was cut off by the return of Sophia who was carrying a sheet of paper in her hand and trying to peer at it. 'Can you read this, Roberto? I can't find my glasses.'

Roberto took the paper. 'She will be home this afternoon. What are these phone numbers, Mother?' He frowned and his eyes roved up and down the sheet. 'The ones in your handwriting? Above the others that have been scored out?'

'She have change of plans. I put the new numbers down, in case of emergency. And then I call her. But there was no need.'

Roberto, still looking thoughtful, put the paper into his pocket. Holly felt uneasy about that and wanted to object, though did not know on what grounds she should. There was something going on that she did not understand.

'Look what I've brought you, Evangeline!' said Holly, diving into a plastic carrier bag and lifting out a half-full bottle of madeira and two glasses wrapped in newspaper.

'The perfect tonic! Just what I need. Pour on, Holly-Berry! There are advantages in having a private room. Though we must watch out for Sister! What fun this is!'

Holly made sure the door was properly closed. They raised their glasses to one another.

'Here's to your leg mending quickly!'

'I think I'll drink to that myself.'

The wine slid smoothly over Evangeline's throat. Ah, that was good. A notch up on Lucozade. She felt in much better fettle today – Mary-Lou had telephoned last night with the news of Holly's return – and had even been up to take a turn around the room with a zimmer. They believed in getting you

185

back on your feet quickly. 'No slackers allowed here!' said the sister. And the physiotherapist had been in to start her on exercises and deep breathing. Evangeline had told her she hadn't been bullied like this for years. Part of her was soothed by it; another part resented it, greatly. Her life wasn't her own any longer, so it seemed; it was under the control of nurses, doctors, physiotherapists – and Sophia Tonelli. Well, she would bide her time and then she would do what she wanted to do, just as she'd always done.

'So tell me what happened!' commanded Holly.

Evangeline skipped over her ordeal quickly, then turned the question back to Holly. 'What have *you* been up to?'

'I went to see my mother.' Holly frowned. Evangeline waited, sipping her madeira, keeping her eyes on the girl's face. Holly looked up. 'I hate her! Isn't that dreadful, to hate your own mother? *Really* hate? Enough to kill her. She's not had much of a life and I guess some people might say I should feel sorry for her. But I can't. And I've grassed on her, to the police.'

'Better perhaps to grass on her than to kill her. Can you begin at the beginning? And before you do you might replenish our glasses.'

Once Holly began to talk, the story came flooding out. Evangeline listened without interrupting.

'If Damian – poor wee sod – is scarred for life, it will be partly my fault. I goaded her and she threw the tea. It was meant for me.' Then Holly put her head down on Evangeline's bed and burst into tears.

Evangeline stroked her hair and talked to her, saying the only things that could be said: that Holly could not take the guilt for the whole family's sins upon her, that she would have to put these experiences behind her, that they were bound to leave scars but that the skin would grow over in time and at least partially heal them. 'We are all scarred, you know, Holly, some of us more than others. Though your wounds have been especially deep.' And nasty, thought Evangeline. Yes, very nasty. She loved this child and did not doubt but that if her mother were to come through the doorway now she would want to throw the madeira bottle at her. And would hope to

186

obliterate her. She had to do one of the physiotherapist's deep breathing exercises to quieten herself and reduce her blood pressure, which she was sure must have soared.

It was at this moment, while Evangeline was comforting Holly, that Anna walked in. Her face, which had been ready to break into a smile of greeting, changed at once.

'What's wrong?' She came quickly to the bed.

'Nothing,' said Holly, lifting her head. She was half crying, half laughing. She blew her nose.

'We thought you might be the Sister come to take us to task,' said Evangeline. 'For illegal drinking. But thank goodness it's you, Anna dear!'

Anna bent over to kiss her.

She looks different, thought Evangeline, examining Anna's face; radiant, I might almost say, as if lit by an inner light. Don't tell me she is in love! But how and with whom? All these secrets that people have, all except me – I am too old for secrets any more.

'Pour Anna a drink, Holly-Berry. She can use my Lucozade glass. This is like old times. Now sit down and tell us all your news, Anna – we want a full performance.'

Anna blushed, very slightly, but enough for Evangeline to note it. She told them about her tour, getting up to mime some of the characters, such as Ralston Cummings, the American – 'New England,' said Holly softly, 'in springtime, imagine!' – and the elderly admirers who waited for her after shows. It cannot be one of them, surely, thought Evangeline; apart from being too old, they sound too insipid. And then she had an inspired guess. And felt alarmed.

'You look extremely well, Anna,' she said. 'I have never seen you look so well.'

Anna blushed again, and smiled, fingering a strand of hair behind her ear, as if she were recollecting a happy moment. She was not fully with them.

Yes, the more Evangeline thought about it, the more convinced she became that her guess was correct.

Anna found herself obsessed by Maximo Tonelli; he invaded most of her waking thoughts and she spent much time at the

187

window watching for glimpses of him. Like a lovesick teenager, as she told herself, and him – laughing as she told him; though to be lovesick was not the prerogative of the young. Why should it be? he asked. In the mornings, when he emerged from the Villa Neapolitana to drive off in his Ferrari, he turned his head up towards her window, though he did not wave, could not, lest he be observed from his own house. Sophia did not come to see him off, they had been married too long for that; she ate croissants and drank hot chocolate in bed in the mornings and did not rise before ten. And Claudio and Giorgio slept late, too. But Roberto, with his sharp, darting glances, was up and about.

An hour after leaving the street, Maximo would ring, from his office. A guarded call, a few minutes, only, consisting of a few uncompromising sentences and phrases. Anna talked freely, he answered in a form of code. *Can we meet today, Maximo? That should be possible, let me see . . . Yes, I see no reason why not. Perhaps at three? That's fine for me. At the motel in Woodlands Road? Excellent! I'll go straight there and wait for you. Shall I register under the name of Grove?* (It was the name of the first place they'd stayed at together – the Grove Country House Hotel.) *Good idea! At three then, Mr Grove.*

Anna had always recognized that she was the obsessive type; when she was involved in something, she had to be totally involved, as in her mime. Playing a downtrodden housewife or a grumpy ex-colonel, she became those people, inhabited their skins and their minds and operated within the parameters of their world. It was another reason that her marriage had failed; she had not been obsessed by Julian, not even in the beginning. But perhaps it was not possible to make an 'obsessive marriage?' It might be too consuming and it might work only if one partner was willing to be consumed by the other. She had no thoughts of marriage with Maximo.

Meeting in a motel room in the middle of the afternoon had all the overtones of a sordid affair, but when she was in the room with him she did not feel at all sordid. The only times that she did were when she had to endure the manager's smile as he passed her the key. She wore dark glasses and a scarf over her hair and had been tempted to wear a wig too, but had

188

decided that might be too melodramatic. The motel was the best they could do, however, even with money, given the circumstances.

'It's a pity you have to live across the road,' said Maximo. 'If only you had a flat somewhere else in town I could visit you there.'

'Don't tell me you seduced me, after all, so that you could get me out of Shangri-la and into a love-nest!'

She had meant it as a joke but he did not take it as such. 'Don't you trust me?' The quickness and intensity of his anger frightened her a little. She protested that she did, but he would not believe her so easily. They had their first row, which shook her more than it did him, she realized, when they had made up and she lay in his arms afterwards. He was used to displays of temper, raised voices, quarrels, the release of emotion; she was not, except in her mime. That had been her safety valve.

They stayed an extra half-hour at the motel. He looked at his watch, sighed, said he must go; he had an appointment at five. He phoned for two taxis.

'I won't be able to come every afternoon, I'm afraid, Anna.'

'No, I know. You're a busy man.'

'And Roberto is acting suspicious. He keeps asking me where I'm going, what I'm doing. He is my son and I love him but he can annoy me very much.' Maximo frowned as he ducked down to see himself in the dressing-table mirror and straighten the knot in his tie. He dressed immaculately, which Anna liked, in freshly laundered shirts and ties that showed no shadow of a stain, and he came to her always newly shaven, smelling of astringent aftershave.

'Don't worry, though. I can take care of Roberto.'

The first taxi was hooting outside.

'You have that one.' He took her hands and drew her to him. They kissed. 'I do love you, my sweet Anna. Even if I cannot offer you . . . everything.'

She nodded.

The taxi blasted its horn again and she fled before it would go, forgetting to put on her dark glasses. She bobbed her head down as she entered the cab, not looking at the driver's face.

She saw the little curl of his lip in the driving mirror up front. The Town Hall, she said. From there she would take a bus home.

As they turned out of the driveway, they passed the second taxi pulling in. The drivers acknowledged one another. We must vary our meeting place, she thought, it would not do for our habits to become too regular. Maximo tipped the motel manager generously, but even so, one could never be sure that he would not talk, and Maximo was well known in the town.

She sat on the left-hand side of the cab, well away from the driver's range of mirror vision, and looked out of the window. The first turning they passed was a cul-de-sac, and in it sat a white car, an Alfa Romeo, if she was not mistaken. They were past now but she knew she had not made a mistake; she saw the same car every morning coming out of the garage of the Villa Neapolitana. And Roberto had been sitting behind the wheel, gripping it with both hands, his shoulders hunched. For an instant, their eyes had connected, and then the taxi had borne her away.

The penetration of Roberto's stare, even at that distance, had unnerved her and when she got out at the Town Hall she had to go and have a cup of tea before catching the bus home. She went into a nearby café and seated herself at a corner table, putting her back to the room, needing time and privacy in which to adjust to this new development.

So Roberto knew: they would have to face up to that. The question was would he tell his mother? It was a question Anna would have liked to have been able to put to Maximo himself but he was gone beyond her reach now and would remain so until he chose to get in touch with her. She could never initiate the contact, was cast in the role of the one who waited. Awaiting his pleasure; that was how many women – probably Evangeline and Holly among them – would see it, and disapprove. In theory, she, too, disapproved, and once when her friend Beryl had got involved with a married man she had told her she was a fool to waste the best months, or even weeks, of her life sitting glued to the telephone, ready to receive him. In the end Beryl had become too demanding and the man had faded away. Beryl had hoped he would leave his wife, of course, when it had seemed obvious to Anna, from what she knew of him, that he would not. He was a contented-looking man whom she could well imagine enjoying the delights of family life. She was more clearsighted about her own situation, and under no illusions, so she told herself. And Maximo was trapped by circumstances as much as she was, set in a cast he could not break. Or was she having such thoughts to comfort herself? Self-deception was easy to slide into when one was in the grip of an obsession. One could talk oneself into believing anything. At times she even indulged in a daydream in which Maximo crossed the road and came to her and said, 'I am leaving Sophia! Let's go!' She smiled wryly and drank her tea. Perhaps he indulged in that daydream, too.

If Roberto *were* to tell his mother, Anna could imagine Sophia, in full cry, coming marching down her drive and over the road to confront her. It would be a stormy interview and the stamp of Sophia's feet would make the floorboards tremble and the sound of her voice would roll and flash throughout the house. Anna felt herself inside Sophia's skin, bursting with indignation and anger. Not resentment though, or bitterness; she thought they would not be part of the canon of Sophia's emotions. She wondered even if Sophia *would* come for she must know that Maximo had not been faithful to her throughout the thirty years of their marriage – 'There have been one or two women, but not many,' he had told Anna, who had not wanted to hear any more details – and they no longer had a sex life together (he had said) and he had a large sexual appetite. Sophia was not so naive as to expect him to remain celibate. She would tolerate his infidelities, Anna suspected, as long as they were not flaunted under her nose. And there might be the rub; to have the 'other woman' living across the road might not be acceptable to her.

Roberto must also be aware that his father had not always been faithful to his mother, perhaps did not even expect him to be. He was unlikely to tell his mother, Anna decided, but likely to use his knowledge as a weapon against his father. Get her out of Shangri-la or give her up! Otherwise I tell all! Anna might have smiled had the idea been less feasible.

'We're closing,' said the waitress, jostling the table with her

191

hip and starting to load Anna's dishes noisily on to her tray.

Looking round, Anna saw that everyone else had gone and chairs had been stacked on the table tops.

Emerging on to the street, Anna realized that she had not left enough time to go home before her evening visit to the hospital. Holly would have gone earlier; they were visiting separately so that Evangeline would have someone afternoon and evening. Anna decided to go to *Pavarotti's* for a pizza. It was nearby, and it was cheap.

Janice served her. 'You're Holly's auntie, aren't you? Thought I recognized you. How's she getting on? Ask her to give us a ring. The place is dead dull without her.'

The girl looked towards the door as it was swept inward. Anna turned her head, too, and saw Roberto Tonelli come striding in with his white trench-coat tails flying.

'Is Pavarotti in?'

Janice shook her head. 'We haven't seen him for a few days.'

Roberto's gaze shifted to the counter. Jackie had stopped kneading dough. Steve leaned against the wall with his arms folded.

'You two got any idea where he might be?'

Jackie shrugged. 'He doesn't tell us what he's doing.'

Roberto stood, frowning, pursing his lips, his hands in his trouser pockets rattling loose change, the trench-coat bunched out behind. Then he looked straight at Anna, slightly raising one eyebrow as if he were asking her to account for herself. She returned his stare without blinking though was conscious of a warm, irritating glow surfacing around her neck and beginning to creep upward. Abruptly, Roberto wheeled about and left. At once the room came to life again, Jackie tossed a round of dough up towards the ceiling, Steve began to chop onions, Janice set Anna's cutlery out in front of her.

'After Mr P for his money he is,' she said as she leant over the table. 'We think he's taken himself off to Spain.' She lowered her voice. 'Well, we know he has. Asked me to go with him, as a matter of fact, and I was tempted, I can tell you, it's getting so cold, isn't it? But my mum said I'd be daft to.

192

Can't blame him going to Spain, though, can you? Not with that guy after him. The Bloodsucker, Steve calls him.'

Anna shivered, in spite of the heat coming from the pizza ovens.

She found Evangeline in cheerful mood. Holly had been reading *Pride and Prejudice* aloud to her in the afternoon. 'I find her responses almost as interesting as the book itself. Her mind is not cluttered with preconceived ideas. What will the child *do* with herself? I keep wondering.'

'I'm working with her in the mornings,' said Anna. It was proving to be a good discipline for both of them; it took Anna's mind off the Tonelli family and Holly's off her own. 'She shows promise. I think she could make a good mime, eventually.'

Evangeline nodded. 'She's got a mobile face and an expressive body.'

'Though whether I should encourage her to go into such an esoteric career I'm not sure. It's not exactly an easy life!'

Better than serving pizzas, in Evangeline's opinion, and, anyway, Holly was young, with many years ahead in which to develop, and who knows what an interest in mime might lead her into? Evangeline had a lot of time for thinking these days, and both Holly and Anna were much in her thoughts. Well, naturally. 'You're the only family I have, aren't you?'

They were interrupted by the arrival of Sophia Tonelli who made an entrance at least once daily. She did not intend to stay long, she informed them; she had just dropped in on her way to visit her cousin Magdalena whose husband had run off and left her. 'He has gone with his secretary, the idiot! What does he think he is doing? He will be bored after he spends three days in the bed with her.'

'I'm sure many secretaries are very interesting women,' said Evangeline. 'In my opinion they are too often underrated.'

Sophia looked at her. 'I do not care if she is interesting. He is a fool, that is all I say. He works for my Maximo. I will ask Maximo to sack him unless he returns at once to Magdalena. She is weeping so many tears into the telephone that I tell her she fuse it unless she stop. She was always feeble, was Magdalena. If anyone put a finger on her or say boo in her face she trembles. Huh!'

Sophia spoke for another twenty minutes about the weaknesses of Magdalena, then she left. Before going, she nodded approvingly at the patient. 'You are looking better each time I come. Soon you go to the home.'

'You're pale, Anna,' said Evangeline, when Sophia had finally gone. 'Are you concerned for the fate of Magdalena?'

Anna met Evangeline's gaze. 'Don't worry – Maximo is not going to run off with me and leave Sophia to cry into the phone. You guessed, didn't you, Evvie? She would not do that, anyway – cry, that is – she would probably come after us with a hatchet! Which she would use on me, not him. It's funny – I suppose I should feel guilty when I see her but I don't. I tell myself I'm not taking anything from her that she wants. I guess it's what the other woman always tells herself.'

'And what is Maximo telling himself?'

'Is he leading me on, do you mean, for ulterior purposes?' Anna smiled. 'I don't think so. In the beginning he might have been, I'm prepared to admit that, but not now. This thing has taken him as much by surprise as it has me. We mesh well together, we're very much in tune, which you might find strange.'

'On reflection, I don't.' Evangeline could appreciate the complementary nature of their relationship. Her observations over the years had led her to believe that people more often wanted in the other person what they themselves did not have, rather than a carbon copy of their own qualities. Who wanted forever to be looking in a mirror? 'I could see that he was much taken by you early on.'

The remark pleased Anna who continued to talk about Maximo Tonelli until the bell rang to mark the end of the visiting hour.

'How *could* you, Anna?' Holly demanded, her eyes ablaze with anger and consternation.

'I love him.'

'But he's . . .' Holly floundered, unable to find a word.

'What do you think he is, Holly? Nothing's ever just black and white, you know.'

'Yeah O.K., *you* know he runs protection rackets and things like that!'

'Do I? I'm not sure that I do.'

'Oh, come on, of course he does! Pavarotti pays protection money to the Tonellis, probably half the other Italian joints in town do, too. Jackie says they're part of the Mafia.'

'That may be overstating it,' said Anna and shrugged. She supposed she shouldn't defend them; she didn't know enough about their business activities, had not wanted to, and was aware that she blanked out thoughts about the aspects of Maximo's life of which she might not approve. He was reputed to be a ruthless business man – though was that not a reputation they themselves had built up for him over the years, referring to him as the King of Naples, the Godfather, even Papa Doc?

She had disappointed Holly. Holly had expected her to be morally beyond reproach.

'I suppose I concentrate on seeing the good side of him.'

'But he's against *us*.'

'I don't believe so. I think he doesn't know what to do about the house and us, now. Roberto knows what *he* wants but not Maximo.'

Holly had heard about Anna and Maximo from Giorgio who had had a word with her on the quiet, over the formica counter, between the pickled onions and the pickled eggs. He had not even told Mary-Lou. 'She's inclined to forget and just come out with things,' he had said, apologetically.

'Georgie says Roberto is brewing up trouble. He's putting the squeeze on his father.'

Anna held her breath. 'And what is Maximo doing?'

'Saying Piss Off at the moment. But Georgie thinks Roberto is coming up to the boil. He's fed up hanging about and wants to get cracking on his dream casino.'

'Roberto and the Dream Casino!' Anna stepped into Roberto's skin; she became smooth, yet smouldering, she bowed the gamblers in, invited them to place their bets, she spun the wheel, watched closely until it stopped, then she smiled – she was the winner, they the losers! She raked in the chips.

'I'm not sure I should play it that way,' she said uneasily, 'in case I invoke it happening!' At least she had made Holly smile. 'Oh dear, what a mess, Holly-Berry!'

Holly flung herself into her arms and hugged her fiercely. 'But why did you take up with him in the first place, Anna?'

'Why did you go with Simon?'

'He was nice – '

'And good? Well, maybe he was, even if he did treat you badly. Maximo's nice, too. To me, at any rate. I love being with him. He makes me feel fully alive. He makes my blood sing. Do you think I'm a fool? Am I talking like one?'

Holly shook her head.

Anna did not sleep that night. She spent much of it sitting by the window drinking tea and staring at the dark windows of the house across the street. In the morning, when Maximo phoned, she told him they would have to stop seeing one another. 'I know Roberto is putting pressure on you and I don't intend to leave Shangri-la. It would seem to be stalemate.'

'Listen to me, my love – I do not give way to pressure. You should know me better than that already. I will not be blackmailed. And I have told Roberto so. He is full of hot air – he will not go to his mother, believe me. He would not dare!'

Evangeline continued to progress and a couple of weeks later was transferred to the nursing home. Visiting now became easier; they could pop in and out two or three times a day, whenever they were passing, to bring books and tempting bits of food, and madeira. Evangeline was in a two-bedded room. 'Imagine, at my time of life – having to share with a stranger!' A few days in a hospital ward she could have viewed differently, but this was meant to be a *home*. Her room mate was incontinent (which she could not help) and rumbled about at nights and snored so loudly that when Evangeline lay awake she found it difficult to concentrate on her book. But there was no choice; single rooms were few and must be waited for. 'It encourages one to watch one's fellow inmates and try to assess

196

who will drop by the wayside first. It even brings thoughts of banana skins into the mind. There is not much about life that is civilized in Zimmerland. And we become preoccupied with such petty things! Like who is getting served first and who will be last and get the cold liver and onions.'

She was not to fret, Holly said; she wouldn't be staying in the place very long. She was to build up her strength and practise walking with the zimmer and when the plaster came off they would bring her home.

Carlo disappeared one day – he had gone back to Sorrento. 'He was not happy,' said Giorgio, who was now short-staffed. 'He missed his mother.' Giorgio offered Carlo's job to Holly and she accepted. She hated the idea of smelling of chips but needed the money too badly to turn it down.

'Just temporary like, Georgie. Until you get someone else. I expect they'll send over a replacement. If they have any boys left in Sorrento.'

She worked faster than Carlo and was good at chatting up the customers and keeping them in a good mood while they waited for the chips to fry. Apart from the smell, the job suited her, just as the one at *Pavarotti's* had, since it left the days free for her to work with Anna and to visit Evangeline. And the shop in the evenings was a lively place with constant comings and goings. She got to know the people in the district better and when it was quiet she had Giorgio to talk to. He was teaching her Italian. And through him she was able to keep abreast of the affairs of the House of Tonelli, and so was aware that Roberto was still furious with his father, that he had not given up his dreams for Shangri-la, was drawing up plans and talking to architects and interior designers and makers of casino equipment. He had even flown to Monte Carlo for the week-end. And had come back with a light in his eye.

'He is obsessed by the idea of the casino,' said Giorgio.

Anna had another out-of-town engagement and would have to be away overnight. It was ringed in red in her diary.

'I don't like the idea of leaving you alone in the house,' she said to Holly. 'Especially with that lout Stefano across the corridor from you.'

Holly arranged to spend the night with Mary-Lou; she could come home with Giorgio then. Mary-Lou had said she was welcome to stay anytime.

Anna's engagement was in a small arts centre as part of a week-long festival of theatre and dance. The atmosphere was lively and she had no surly caretakers to bother with. After the performance Maximo joined her and they drove off to a secluded hotel deep in the countryside. Neither of them had left telephone numbers behind.

'We can be out of reach for one night,' said Maximo.

In the nursing home they didn't like their ladies and gentlemen to stay in their rooms during the day; they preferred to have them rounded up in the sitting room where they could keep an eye on them all at once. Well, they had enough to do, hadn't they, what with running up and down with trays of ham salad and semolina pudding, and stripping sodden sheets from beds and wiping up the lavatory floors after the men who were incapable of standing up and aiming steadily, but still insisted on trying to and wouldn't listen to Matron who said there was nothing to be ashamed of in sitting down, was there? Apart from all these other duties, the auxiliaries (untrained) had the job of leading the inmates in and out of their rooms. *Come on now, Rita! Come on, Henry! There'll be something nice on the telly, you'll see. Now you're just being anti-social, Peregrine. Evangeline, hang on to my arm, there's a good girl* . . . Only Christian names were used – just as in a family, said Matron – which upset some of them who hadn't been addressed so familiarly for years. 'Mr Basildon-Jones, *please!*' But everyone called him Peregrine. Or Perry.

And so, every morning, and every afternoon, after they'd had their naps, they were wheeled, propelled or half-carried into the sitting room and placed in the ugly high-backed chairs which lined the walls. The incontinent brought their bottles with them. Tartan rugs were wrapped round withered legs. And then the monstrous television set was turned on. It was too loud even for Evangeline who acknowledged that her hearing was not perfect. She always tried to get the seat nearest

198

the door, a position favoured by no one other than Peregrine. They fought over it, in a civilized way. First there, first served. 'We might have a zimmer race,' said Evangeline, as they headed up the hall together. She was pleased to find that she could beat him, now that her plaster was off.

She was luckier than most as the matron did not tire of telling her, with her leg having mended so well and her regular visitors. Mrs Tonelli was very attentive, wasn't she? Seldom missed a day. Matron was very impressed by the Tonellis.

'Is the nursing home owned by the Mafia?' asked Evangeline.

'Whatever do you mean, Evvie! You do have some wicked ideas, don't you?'

One or two, admitted Evangeline, though not wicked enough. She had one, though, that she was entertaining which she was sure Matron would consider to be quite wicked. She intended to put it into action on the evening that Anna was out of town.

At eight-thirty, they had drinks of their choice – 'Not madeira, though!' said Matron, wagging her finger at Evangeline – and digestive biscuits, sometimes chocolate-backed, on Sundays and holidays, or else plain. Evangeline drank her cocoa down quickly that evening, was first away to the bathroom and first in bed. She was sitting up reading when the auxiliary came in to see if she needed any help undressing.

'No, thank you, dear. I've managed very well on my own.'

'You were quick off your mark tonight, weren't you? Must be a good book.'

'Excellent.'

'Is it a romance?'

'Yes. The heroine is called Emma.'

'Sit and have a nice read then.' The girl put the sides up on the bed and then went out, shutting the door behind her. Evangeline was alone in the room; the other occupant had become too difficult and had had to be sent back to hospital. She'd kept ringing the bell during the night and asking for gin slings and during the day had caused problems by turning off the television set and standing in front of it to announce that she was Princess Diana. 'Just call me Di.' Her name *was* Diana. 'I can tell you all about Charlie. He isn't half a one in the sack, let me tell you!' And she'd wink, very lewdly, which had caused Peregrine, who had not managed to pick up everything she said, to say in a loud voice, 'My God, I didn't know they let trollops in here!' It was a bit of a joke to begin with, as the matron said, but after a while it began to get rather tedious and often Di would switch the television off right in the middle of a quiz game just as it was reaching the moment of climax.

It was the matron's night off. She was going to the cinema to see Rambo the Twelfth, or some such thing. She liked to keep her ladies and gentlemen informed about what she was doing on her nights off and the next day would report back on the film. (She had seen *Crocodile Dundee* five times.) It made them feel they weren't missing out so much, she said to the auxiliaries, kept them in touch with the outside world. After ten o'clock only two members of the staff were left on duty, a nurse and an auxiliary. They sat in a little back room with their feet propped up on cardboard boxes full of toilet rolls and watched television on a portable set. Above their heads was the row of bells which would go off if anyone was in difficulty.

Evangeline listened to the sounds of the house settling. When all was reasonably quiet – it was never completely quiet, with people coughing and snoring and beds squeaking – she pushed back the covers, undid one side of the bed and very carefully swung her feet down to the floor. She slipped them into her fur-lined boots, not bothering to stoop and zip them up, and took off her bed-jacket. She was fully clothed underneath. Quietly she opened the wardrobe door and brought out her coat and hat and put them on. So far so good, Hudson! The thing was to move cautiously and not to panic and try to hurry. Her handbag was on the dressing table. It would be too cumbersome for her to carry. She'd need both hands free. She took only her purse and the keys of Shangri-la from the bag. Now where should she put the note? She looked round the room. On top of the pillow, she decided, as a stand in for herself. She arranged the top sheet so that the note would not be seen until the girl came in to strip the bed back in the morning.

Then, with the aid of the zimmer – blessed zimmer! – she made her way towards the door. Easing it open, she peered out into the underlit hall. They were almost as bad as the French with their light bulbs. There was no one about. She edged out, closing the door at her back and, step by step, shuffled up the hall to the corridor which branched off to the right. She was lucky that she had a room on the ground floor. As she reached the mouth of the corridor, she heard footsteps. She stopped to listen, bent over the walking frame. They were old footsteps. Shambling along. Going to the lavatory. Sounded like Peregrine's cough. She waited until he had gone into the toilet then she continued along the corridor to the side door.

It was locked and bolted, as she had expected. She put down the zimmer and took hold of the heavy key with both hands. As it turned in the lock it juddered her shoulders. But she was all right. No harm done. The bolt was easier; the snib slid back smoothly. And now the handle, and a tug, and the door was open and she could smell the night air and see the street lights and hear the cars passing along the road. Freedom! As they said, it was heady stuff. Don't let it go to your head now, Hudson!

Keeping cool, she recovered her zimmer and set off on the next lap of her journey.

'Mary-Lou wants me to take her to Tenerife for Christmas,' said Giorgio unhappily.

'Well, why don't you?' asked Holly, lifting a chip from the basket and then tilting her head back, dropped it into her mouth.

'The family wouldn't like it. We always spend Christmas together.'

'Maybe you'll just have to thumb your nose at them this year. Mary-Lou's getting restless.' Holly elbowed Giorgio. 'Here's your kid brother coming.'

Giorgio looked up.

'*Caio*, Giorgio!' said Roberto. He nodded at Holly.

'Fish supper?' she asked. 'Salt and sauce? Sauce is on the house, isn't that right, Georgie?'

'Sure thing.' He gave a cracked smile and massaged the back of his left hand with the palm of his right.

'I've just eaten at Claudio's,' said Roberto, sounding surprisingly friendly. Holly hadn't expected a response. He even leaned an elbow on the counter without seeming to worry that he might get a grease stain on his trench-coat. 'You're staying with us tonight, I hear?'

'With Mary-Lou and Georgie.'

'Miss Pemberton away?' His question appeared casual but, immediately, Holly was on her guard. So that was what he'd come snooping round for! She floundered, though, when she tried to find an evasive answer.

'She's got a show,' she said lamely.

He probed no further; in fact, appeared to lose interest. He asked Giorgio how business was doing and then was off. They watched him get into his Alfa and drive away.

'Didn't stay long, did he?' said Holly. 'Thank God!'

Giorgio grinned.

Holly glanced up and saw that it was five minutes to eleven on the wall clock. Next day, she was to remember that.

'It's such a relief not to have to see you in that awful motel!' said Anna. The worst aspect of that, she had found, was that it reduced their relationship to being only a sexual one; it allowed no time for companionship and relaxing together without time pressing, as they were doing now. They had lingered for three hours over their meal. They had so much to talk about, gaps in their lives to fill in for one another. He wanted to know about her parents, how she had lived as a child. She knew more about him, he said; she could see it all spread out before her eyes when she looked out of her own window.

'Yes, I'm sorry about that motel.' He touched her hand. He touched her frequently, at all times. It was something she warmed to. Her parents had not done much touching of one another, although there had been a great deal of affection

202

between them. 'We'll have to work out some better ways of meeting,' he said. 'Coffee?'

He signalled to the waiter. They were the only guests in the hotel; it was mid-week and out-of-season. It was like living in a private country house, thought Anna, with a bevy of servants on call. She felt relaxed to the point of indolence and the rest of the Tonelli family seemed far, far away, except for Roberto whose shadow she was still aware of on the extreme edge of her horizon, like a grey blur.

'Do you think Roberto suspects you're with me tonight?'

'Probably. But he's backed off since we had our row. Don't let's think about Roberto tonight. Don't let's think about anyone but ourselves.' Maximo looked at his watch. 'Eleven. It'll soon be our bedtime.'

Evangeline was feeling pleased with herself. She had managed to negotiate the nursing home drive and inch her way along the road without meeting anyone or hearing a voice shout behind her, 'Evangeline, come back here, you naughty girl!' She chuckled when she thought of them finding her bed empty in the morning. Once she turned in at the drive of Shangri-la she began to feel safe. She wouldn't go back now even if they were to catch her. They couldn't force her; they wouldn't be within their legal rights. She was a voluntary, paying guest at the nursing home. Guest! Home! What a lot of twaddle they talked! Why couldn't they be honest and say inmates and institution and be done with it?

Shangri-la loomed large and black in front of her. Not a peep of light showed anywhere. She had to be extra careful going up the steps – the last thing she wanted was another broken leg! This was one of the most difficult parts, but she made it. Fitting the key into the lock, she turned it and the door opened and she lifted the zimmer and first one foot and then the other over the step and she was inside!

Her hand fumbled along the wall, found the light switch and clicked it down. Nothing happened. She tried again. Still, no light. The bulb must have burnt out or else the boys had pinched it for their room; that had happened before.

The fanlight above the door and the cupola overhead let a

203

little light through. She waited until her eyes had adjusted then began to grope her way round the edge of the hall, striking the wall every now and then with the feet of the zimmer when she went too close. The grandmother clock struck the quarter hour. She smiled as she paused to listen to it. The note lingered on in her head. It must be a quarter past eleven. She reached her rooms.

The light bulbs were working there, thank goodness! When she switched on the light in the sitting room and saw the tidyness of it she had a slight shock – could this be her room? Damn Sophia Tonelli! What a nerve the woman had thinking she was queen of all she surveyed! But the mood passed at once. She hadn't looked at the newspapers and magazines for years; it had probably been time to have a bit of a clear-out. The bedroom was more annoying and inconvenient for it meant she was going to have to do something about the bed. She solved that by deciding to sleep without sheets; it wouldn't do her any harm for one night and she could just pull the blankets and eiderdown up. She was *home!* That was the important thing and she was away from Zimmerland and no matter what happened she would never go back and sit in a ring with a tartan rug over her legs and watch *Neighbours* and *Coronation Street*.

She was exhausted now, and no wonder! It had been quite a journey. She took off her hat and coat, stepped out of her boots and eased herself on to the bed and dragged the blankets round her. Then, putting out her hand, she extinguished the side light.

She felt warm and perfectly comfortable. Wouldn't Holly and Anna get a surprise when they came home and found her? As she was drifting off to sleep she thought she heard footsteps going past her window and round the side of the house, but decided she must have imagined them. She had never been the nervy type who thought that every creak in the night was a burglar.

She slept.

At ten minutes past twelve, Holly and Giorgio heard the first fevered wail of sirens. They raised their heads. The sound swelled and in the next instant a fire tender went hurtling past in the street outside, and then another. The flash of their blue lights shot through the plate glass window of the shop. The noise went on, and on, filling the night. A third fire engine passed. And then a police car.

Holly and Giorgio went to the door but could see nothing. Holly thought she saw a glow in the sky but Giorgio said that that glow was always there: it came from the sodium street lights. While they stood another police car passed, its siren also screaming.

'I hate that sound.' Holly covered her ears.

'It must be a bad fire,' said Giorgio.

They went inside to clear up but before they could start two boys came in to see if they'd any chips left.

'There's a big fire a few streets back,' said one of them, while Holly shovelled up the remaining chips. 'One of those big houses.'

At that moment, the phone rang. Giorgio answered it.

'Oh, it's you, Mary-Lou.' His face spread into a slow smile. He really loves her, thought Holly; how amazing. *'What?'* His smile was ebbing, his jowl slackening. A pucker brought his heavy eyebrows together. 'The *women's house . . .*' he said and looked over at Holly.

THIRTEEN

'American pizzas *are* better than the ones Jackie used to make,' said Holly. 'More cheese. More everything. 'Course Pavarotti was a skinflint. Wouldn't give his customers a mushroom more than they'd paid for. Mind you, he did have to make his protection money for Roberto Tonelli.'

At the mention of Roberto, their mood changed.

'I hope he rots in hell,' said Holly glumly.

'I doubt if he will,' said Anna. 'He's probably flourishing. And the casino will be rising up into the sky, brick by brick, second by second.'

They seemed to see it rise before their eyes, in the middle of the red formica table. Holly saw it, gilded and domed, like a cross between the Taj Mahal and the Vatican.

'Pity they didn't manage to nail him!' she said, savagely attacking her pizza with her knife and fork. She hacked a mushroom slice in two, pierced a wafer of salami, gouged out a shining black olive and dropped it into the ashtray. Anna held on to the table to stop the sauce bottles rattling.

The investigators called in after the fire had found evidence of arson. When Anna and Holly were questioned they had both, separately, pointed the finger at Roberto Tonelli. He had the motive. Everyone knew he had. But Roberto had an alibi; his cousin Gino, who was a solicitor, swore that he had been with him in his apartment from five minutes past éleven that evening until one in the morning. They had played backgammon. The board had still been out when the police called. Roberto had left at one o'clock after a phone call from his mother telling him of the fire. He had been very shocked, Gino said.

Roberto had left Giorgio's at five minutes to eleven: this allowed ten minutes for him to be in transit, if Gino Tonelli's testimony was to be believed. It took seven minutes fast driving to travel from the chip shop to the apartment of Gino. Manifestly, it was not possible for anyone to take in a detour to include parking somewhere out of sight, stealing up the drive of Shangri-la, entering the house by the kitchen door, dousing the floor with paraffin and then making his escape.

Roberto had been even more shocked the next morning (as had everyone else) when it was discovered that Evangeline was missing from her room in the nursing home. Holly had been drinking coffee with Mary-Lou in the Villa Neapolitana when the matron had come running up the drive holding a piece of paper in her hand. It was a note in Evangeline's handwriting. 'Gone home,' it said. 'Sorry for any inconvenience caused.'

'I cannot take the responsibility for it,' said the matron, still panting from the exertion of her run. 'She was in our home of her own free will. We cannot keep them prisoners. We double lock the outside doors, we do all we can. But they can be quite cunning, these old people, like children . . .'

The Tonelli family – all but Maximo who was away on business and did not yet know of the fire – gathered in the hall amongst the madonnas. Holly stood with them, stunned, unable to speak, to think, to feel, even. It was left to Sophia to react.

'Oh, dear God, dear God,' she wailed, her voice rising up the marble staircase to the cupola. She faced her favourite madonna – the Lippi – and crossed herself. Then even she fell silent.

Roberto was the first to move. He turned, his face the colour of ashes, and went running up the staircase as if the hounds of hell were snapping at his heels. Later, he was seen entering the side door of the church with his head bowed. By the following day he was walking with his head up again and was back on his rounds with his white trenchcoat tails flying.

Holly pursued him round the town on Evangeline's old bicycle, and waited for him in the street outside his office. She cornered him one evening when he came out, alone. She had

207

her sharp pointed scissors in her pocket.

'You killed my grandmother,' she shouted into his face. *'Murderer!'* A man and a woman passing by stopped to look round.

'Shut up, you little fool!' hissed Roberto and tried to push past her. But she stood her ground, her hands tightening on the scissors. Her body felt strong tonight: his, racked with guilt, was weak. 'It's a damned lie,' he said, keeping his voice down and his face close to hers.

'You're the damned one.'

'I was nowhere near Shangri-la that night. I was at my cousin Gino's. So watch what you say or I'll sue you.'

'It's the God's own truth and you know it! You can't look me in the eye, can you? Could you put your hand on the Bible and swear you didn't fire our house? Your soul'd rot in hell if you did!'

She saw his eyes blench. I could run him through with the scissors, she thought, I could stab him in the throat, and watch his blood gush out. Then she heard Evangeline's voice as clearly as if she spoke behind her. 'You don't want his blood on your hands, do you, Holly-Berry?'

Holly pushed her plate aside and began to drink her capuccino.

'We'll need to go easy on the pizzas,' said Anna. 'Mimes can't afford to put on weight. Especially when touring. Not that you need to worry about getting fat!'

The pizza manageress was approaching their table carrying in front of her, like a mace, a menu two feet long. She parted her lips in a glossy smile. Everything all right? Had they enjoyed their pizzas? They were great, said Holly. Then the manageress asked if they would mind sharing their table with another lady? A large woman with many shopping bags was following in her wake. 'We're pretty busy, as you can see.' Behind the 'Please wait here to be seated' sign a line of people stood.

'Of course not.' Anna removed her jacket from one of the spare chairs.

The woman heaved herself into the chair. She was friendly

and liked to talk and had soon found out where they were from and what they were doing here.

'My, isn't that interesting? I'll have to come along and see you.'

'We're only playing here tonight,' said Anna. 'Then we move on.'

'We're touring New England for six weeks,' said Holly.

'Won't that be kinda tiring? Different bed every night?'

'Holly loves motels,' said Anna and tried not to think of a certain motel visited for stolen hours on winter afternoons.

'Is that a fact?'

'It's just like having a little house complete with everything you need,' said Holly. 'And the bathrooms are fantastic!'

'Well, well! Can't say they've ever done much for me but then I like my own bed. But everybody likes different things, don't they? Wouldn't do if we were all the same.'

'And when the six weeks are up we're going to travel all over the rest of the States and Canada, on spec,' said Holly. 'I'm dying to go to California and New Mexico and Nevada! We're going to try to get engagements on the way. We might even do some street theatre.'

'Play outside in the street?' The woman looked at Anna, as if she could not imagine it.

'Probably just out west,' said Anna, with an apologetic smile.

The woman nodded. 'Anything goes out there. Places like L.A. and Frisco.'

'We've come away for a whole year,' said Holly. 'We've rented out our house back home.'

Evangeline's annuity had been worth more than they'd expected; with the money it raised they were able to buy a three storeyed Victorian terraced house on the other side of town. It was in an area that had gone down over the years but was now reputed to be on its way up, so Evangeline's lawyer, Mr Partridge, told them. Young couples with good salaries and even better prospects were buying the houses and all the usual signs could be seen: hanging flower baskets and egg-yellow doors and parking spaces at a premium. The nearby factory, which had once manufactured paper, had been converted into desirable one- two- and three-bedroom apartments.

'Definitely a good buy,' said Mr Partridge of their house, as they stood in its garden, knee deep in weeds, gazing up at the cracked window panes stuck over with brown paper and at the guttering which leaned out from the walls. 'It'll need a little doing up, of course. But you might as well be in with the uppers rather than the downers.'

'All this upping and downing!' said Holly. Neither she nor Anna could believe that they belonged with those whom they had heard classed – by Mr Partridge – as upwardly mobile. To stay on their feet would be enough for them, said Anna, which did not preclude their having ambitions.

The house had been inhabited for the past fifty years by a man who had let out rooms and had lived in an advanced state of squalor in the basement. They had had to wear masks over their faces, like surgeons, when they cleared it out. They spent the rest of the winter renovating the house, as well as rehearsing for their coming tour of North America. Both forms of hard work had helped them to get through the first terrible weeks following the fire. They would slog on until midnight, stripping and plastering and painting, and fall into bed exhausted. When spring came, they had a fresh, sweet-smelling house. They each had a separate floor for living, with their own bathrooms, and a communal kitchen and studio in the basement. They never went back to their old street. And Holly didn't see Mary-Lou again either – soon after the fire she left Giorgio (and Alexis) and ran off with a gold-spangled drummer.

'Guess it's time to go,' said Anna, consulting her watch.

They said goodbye to their table companion who wished them well and went to pay the cashier who told them to have a good day even though it was more than half over, as Holly observed, when they stood on the sidewalk in the golden sunshine of a late afternoon in May. Shreds of blossom still clung to the trees which lined the street. It was a small, drowsy town.

'I can't believe I'm actually here,' said Holly, tilting back her head to look at the white spire of a wooden church. Small cotton wool clouds drifted across the bright blue sky. 'I must send a postcard to Pav's.'

They stopped on their way down the street so that she could buy one. She wrote the message quickly: 'Greetings from the US of A. The pizzas are brill. Eat your heart out, Jackie! I'll keep my eye open for Michael Jackson for you, Janice. Love Holly.' She dropped it into the box.

The little theatre where they would perform that evening was at the end of the main street. On the board outside the announcement read: '*Anna Pemberton, leading European mime, assisted by Holly O'Malley, at 8 tonite.*' Holly was playing small parts in two of the sketches and also acting as stage manager, setting out the props, playing the music and so forth. If necessary, she would take the money at the door, too. She ran her finger over her name.

'That's you all right!' said Anna.

They went inside and Holly began to set up for the performance. Anna retired to the dressing room where, first of all, she spread out her towel to create her own space. Then she laid on it her items of make-up. Seating herself in front of the mirror rimmed with light bulbs, she began on the ritual of making-up. She smiled at the lit image of herself. She loved having Holly with her; it was so much pleasanter than travelling alone, yet she had never thought she would want to work with another person. But then she had never felt lonely, not really lonely, before knowing – and losing – Maximo Tonelli. As she looked into the mirror she could imagine him standing behind her, his dark eyes engaging hers. She could imagine the feel of his hands on her shoulders and trembled a little, putting up her own hands to cover the places where his might have lain. The sense of his physical presence was still strong. Back home, going out to face her audiences, she would glance quickly at the front row, half expecting to see him sitting in the middle, his eyes turned like lamps full upon her. And then she would have to rally herself quickly and enter into the skin of the character she was about to portray.

She brushed out her hair, making the strokes long and

211

vigorous, pulling her head to one side. The adrenalin was beginning to pump through her system and by the time she was ready to go on stage her body would be brimming with energy and vitality. Excitement surged in her, as always.

'Anna,' said Holly, putting her head in. 'It's Mr Cummings.'

Anna got up to shake hands with Ralston Cummings.

'Nice to see you again, Anna! Glad we were able to get the tour together. How's our old friend Maximo? Sorry he couldn't make it.'

'Yes, he was busy.' She managed to speak of him calmly though she could detect a faint tremor in her voice. Or perhaps it was just inside her.

'Pretty high-powered business man I'd guess?'

Anna nodded.

She had not seen Maximo for five months, not since the day of Evangeline's funeral. And that had been a glimpse only, without a word exchanged.

The day before the funeral, they had met in the motel in Woodlands Road for the last time. They had sat in their coats on the bed, with the curtains drawn and the overhead light on. Anna had shivered, even though the room was warm. Since returning to see Shangri-la gaping open with its jagged black wound still emitting puffs of greyish smoke into the sky, she had felt cold right to the centre of her being. She stared down at her hands where they lay on her lap, the fingers locked tightly together. She could not bear to look up, and into Maximo's eyes.

'Look at me, Anna,' he said softly and, putting a finger under her chin, raised her head.

The tears came then, spilling out of her like a fountain, and he enfolded her in his arms, rocking her to and fro. Until then she had been unable to weep, even when she'd stood in the street looking at the smoking remains of their house. She had felt stunned. She had thought she must be hallucinating. She had turned and looked at the shining house across the way, its mirror image. And then she had realized it was no longer that. The glass, after all those years, had been finally shattered.

Sophia had come and taken charge of her and led her across

the road and given her hot sweet tea and talked to her and Anna had heard but not listened and had sat on a pink and gold settee with her arm around Holly and thought, Evangeline is dead, she was burned in a fire. Holly had wept but Anna had not.

'Anna love, Anna love.' It was all that Maximo could find to say.

'It was Roberto, wasn't it?' she asked.

Maximo did not answer. She could not expect him to. But when she looked again into his face she saw the pain reflected in those dark, sad eyes.

'I know I have to take some responsibility for the sins of my son. Did you not tell me that once?' He smiled briefly and shook his head.

They stayed there for some time, holding one another, without speaking. Both knew that it would be for the last time since Roberto's crime would stand between them. And the blood of Evangeline.

They put 'Funeral Private' in the newspaper announcement this time, wishing to make sure that no one other than themselves would attend. 'Evangeline Harriet Hudson,' Anna had dictated to the clerk at the newspaper office. 'Dear friend of the late Dorothea Wilberforce, and of Anna Pemberton and Holly O'Malley.'

Anna and Holly sat side by side in the chapel, staring at Evangeline's coffin on top of which rested their two wreaths. One had come from the Tonelli family – with sincerest condolences, written in the hand of Sophia – but Anna had asked the undertaker to leave it behind. Organ music by Purcell wafted round them.

Hearing the door squeak behind them, feeling a rush of cold air, Anna glanced round and saw, advancing up the short aisle of the crematorium chapel, wearing dark glasses and a dark suit and a blindingly white shirt and black tie, which he was fingering, just below the knot – Maximo Tonelli. Her throat thickened uncomfortably and she almost cried his name aloud. *Maximo!* She almost thought she had. She seemed to hear it echoing up to the domed ceiling. He held out his hands as if

213

asking her to accept his presence. He then slid into a seat in the back row and bowed his head. Anna turned back as the chaplain came glissading in through the side door. The same chaplain who had officiated at Dorothea's funeral. They had been too shocked to consider what else they might do for Evangeline. They had decided to take the easiest way out.

The chaplain said his piece about giving thanks for a long and bountiful life, then displaying his wolf-like teeth, said, 'And now, I believe, Miss Pemberton, you would like to recite some poetry in honour of our dear departed friend Evangeline?'

Anna started, not having expressed any such wish, but feeling compelled now to comply, rose and stepped forward. She faced her small audience. She could hardly bear to look into Holly's face and see her grief.

Maximo drew down his dark glasses and gazed at Anna intently. She allowed her eyes to engage with his. She felt steady now.

Some lines of Sylvia Plath's came to her from a poem entitled *Edge*.

'The woman is perfected.
Her dead

Body wears the smile of accomplishment,
The illusion of a Greek necessity

Flows in the scrolls of her toga,
Her bare

Feet seem to be saying:
We have come so far, it is over.'

She stopped. For a moment there was silence and then the music which they had chosen four months before for Dorothea's funeral – Schubert's *Trout Quintet* – burst forth from the loud speakers and went rushing and burbling through the chapel. The chaplain raised his hands in what might have been intended as a benediction, then made his escape through the side door. The coffin began to slide backwards, on its last journey. It seemed too much, thought Anna, that Evangeline's body should have to endure ordeal by burning twice.

She gave Maximo a final glance then rejoined Holly in the pew. Holly groped for her hand and Anna gave it and they remained sitting there until the music ended and quietness settled around them.

When they got up to go, they saw that the chapel was empty, but for themselves.